High class hij[...]
Praise for the previous
DEBUTANTE DROPOUT MYSTERIES

"[...]

Publishers Weekly

"Andrea Kendricks is a society sleuth with wit
and verve. One hundred percent fun."
Mystery Scene Magazine

"Smooth, sassy, silly, slick, and sexy."
Sauce Magazine

"Susan McBride kept me laughing all the way
through this delicious romp of a mystery."
Tess Gerritsen

"Susan McBride has an engaging new heroine in
Andrea Kendricks, a young woman whose approach
to crime-solving is asking herself WWND?
(What Would Nancy [Drew] Do?) . . . In a genre
where every char[...]
her plucky inc[...]

D1586208

The Debutante Dropout Mysteries
by *Susan McBride*

BLUE BLOOD
THE GOOD GIRL'S GUIDE TO MURDER
THE LONE STAR LONELY HEARTS CLUB
NIGHT OF THE LIVING DEB
TOO PRETTY TO DIE

Too Pretty To Die

A DEBUTANTE DROPOUT MYSTERY

SUSAN McBRIDE

AVON

An Imprint of HarperCollinsPublishers

AVON BOOKS
An Imprint of HarperCollins*Publishers*
10 East 53rd Street
New York, New York 10022-5299

Copyright © 2008 by Susan McBride
ISBN: 978-0-06-084601-5
www.avonmystery.com

First Avon Books paperback printing: February 2008

Avon Trademark Reg. U.S. Pat. Off. and in Other Countries, Marca Registrada, Hecho en U.S.A.
HarperCollins® is a registered trademark of HarperCollins Publishers.

Printed in the U.S.A.

10 9 8 7 6 5 4 3 2 1

Acknowledgments

While writing *Too Pretty to Die*, I went through a pretty scary patch in my life, and I wondered if I'd be able to focus enough to finish the book. Somehow, I did. And I'd like to dedicate every word to the wonderful people who got me through the worst. Thanks in particular to my amazing mom, Pat McBride, the love of my life, Ed Spitznagel, and my fabulous "second mom," Alice Spitznagel, who took such good care of me and made me laugh instead of cry. I am blessed with terrific friends who did their share of hand-holding (many from long distance), and I adore you all. To my readers who sent well wishes, thank you so much. To the doctors, nurses, and rad techs who made me well again: y'all rock. Finally, to the women who battled breast cancer before me—and alongside me—and after me: I am in awe. I have a whole new set of heroes, and every one is a regular person who had to suddenly become extraordinarily brave.

This one's for you.

"I'm tired of all this nonsense about beauty
being only skin-deep.
That's deep enough. What do you want,
an adorable pancreas?"
Jean Kerr

Too Pretty To Die

Prologue

She used to be so pretty.

Perfect, some would say.

Her eyes had always been so blue and wide, her smile so bright; her skin without a blemish. She'd never gone through an awkward stage, having blossomed from beautiful baby and skipping through puberty without a hitch; ending up the fully spun butterfly everyone knew she'd become.

She was the one who Daddy had called "my own little Grace Kelly," showing her off at the country club when she was a toddler in rompers and saddle shoes. Even in grade school, the boys from St. Mark's had tripped over themselves to be near her when they'd mixed with the Hockaday girls at dances. Her mailbox had always overflowed with love notes on Valentine's Day, many from names she didn't even recognize.

She'd grown accustomed to being adored, and thrived on it. She figured her looks were her gift, and there was nothing wrong with that. Some savants played piano like Mozart or painted like Chagall. Miranda knew that her talent was in keeping up her appearance. And it had been so easy for her, really.

Sure, she'd had to deal with Venus envy. Girls hated her for no other reason than that she was prettier. But there would always be people who wanted what they couldn't have, wouldn't there? If people didn't like her, it had more to do with them than her, or so her mother had always suggested.

Such was life, and Miranda had fast learned how to shrug off the jealous whispers. She'd been blessed where it mattered most when the eyes of Texas were upon you: her shiny chassis.

And she'd never, ever taken it for granted.

If she'd been pug-ugly, she wouldn't have been a Pi Phi at UT-Austin, and she certainly wouldn't have been a Symphony Deb (okay, maybe she could have, since her daddy had practically paid for the entire string section with his annual donations).

She'd surely never have won Miss Dallas or first runner-up at the national pageant.

Homely girls didn't wear sashes, and they damned sure didn't get tiaras unless they bought them at Oriental Trading.

When she'd graduated from UT, she'd gotten a gig right off the bat doing on-air consumer reports at KXAS-Channel 5 in Big D, before the news director had claimed she was being underutilized and moved her to the anchor desk. And, really, it had everything to do with all the viewer e-mails about her Southern charm, the breezy way she read the teleprompter, and her movie-star looks, and not a whit to do with the fact that she was sleeping with her married boss—call her naïve, but she'd believed him when he said that he loved her and planned to leave his boring wife.

My God, but it had been so easy when she was beautiful, when all she had to do was smile and the world fell on its knees to please her.

She used to pray to God every night, thanking Him profusely for blessing her with good features. Her mother had raised her to think of others, too; so she'd prayed as well for the ungainly, the gawky, the brace-faced, and pimply, because, Lord knew, they could always use the help.

Now her prayers had changed.

They'd become more like an SOS.

Thirty-one years old, and she'd been ruined for life.

She was a freak, a loser, a big, fat (okay, skinny) nothing.

Through moist eyes, she read the letter from

the Caviar Club one last time before she crumpled it into a ratty ball and tossed it across the room. It bounced off the open screen of her laptop and dropped to the carpet.

So that's how it ended?

With an impersonal note?

After all the lip service when they'd embraced her about how special she was, how extraordinary on the inside and out?

Tears slid down her cheeks, and she brushed them off, angry and disappointed at once.

Screw them all! she thought.

Even *him*. No, especially him.

She'd barely heard a peep from the man she'd been seeing, not since Dr. Sonja had turned her into a pariah. Then, wham, he'd sent a text message earlier in the afternoon saying, NEED TIME 2 THINK. GIVE ME SPACE, OK?

Space?

Wasn't that the precursor of the infamous "can't we just be friends" brush-off, dating back to junior high?

What had happened to all the gushy messages before Dr. Sonja turned her into a freak? Had his professed adoration been a lie? And how had he found out? She hadn't told him, not personally. So how had he learned?

Someone must've spread the word, and Miranda was fairly certain she knew who was responsible, despite how hard she'd tried to keep her disfigurement under wraps, wearing dark glasses and a scarf around her hair every time she ventured out, telling fibs, avoiding everyone as best she could.

Pretty soon it wouldn't matter what disguise she donned or how many excuses she made up. The world would know what she'd become: the Park Cities' version of the Hunchback of Notre Dame.

She'd forever be known as the Ugly Chick with Botched Botox, or how about, Your Friendly Neighborhood Sideshow Freak?

She'd no longer be Dallas's "Most Beloved On-Air Personality," that was for darn tootin'.

Because she wouldn't be on-the-air anymore; no one would want her.

It didn't matter that her co-anchor, the smarmy Dick Uttley, looked like he was 101. He had a million tiny creases from a fifty year nicotine habit and the broken capillaries of a lifelong drinker. But did he ever get e-mails about his hairstyle or the color of his lipstick? Did anyone care that he'd cheated on his wife about a hundred times with every intern at the station?

Noooooo.

If Dick had been the one scarred by a permanent eye twitch and an Elvis sneer, the viewers likely wouldn't have even noticed.

But they expected Miranda DuBois to be perfect. They demanded that she look gorgeous from the tip of her pedicured toes to the roots of her shiny blond hair.

The only trouble was, she would never be perfect again.

Her breaths became rushed, and she felt dizzy, on the verge of hyperventilating.

Oh, God, she couldn't breathe!

She gulped down the last of her gin and tonic, struggling up from her Barcelona chair only long enough to pour another—minus the tonic this time.

"Just try a little around your eyes, Randa, and let's do your laugh lines. Then you'll look as perfect as you did when you were twenty," Dr. Sonja had cajoled her, and who wouldn't have listened? Sonja Madhavi was cosmetic dermatologist to all the pretty people in Dallas. Everyone and her pedigreed pup had Dr. Sonja show up for glycolic peel parties and Botox bashes.

So she had done it, too, like a sheep.

The one truly bad thing about being born with pretty genes was seeing that first wrinkle and glimpsing the future.

She'd been afraid of growing older, knowing how women who aged disappeared from TV news like old soldiers who'd faded away. She'd decided, what the heck? Enough of her friends had gone under the needle and raved about it. No one ever talked about the "what ifs," as in, "What if Dr. Sonja hit a nerve or injected a bad batch of botulism?"

What a fool she'd been!

Now she was a walking example of those "adverse reactions" that Dr. Sonja had so quickly glossed over. Who ever paid attention to the warning labels until it was too late? What woman truly cared that the FDA hadn't put its stamp of approval on a product if it was featured in *Vogue* and lauded by doctors in France and Italy?

Those French were always ahead of everyone else in matters of beauty. They were willing to take risks, throw caution to the wind. It wasn't fair. Why should they have dibs on everything?

But she should've read the fine print. She should've erred on the side of caution instead of being so fast to jump on Dr. Sonja's better-than-Botox bandwagon; should've wised up to the fact that Dr. Sonja had never seemed to like her.

If she had, things would be different.

As it was, she would never be the same.

It had been three weeks since her injections, and she'd had to call in sick at work, claiming "female troubles," which prevented any of the producers from asking probing questions. They had the weekends-only anchorwoman sitting in temporarily "while Miranda DuBois takes a much needed vacation," or so they told viewers.

But what she had was a case of botched wrinkle filler: a serious tic in her left eye that wouldn't stop, and a droop in the corner of her mouth, so she appeared the drooling idiot. She'd been to Dr. Sonja's for a follow-up, begging her to fix things, but Dr. Sonja had blamed her, said she must be overly sensitive, and told her to wait it out.

Wait out ugly?

Good God!

What if that took forever?

She had on-air news to read, celebrity charity events to chair, commercials and public service announcements to tape, not to mention countless promotional gigs for the station.

But Dr. Sonja didn't care. She'd stopped returning her phone calls, was intentionally avoiding her, despite Miranda threatening to report her to the BBB and the AMA if she didn't do some kind of quick fix. And she would do it, too.

She had never felt so abandoned.

Oh, Lord, she would die alone, wouldn't she?

Forget the tiaras and sashes! She'd be lucky if any single, attractive, heterosexual male would pay attention to her ever again.

The one man she'd believed loved her—who used to ring her cell spontaneously to whisper dirty little come-ons, who'd made a million excuses at work and at home so he could squeeze in a half hour at her place in the mornings or at night—had vanished off the radar after her face was ruined.

She knew she could make his life a living hell if she wanted to; hurt him as much as he was hurting her. And she might—she could—but she wasn't sure he was worth it. He had never really been hers.

It was the sign of things to come, wasn't it?

She could already see the future, and it was as ugly as she was: being forced to move out of her pretty duplex on Preston near the country club and into the guest house of her mother's Highland Park manse, undatable and unable to pay rent when she got permanently canned, because what TV station in its right mind wanted an anchorwoman whose features frightened small children?

Talk about a double whammy.

She was unattractive *and* pathetic.

Maybe she should just choke down the bottle of Xanax in her medicine cabinet, chase it with the gin, and be done with it, so she wouldn't have to live with the sight of her mangled self another day.

Only, Miranda DuBois had never chickened out on life before. She'd always found a way to land on top, no matter what it took. What she wanted wasn't her name on a marble slab in Sparkman Hillcrest Memorial Park.

Why should she be the one to chuck it all?

Would that make things right?

Miranda drained her drink and slapped down the empty glass on the table beside her, wiping at her mouth with a silk sleeve.

What she wanted was payback.

If anyone knew about revenge, it was a pageant girl. She hadn't suffered through butt tape and sequins all those years for nothing.

She would make that quack suffer, just as she was suffering.

Hell, she'd get *all* the insensitive jerks who'd given her the cold shoulder. And she had plenty of ammo to do it.

Her quest would start tonight with the good doctor.

Sonja Madhavi wouldn't know what hit her.

Chapter 1

"Aw, c'mon, Andy. Don't be a chicken. Everybody's doing it. What's the big deal?"

I'm not exactly sure why Janet had followed me into the opulent powder room in Delaney Armstrong's enormous Bordeaux Avenue manse, except to torment me, as she was supposed to be mingling with the loitering ladies swarming the living room: upper crust women in their twenties and thirties, sipping Chablis and waiting for a turn with *über*-dermo Dr. Sonja Madhavi, there to inject the beauty-obsessed with her latest age-defying cocktails. My only consolation was that Dr. Sonja hadn't brought her fat vacuum to liposuction any thighs or bellies. That would've had me running straight out the front door and not just to the can.

If I strained my ears, I could discern the hum of yammering voices alongside the bass of "Hot

Stuff" by Donna Summers, being that disco was the night's background music. No one had asked, but if they had, I'd have kept disco dead and buried.

I was no *Saturday Night Fever* diva, but a rock chick to the core.

Yet another reason why I'd rather have been just about anywhere else at the moment and felt extra grateful for my temporary refuge in the loo.

I'd endured enough Abba and eyeballed enough shallow women wearing Gucci, Fendi, and Prada to satisfy my quota for the year, and I certainly had no intention of experiencing Dr. Sonja's party favors, since that would mean subjecting myself to a syringe full of God knows what. I'd heard tell that she made up some of her "beauty remedies" on the stovetop in her kitchen. Kind of like an upscale meth lab for the chic.

The idea gave me shivers, but it obviously didn't do much to scare off the long list of Dr. Sonja's clientele. Even the *Morning News* had dubbed the exotic-looking doc who wore miniskirts and platform heels "Big D's Own Fountain of Youth."

Like a bad case of the flu, Dr. Sonja's "Pretty Parties" had spread across the city, infecting every wrinkle-fearing, couture-wearing woman in Dallas's in-crowd from age fifteen to 115.

It was worse than the Tupperware plague of the 1980s.

Plastic wasn't my thing, not the kind you stored leftovers in or the type that meant reshaping body parts with knives or needles.

Call me crazy—and plenty of folks around Big

D did—but hardcore superficiality gave me the heebie-jeebies, not surprising considering that I, Andrea Blevins Kendricks, would forever be known as the "debutante dropout" after bailing on my own cotillion, and deemed fatally etiquette impaired by the city's blue bloods, despite being reared by the High Priestess of High Society and Matron of Good Manners, my Chanel-wearing mother Cissy Blevins Kendricks.

So why the heck would I want to inject myself with some funky substance just because all the appearance-obsessed females in town were doing it? If peer pressure—and dire threats from Cissy—hadn't inspired me to don white and debut at eighteen, it sure as heck wasn't going to work now.

"Baawk, baawk," my so-called pal, Janet Graham—the culprit responsible for my presence at this particular Pretty Party—squawked in her best chicken imitation, even flapping her elbows to get the point across.

I loaded up my verbal slingshot.

"If everybody jumped off Reunion Tower with Sub-Zero fridges strapped to their butts, would you do it, too?"

I flung the words at her and stared her down, waiting for her comeback. Oh, and she'd have one, too. I could bet my rarely touched investment portfolio on it.

Janet never lacked for words. She edited the society pages for the *Park Cities Press* newspaper, the rag that covered the upscale Dallas neighborhood I'd grown up in, and she wrote much of its contents. Janet knew everyone who was anyone in the city, and she always had something to say about each one of them (the choicest cuts saved for private snarking sessions).

"I see," was all she said at first, and cocked her head, sending ringlets of bright red hair cascading over her shoulders—a new and very feminine look for her, as she usually went for no-nonsense cuts. She studied me with eyes made all the wider by her black-rimmed "smart girl" glasses. "So, my self-confident compadre, you wouldn't try a little of Dr. Sonja's super-new wrinkle eraser? Not even to wipe out those lines between your brows?"

Lines?

"What lines?" Instinctively, my fingers went up to poke the terrain north of the bridge of my nose.

"The ones you've had since high school, Andy." She sighed and smoothed the lapels of her 1940s style jacket, armed with shoulder pads that had the wingspan of a 747. "You always scrunch up your brow when you contemplate something, and it's given you premature creases." She sighed again, agitated, "You're doing it right now."

I ambled over toward a mirror, as there were several large gilt-framed ones hanging on the velvet-papered walls in Delaney Armstrong's gargantuan downstairs hall bathroom. The whole mansion was overstuffed and ostentatious enough to look like an old-fashioned bordello (not that I'd ever seen an old-fashioned bordello, but I had been in a strip club once that had red velvet ceilings and chandeliers).

Did I mention that Delaney was the hostess for this evening's soiree plugging Dr. Sonja's miracle cures? And that I'd been tricked into coming by La Femme Janet, who'd invited me out for a friendly "let's catch up" dinner, only to pull one of her "oops, I nearly forgot, I have to cover this teensy-weensy event for the paper. It'll just take a sec. Want to go with me?"

Grrrr.

She was almost as bad as my subversive Mummy Dearest, and I was far too gullible for my own good. I would never learn, would I?

I squinted at my reflection, contemplating it so thoroughly my brow was pleated like an accordion. Even when I forced a blank expression, the pleats didn't erase, not completely.

Well, shiver my splintered timbers.

Janet was right.

I did have a permanent pleat between my eyebrows.

Why had I never noticed?

I saw my redheaded chum smile in the silvered glass as she showed off pearly whites that belied her own fortuitous upbringing: we'd both attended the Hockaday School for Girls, though Janet had been ahead of me by a few years. Still, she'd been a rebel in her own right, and I had admired her for it, more so when I'd committed my own heinous act of rebellion (namely, skipping out on my cotillion).

"Maybe I like my lines," I grumbled, and I wanted to mean it, even if I didn't feel the sentiment wholeheartedly. Did frowning make wrinkles worse? I wondered, and turned my back on the mirror.

"You like your lines?" Janet laughed. "C'mon, sweetie, don't lie to me. No woman in her right mind wants to look like a Shar Pei."

What about left-minded women? I wanted to ask, but instead said, "There's nothing wrong with growing older naturally."

So long as my wrinkles didn't bother my boyfriend, Brian Malone. At least, I assumed he didn't mind that I wasn't as crinkle-free as polyester. But if he did—if he was that superficial, which he wasn't—he wouldn't be worth it, would he?

"It doesn't matter anyway. I'd never shoot up my creases with sheep poop," I declared, and Janet crossed her arms over her brass-buttoned chest, looking skeptical.

"Doesn't hitting forty scare you, Andy?"

Forty?

Hello? I had nine more years to worry about that. Though Janet was closer still, possibly the cause behind her sudden interest in Dr. Sonja's crease-eradicating potions.

"How does the saying go? That getting old is better than the alternative," I responded, in lieu of a real answer.

"Tell that to all the teenage girls who are already getting peels and Botox to stop the lines they haven't even earned yet," Janet said with an arch of sculpted eyebrows, and I shook my head at how absurd that sounded.

Okay, so it was trendy for teenagers to have antiwrinkle gunk injected into their faces as "preventive" measures ('cuz, God forbid, they should live past thirty and develop crow's-feet). So plenty of society matrons in my mother's crowd threw Pretty Parties where Dr. Sonja came armed with her syringes and filled their faces with concoctions made from human placenta and cow fat. I'd been raised in a world where middle-aged wives were routinely dumped for newer models, so I could understand harboring that kind of fear.

But I was neither a self-conscious teenager nor a youth-obsessed society matron; and, though I'd recently hit thirty-one and had the creases to show for it, I was not about to have foreign substances shot beneath my skin so I could purportedly shed a few years.

Did anyone really know what that goo would do in time? Maybe it would harden like concrete and turn once-human faces to statues.

Besides, I liked to think when I expressed an emotion, my facial muscles followed suit. I knew too many women who smiled and looked as numb as movie zombies.

Hello? Can you say 'Cher'?

Or this evening's hostess, Delaney Armstrong, a fellow prep school alum from the Hockaday School for Girls. She'd never been beautiful in the classic sense, but bright-eyed and energetic: the kind of girl who'd taken charge of things, like pep rallies or dances or club meetings. Delaney's square-jawed features probably would've aged very attractively. Only Delaney hadn't allowed for growing old naturally. She'd had so much dermabrasion, peels, and Botox that her entire face appeared frozen and vaguely swollen. Her once nut-brown hair had been dyed pale blond and highlighted to within an inch of its life. Her lips looked like someone had inflated them with a tire pump.

I'm not sure whose idea of beautiful that was.

Perhaps Delaney's hubby liked having a wife who could double for a wax statue at Madame Tussaud's. If I ever met the man, I might be tempted to ask.

"Dr. Sonja's giving everyone freebies," my insistent pal, Janet Graham, tried again, as if that would entice me. "She wants to get everyone good and hooked, so they'll keep running back to her office for more."

"Pass," I told her.

I had no intention of letting Dr. Sonja fill up my cracks with spackle made from squid intestines, not even if it was on her dime.

The whole fast-food mentality of the anti-aging business creeped me out immensely.

The hip and trendy cosmetic dermo had even opened up several Pretty Place clinics in various upscale shopping malls around the city. So, after you bought your size two, low-rise, boot-cut jeans at the Gap and picked up a salad to-go from La Madeleine, you could pop into The Pretty Place for wrinkle shots and a brow wax.

How convenient.

"You're really not curious to try a little?" Janet bugged me, shrugging when I said most assuredly, "No."

"Well, I'm thinking of having my lips done," she said, toddling over to the nearest mirror on stiletto heels and then proceeding to pout at her reflection, resembling a demented fish more than Angelina Jolie. "What d'you say, Andy? Could I use a little plumping?"

"Pillows should be plumped, not lips," I groused. Janet looked perfectly fine to me. She'd always had her own sense of style, never playing to what was trendy or popular. So what had gotten into her? Why would she suddenly want to look as artificial as the Park Cities socialites she wrote about?

"You can say that, Andy, 'cuz you've got good lips. Mine are as thin as a bird's."

"I didn't know birds had lips."

Janet nudged me. "Stop it, Andy. I'm serious."

"You can't be," I said, because . . . well, she couldn't be. It was so not like Janet Graham to fret over less-than-ripe lips. She was more apt to get worked up over sexism or racism, or drivers on Central Expressway who talked on their cell phones and applied mascara while weaving from lane to lane. So why was she suddenly so concerned about appearance?

"I'm dead serious," she assured me, squirming uncharacteristically. "What's so wrong with wanting a sexy mouth?"

I wished I didn't believe her, but I did.

She had the most earnest look on her face, maybe even a little sad, like a woman who was questioning her self-worth and finding it lacking; though it was hard for me to believe that someone as independent and tough as Janet Graham would ever lack in self-confidence. I'd watched her blaze through Hockaday with her ever-changing hair colors and artful adjustments to our uniform of white blouse and plaid, never pushing the envelope far enough to get in trouble but making it clear that she wasn't like everyone else.

She wasn't just a breath of fresh air, she was positively tornadic, knocking down everything in her path, never letting anyone tell her "that can't be done," and leaving a lot of stunned glances in her wake.

I'd been two years behind her, but had felt every bit the outsider that Janet seemed proud to be, so I couldn't help but admire her. I had cheered from the sidelines as she'd left Big D in pursuit of a career in the theater, returning less than triumphant after mere bit parts on soap operas and off-off-Broadway shows that closed within hours of opening, and taking on a stint as a society reporter with the *Park Cities Press* on a lark, only to realize she was damned good at it.

Janet wore vintage clothes, dyed her hair red as a fire engine, and had all of Dallas society at her fingertips. Literally. She could speed-dial Mrs. Ross Perot or Mrs. Jerry Jones via cell phone if the mood struck her.

So why the heck was she suddenly worried about thin lips?

Janet had never put a lot of stock in her appearance, beyond looking like, well, herself. She wasn't like the dozen society snobs in Delaney Armstrong's living room who practically lived and died by the sword (or, rather, by the scalpel); who thought that winning meant the tiniest nose, the roundest breasts, the fullest mouth, and the thinnest thighs.

If Janet wasn't out to one-up other women in the eternal "who's the fairest of them all" debate, then it had to be because . . . oh, gosh.

"You've got a man," I blurted out, because it was the only thing that made sense. Why else did a normally sane and rational woman suddenly turn nonsensical?

Her eyes went wide, and her mouth—with its perfectly normal-sized lips—hung open just a spell, long enough for me to figure I'd hit that sucker on the nose.

"You've met a man who thinks Angelina Jolie is the feminine ideal," I went on, sure that I'd figured it out, brilliant detective that I was (well, I'd read enough Nancy Drew and Sherlock Holmes in my growing-up to qualify for a GED in Detection, at least). "So you want fat lips to please him."

"Andy, you know me better than that," she remarked with a lift of her chin, only to tag on, "I'm just maybe a little too caught up in something I'm working on, for the paper. It's got me to thinking about perception."

"Perception?"

"Looks, perfection, what men want from women, how others view us, what makes someone attractive. Lots of things." Her eyes clouded for a moment, then she shook it off. "I can't say more about it yet, Andy. But I will reassure you that I will not change any part of my body to please anyone but myself."

Uh-huh.

I'd told myself that same story before I'd fallen for Malone. It was easy to make all those feminist proclamations before your heart completely turned to mush. Look at what Ted Turner had done to Jane Fonda. Nothing on that woman was real anymore. And good ol' Ted had dumped her for a younger model regardless.

So had Janet found her own Ted? After so many years of being single—and professing she would remain so forever?

Hmm.

But I didn't debate her or interrogate her. I'd find out any scoop soon enough. It was inevitable. Janet was a gossip columnist, for heaven's sake. Eventually, she'd have to spill her guts.

"Then promise me you'll leave this Botox bash tonight without going all Morgan Fairchild on me, okay?" I said, and put a hand on her padded shoulder.

"Good God, girl, that's why I invited you to tag along with me," she quipped. "To remind me that I'm not like them. I just write about 'em."

"Did you say you *invited* me?" I parroted. "Wasn't it more like *tricked me.*"

"Semantics." She wiggled bejeweled fingers— Janet did so appreciate good costume jewelry. "You give me strength, my friend, so I will pass on Dr. Sonja's freebies and do a little more research before I make a decision. I don't need to jump into lip plumping right this minute. What I do need is a decent steak and some onion rings."

"Now you're talkin'." I grinned.

The aliens from Planet Superficial that had momentarily possessed my friend's brain had released it with no obvious residual damage.

Phew.

After a final glance in the mirror—and a quick primping of her curly 'do—Janet turned to me, suggesting, "How about we take off now and go get that dinner? I don't need to stay till the end for the door prizes. I've seen enough here to write my story. Besides"—she shrugged—"if I hang around any longer listening to well-to-do women bitch about boob jobs and face-lifts and liposuctioned thighs, I think I'll have to throw myself under the nearest Mercedes. I might have to chronicle the self-absorbed insanity of the rich and plastic, but I don't want to catch it."

Ah, now there was my comrade who liked to color outside the box. It was good to have her back after that *Nip/Tuck* moment.

I grinned. "That's the Janet Graham I know and love."

She nudged my arm, and the familiar spark returned to her eyes. "How does Bob's Steak and Chop House sound? You can't even tell there was ever a fire," she added, because there had been one, a year or so back. But it wasn't because of overcooked tenderloin.

It sounded lots better than hanging out at Delaney's with a bunch of wine-sipping women lining up for needle sticks.

Yuck.

"Give me smashed potatoes over a vial of cow placenta any day," I said, and headed out of the quiet of the posh loo, catching the opening beat of the Village People doing "YMCA" and praying we could slip past the living room unnoticed.

As I led the way toward the front door, I buttoned my jacket to ready myself for the cool November air, ignoring Janet's whispers about slowing down.

We were so close to getting away, I could smell freedom as clearly as I could Delaney Armstrong's overpowering White Linen perfume.

"I should probably let Delaney know we're leaving," she whined, glancing behind her. "She was kind enough to add me to the guest list so I could research a story."

"Make up your mind," I said, and paused as she contemplated whether to keep moving or head back to bid Delaney farewell.

While I tapped my foot on the floor, I stared at Delaney's family portrait, hung above an elaborate Italian console in the foyer, in which the Armstrong clan posed in their English garden out back. Delaney smiled so tight it looked like it hurt. Beside her sat her husband Jonathan, who had *GQ* looks from his thick brown hair to the cleft in his chin. On either side stood their twin girls, wearing matching lavender dresses.

Glancing at the picture-perfect tableau made my teeth ache.

"All right"—Janet turned back toward me— "you win. I'll just give Delaney a jingle in the morning to say *merci*."

"Let's boogie then, chickie!" I caught Janet's wrist, eager to hustle her out of there, and we would've surely snuck out unchecked if at the very moment I reached for the nickel-plated handle, the door hadn't pushed wide open, nearly butting into my nose as a woman in pink barreled in.

She was drunk as a skunk, stumbling forward on tottering high heels, big poof of blond hair flying, waving something dark in her hand—a clutch purse?—and leaving the reek of gin in her wake.

"Ooooph," Janet gasped, running into my back as I came to a cold hard stop.

Who the heck would be nuts enough—or, rather, smashed enough—to crash Dr. Sonja's Pretty Party, one being covered by the society editor of the *Park Cities Press*, no less?

I caught the crasher's profile as she charged toward the living room, and a familiar name rose to my lips. I was sure I was wrong, until I heard the slurred voice as she howled, "You quack, you ruined my face!"

Nope. I was right on the nose.

Miranda DuBois, I knew without a doubt, co-anchor of the Channel 5 evening news, famous for her dimpled smile and ample cleavage; but, long before that, a classmate at Hockaday, one of the pageant girls I'd avoided like the plague. Not that she wasn't nice enough, but it had always felt more like saccharine than sugar to me.

"Look at me . . . I'm a monster! My life is ruined!"

By the sound of her raving, I guessed that the long-term effects of bleaching her hair had damaged her self-control.

The woman was acting totally bonkers.

"Oh, my, now *this* is what I call a story," Janet murmured as she stepped around me to get a reporter's eye view of the goings-on.

Despite my best intentions, I followed in Janet's wake, reaching the threshold of the living room in time to glimpse Miranda shaking her tiny black purse around the room and sputtering about exposing the truth and making them—whoever *they* were—pay for what they'd done.

Once I got close enough, though, I saw that it was no clutch bag Miranda was jabbing in the air.

In case my eyes weren't to be trusted, my ears picked up the gasps of "She's got a gun!" as the less-than-sober Ms. Miranda DuBois took aim at Delaney . . . then at the mustached blond dude who'd come with Dr. Sonja . . . and finally pointed the tiny pistol right at Dr. Sonja's heart.

The women started shrieking and dodging for cover in a blur of autumn-colored cashmere and wool.

"Get down!" Janet cried, and grabbed my shoulder, pushing me toward the floor with her just before a shot rang out.

Chapter 2

★ If I'd been smart, I would've hightailed it out of Delaney's place ASAPP (As Soon As Pistol Popped). No one would've thought less of me. Heck, no one would've noticed had I gone, since I'd hardly been the life of the Pretty Party.

Only I didn't do the wise thing. I did what I usually did: opened my mouth when I shouldn't, raised my hand when I should've kept it firmly entrenched at my side, and generally played Dudley Do-right.

Ugh.

Which explained how I ended up driving a drunk and unhappy Miranda DuBois to her duplex après the fiasco at Dr. Sonja's Botox bash.

My buddy Janet Graham deserted me—and aborted our dinner plans for Bob's Steak and Chop House—instead calling a cab and hightailing it to her *Park Cities Press* office. She had a juicy story to type up and was determined to get it into tomorrow's edition. If she waited until morning, it would have to go in the second biweekly edition, not out for three days, and by then it would be old news.

There was little Janet hated more than being old news.

So I got left behind and stuck with Miranda.

Call me a sap, but after witnessing the goings-on, I felt suddenly protective of Hockaday's prettiest graduate. I felt sorry for her, even.

Strange, because she'd doubtless felt sorry for me back in prep school, since I wasn't anyone's idea of "most beautiful" or "most popular." She'd been the golden girl, the kind of woman every guy wanted to be with and every woman wanted to be; while I'd been gawky and more of a loner. I was the artsy kid, the one with glue in her finger-nails and paint in her hair.

I was still artsy.

Only, Miranda DuBois was hardly the golden girl anymore.

The woman was obviously in the midst of a meltdown, and could well have killed a woman had her aim been square. Assuming her driving would be equally erratic, I didn't want to be a party to the former Miss Dallas propelling her Jaguar off the road and into a tree.

So I retrieved her keys from the ignition—she'd left her car running right out front—and I handed them over to Delaney Armstrong, who promised to have someone drop the silver Jag off at Miranda's by morning.

Personally, I could not have cared less what happened to Miranda's fancy vehicle. My brain was still trying to wrap around the sight of my former classmate having a nervous breakdown in front of a dozen women who'd be on their cell phones all night, spreading the word about Miranda's messed-up face and lousy gun handling.

I assumed that Miranda had at least a few snooty friends among the party guests, and I expected one of them to step forward and assist the broken-down beauty queen. But when no one volunteered a shoulder for Miranda to lean on, I stupidly offered an ear and a Kleenex, reaffirming my title as "Collector of Strays."

I couldn't turn my back on a wounded creature, even the dumbest of the two-legged variety.

Besides, Miranda could hardly stand upright without assistance, much less drive a car, and her state of mind was too questionable to just stick her in the back of a taxi and send her off alone.

I figured that once I got her safely to her door, I'd call her mother. Or, rather, have my mother call her mother. Cissy had been pals with Deborah Santos since their own stint at Hockaday, many moons ago. Debbie had been married more times than Erica Kane on *All My Children*, but she'd always doted on her only daughter. In fact, when I'd exasperated Cissy, she used to sigh and say to me, "Why can't you be more like Miranda DuBois? That girl respects her mother."

Only I wasn't sure how to get in touch with Miranda's mummy, since she wasn't exactly listed in the yellow pages and more often than not was gallivanting around the globe to her villa on the Riviera or her palazzo on Lake Como or her beach house in Costa Rica.

I wanted to find her, though, if I could, as Miranda needed someone with her who truly cared . . . and who might possibly drop her off at her therapist's for a new Prozac prescription first thing in the morning. I'll warrant someone like Miranda had her shrink on speed dial. The bigger the ego, the more fragile the psyche, wasn't that how it went?

And Miranda's psyche had shattered tonight like Tiffany glass, scattering into a million sparkly pieces.

Following her bungled attempt to put a bullet in Dr. Sonja—or, at least, threaten her with a bullet—she'd dropped the gun, broken down in tears, and sobbed about Dr. Sonja ruining her life and her career.

When I came up off the floor after the gunshot, I'd seen little beyond Miranda's tragic figure kneeling in the midst of Delaney's living room, her head in her hands; the dozen women who'd taken refuge behind furniture emerging to surround her, all the while yammering like squawking geese.

I'd heard Delaney profusely apologizing to Dr. Sonja, who'd been busy herself, packing up her syringes and potions and lotions and vanishing with her hard-bodied sidekick before the air cleared.

One of the other guests must've removed the .22 during the melee, because it was no longer on the floor near Miranda by the time my reflexes kicked in and I went over to help her stand. I figured someone had snagged it for safekeeping, which wasn't a bad idea.

That was the first chance I'd had to get a good look at Miranda's tear-stained countenance. She was still slightly bruised and puffy around the eyes and mouth, but that wasn't the worst of it. Her left eye had a chronic tic, and her mouth drooped noticeably on one side.

No wonder she'd been off the air for a couple weeks. Anchor babes were required to look perfect, even if their male sidekicks had receding hairlines and age spots as big as Australia.

What exactly had happened to Miranda? I'd wondered. Were the ill effects permanent? Could she ever return to TV?

And was Dr. Sonja truly to blame?

If so, why didn't Miranda just sue her, instead of coming after her with a small caliber weapon in front of witnesses? For Pete's sake, people sued over coffee that was too hot. Having your face screwed up by a dermatologist who played God with people's exteriors would hardly be considered frivolous.

Still, we were in the great State of Texas, and some well-armed Texans thought with their trigger fingers instead of their common sense. Following that rationale, I could fathom why a beauty queen who'd lost that which was most precious to her—namely, her beauty—might go ballistic. It was the sort of scenario I could picture playing out in a TV reality show.

Only this was real life. Or as close to reality as life got in Big D.

Poor Miranda, I mused, as I glanced aside at the passenger seat of my Jeep, thankful to hear her loud snores, after listening to her cry for the first five minutes and moan about being too ugly to get a TV gig anywhere but Dog Bite, Alaska.

Was there really such a place?

Part of me had wanted to slap her, telling her she was lucky she had all her limbs and her senses (well, except the one that would've helped her out most about then, namely the common type), and that folks with eye tics and mouth droops could live perfectly normal lives.

Though I knew I'd be wasting my breath.

Thankfully, after she nodded off I didn't have to listen to her blubber about her disfigurement, nor did I need to make futile attempts at idle conversation. I mean, what did one talk about with a woman who'd just tried to shoot someone? Something like, "Hey, Miranda, did that OPI nail polish chip at all when you tried to mow down your dermatologist?" Or how about, "Is it harder to keep your balance when shooting a gun if you're wearing Jimmy Choos?"

Stop it Andy, I told myself.

I'm sure Miranda didn't find anything about this evening remotely amusing.

She looked almost angelic with her blond head tilted back, her mouth wide open, blissfully passed out.

I wondered if she'd even remember what she'd done in the morning.

At least she wouldn't be waking up in jail, I mused, figuring Miranda was lucky that Delaney Armstrong hadn't called the police, luckier still that Dr. Madhavi hadn't wanted to press charges, considering she'd been the target of Miranda's tiny black .22. The only real damage was to the frame of a Picasso print hanging above the fireplace mantel . . . and to Miranda's reputation.

Though I begged Janet Graham to be kind to Miranda in whatever ink she splashed across the *Park Cities Press*, I had no doubt my friend's mind was already at work, mentally penning a juicy column headlined in bold with something notorious, like: Pageant Princess Plugs Picasso at Pretty Party!

The rest of the party guests hadn't seemed frazzled so much as titillated.

If we were anywhere but Texas, the sight of a firearm might've inspired swoons and heart attacks, though I'd wager half the women in the room owned a pistol and knew how to use it. I knew for a fact that Delaney Armstrong used to go hunting with her daddy and had bagged a twelve-point buck when she was still in a training bra.

Carrying concealed was almost as common these days for Dallas ladies as carrying concealer. "Don't leave home without it" didn't mean your American Express card. No, siree, Bob. It meant your Smith & Wesson, baby.

Though I don't think I've ever been to a private party where anyone had been shot at before.

Oh, wait, except for Dina Willner's birthday in

fourth grade when her brother and his friends played Commando Ninjas and popped out of the bushes, tossing Japanese throwing stars at us girls as we rode in circles on rented ponies. I wasn't the only one who had emerged with at least one black eye.

Speaking of black eyes—the metaphorical kind—I gently shook Miranda's shoulder and told her, "Wake up, we're here."

She grunted, then let out a cat-sized yawn.

I had parked smack in front of Miranda's duplex, and noticed that the windows were lit and her garage door wide open. I wondered if she'd even had the presence of mind to lock up before she'd torn over to Delaney's and parked her Jaguar cock-eyed: half on the driveway and half on the lawn.

I found my answer soon enough, as I pried Miranda down from the Jeep's passenger seat and maneuvered her toward the door.

Funny how a 110-pound woman (max) could feel like a ton of bricks when you were propping up every ounce of her and dragging her forward. I wasn't sure I'd be able to get her inside without dropping her on the sidewalk, though somehow we made it.

Lo and behold, the front door wasn't locked—thank God, because I'd left Miranda's keys with Delaney—so I flung it wide and drew a staggering Miranda through it. I guessed the bedrooms were upstairs, but had no desire to push or pull Miranda up the steps.

So I propelled her as far as the powder-puff-pink

living room and plunked her down on the sofa, where she collapsed like a spineless jellyfish.

I eased off her pink blazer and propped her up with pillows, urging her to stay conscious until I could get her to swallow two aspirin and a little water. That had been the cure-all for hangovers during my college days, though I won't claim it was a sure-fire remedy. Besides, I didn't know how to make coffee, and I didn't figure that caffeine would be the best thing for Miranda at this point. I wanted her to sleep it off, not stay awake all night, beating herself up for losing it in front of a dozen of the Park Cities' mouthiest females.

When I was done with my Florence Nightingale routine, Miranda looked at me, her eyes fluttering—well, the one eye did that nervous tic—then grabbed my hand and started babbling.

"If I'd really wanted t'do it, I could have," she confessed, slurring the words, and I squatted down closer to listen. "I could've nailed her in the heart, if she had one." She paused to lick her lips, and I noticed again the droop of her mouth, like an upside-down sneer. "But I'm not gonna shoot bullets into her . . . or any of them. That's not how I wan' this to end." She laughed, but her eyes welled with tears. "How does that go, somethin' about how the truth will set you free? If I go down, I'm taking them with me. Then it'll be all over, Andy. And I mean, all over. You'll see."

"Shhh," I said. "Try to sleep, okay? You'll feel better in the morning."

My God, I sounded like my mother.

But she seemed to listen. She nodded groggily

and shut her eyes, pushing her cheek into the sofa pillow.

I did my best maternal act and pulled a fuzzy throw around her, jostling her laptop in the process and causing the screen to glow with a photograph of Miranda and some faceless dude in a big-time clench, the sun setting behind them so they were little more than dark silhouettes.

But will he still love her tomorrow? I mused as I put the computer in sleep mode, which turned the monitor black.

I went around dousing enough of the lights so Miranda could resume snoring. If she could sleep this one off until morning, it would be best for everyone.

After I'd waited all of fifteen seconds for her to drop off, I phoned my mother, hating to ask her for any kind of favor, even if it wasn't for me. It would mean that I owed her. And owing Cissy Blevins Kendricks was akin to indentured servitude. She'd call in her marker, and I'd end up peddling cookbooks in the Junior League's booth at their Christmas bazaar.

Again.

I sucked it up, regardless, and hit her number on my cell phone's speed dial.

She answered somewhat breathlessly after four absurdly long rings.

"Yes, yes, what is it?" came her familiar drawl, albeit sounding less than pleased to hear from me.

Heck, it was barely nine o'clock on a Friday night. Surely, I hadn't awakened her. What grown-up went to bed before the evening news on the weekend? Maybe she wasn't feeling well, I decided, though she'd looked just fine the other evening when Malone and I had gone out to dinner with her and Stephen— her former IRS agent and ex-Navy boyfriend.

"Mother? Are you all right?"

It sounded like she had to catch her breath before she told me, "Yes, dear, I'm fine and dandy. Just, ah, in the middle of something rather sticky."

"Is Stephen there?" I took a guess.

"Why, yes, he is," she said, and I heard a muffled noise (grunting?) on her end. "He's assisting me with this little, ah, project, as a matter of fact. Hang on a minute." The phone clattered, as if she'd dropped it, then I caught her advising, "Ah, no, no, darling, you're too far to the left. Move it more to the right. Oh, yes, yes, perfect . . . right there. Now hammer it home."

I couldn't help wincing. "Um, Mother?" I tried, but she wasn't listening.

"Yes, yes, that's it! Glorious!" she cooed to someone other than me.

What the heck was going on?

Heavens to Betsy, had my impeccably coiffed, Chanel-and-pearl-wearing mother just gotten down and dirty?

"Geez, um, you do sound busy, and I don't want to be a bother," I babbled, squishing my eyes closed to cleanse thoughts that had ventured into an icky place I didn't want to go. "If you're otherwise occupied, I can call back. . . ."

Because that's exactly what I wanted to do. One more of her double entendres and I'd never be able to look her or Stephen in the eye again without blushing.

"What?" she piped up, finally tuning back in. "Oh, no, sweet pea, we're almost done, although it was trickier than I'd imagined. I'm so out of practice, doing anything so hands-on." I winced, afraid to hear more, but Cissy continued. "Particularly since Stephen's drill ran out of juice, and he had to do the screwing manually—"

"Stop, please, stop," I begged, not even wanting to know what that meant, though wilting flowers and Viagra came suddenly to mind.

I plunked down into a puffy pink chair, feeling like I was drowning in a sea of Pepto-Bismol; though I could probably have used some to settle my queasy stomach. First, I'd had to endure the Gun Fight at the Botox Corral, and then I'd been forced to listen to my mother as she and Stephen reenacted an unedited sex scene from *Cocoon*?

Help me, Rhonda.

"Andrea, you sound odd, dear"—Cissy sounded more her normal self—"whatever's going on with you? Have you been drinking?"

Don't I wish.

I cleared my throat—and rid my head of the nightmarish vision—and managed to squeak out, "I just wanted to ask you a favor. You see, I'm at Miranda DuBois's duplex, and she's in bad shape after she fired a gun at Dr. Sonja over at Delaney Armstrong's, but if you and Stephen are busy—" Um, how did I put this? "—playing 'hide the monkey wrench,' I'll figure things out by myself."

"You're at Miranda DuBois's?" she asked, more akin to a gasp, as I imagined that was something she'd often wished to hear me say. She'd always wanted Miranda and me to be tight friends, the way that she and Miranda's mother were. "What do you mean she shot at Dr. Sonja at Delaney's? Did Delaney leave her off the guest list? Hell hath no fury like a woman snubbed."

Close, but no cigar.

I sighed, about to explain further, when Mother sputtered out another question.

"Did you say 'hide the monkey wrench'? For heaven's sake." She made those *tsk-tsk* noises that every mother does so well. "If you're implying that Stephen and I were engaging in an act of intimacy when you called, you're way out of line."

"But—" I started, wanting to add, *You were the one babbling about Stephen's drill and manually screwing*. But she didn't let me finish.

"Goodness gracious, he was helping me put up a new curtain rod in the sun room, but his drill broke and he had to use the Phillips," she explained, and not sounding at all happy at having to do it. "You young people today"—she sighed—"you have such one-track minds. Too much smut on MTV."

"I don't even watch MTV," I said in my own defense, wanting desperately to get off the subject of rods and drills altogether. "Miranda DuBois," I reminded her. "She's passed out drunk and all alone, and I don't want to leave her, not after the episode at Delaney's. I was hoping you could phone her mother and get her over here. . . ."

"No can do," Cissy said in Southern singsong.

No can do?

Those were words I didn't often hear from Her Highness of Highland Park, the woman I always thought could do *anything*. Was she being snippy because I'd jumped to the conclusion that she and Stephen had been canoodling?

"Mother, if you don't want to help, just say so," I ran off at the mouth, my cheeks flushed. "I'll phone Mrs. Santos myself."

"Oh, no, you won't," Cissy said, "because she's not home. She's not even in the country. Debbie's in Brazil, incommunicado, taking a two-month vacation. She's at Club Suture. She needed some time to relax in the sun."

Ah, Club Suture.

The code for "having some work done."

'Tis the season, I mused.

And Brazil was a hot spot for those wanting a face-lift, liposuction, rhinoplasty, or boob job on the QT. It ranked up there with Dallas and L.A., vying for rights to the title of "Plastic Surgery Capital of the World."

If you were lucky, your Brazilian surgeon would give you a face-lift for half the cost of having it done in Big D; then he'd arrange for you to recuperate for a month afterward at a spa on a beach without the noise of TVs, laptops, or phones, being waited on hand and foot by dark-skinned boys in Speedo bikinis.

Those South Americans knew how to do it up right, I decided. If I were wrapped in gauze from head to toe, drinking liquid meals through a straw and too bruised to move, I'd at least want something nice to look at through my swollen peepers.

"Why don't you call one of Miranda's friends?" my mother suggested, and I groaned.

"That'd be great, if she had any pals after tonight," I said. "No one wanted anything to do with her after she took a potshot at Dr. Sonja and hit the Picasso instead. What's even more shocking is that Miranda's not sleeping it off in a jail cell."

"Oh, dear, yes, she's very fortunate indeed"— my mother sniffed—"if anyone had put a bullet in my Picasso I'd have them arrested in a blink. Unless it was one of his napkin doodles, which aren't worth the price of framing, if you ask me."

Which I hadn't.

"It wasn't a napkin doodle, and besides, it only damaged the frame. The sketch is just fine," I said, and realized I was basically making excuses for a crazy woman whom I'd never even liked. Ah, well, someone had to do it, right? "I don't imagine anyone really believes Miranda wanted to kill the good doctor." Not on purpose, anyway. "She just needed to release some steam."

Some people did yoga. Some got drunk and threatened their cosmetic dermatologists with loaded .22s.

"Why don't you stay with her, Andrea?" the Ann Landers of Beverly Drive advised, and I sat upright in the pink seat, about to howl in protest. Before I had a chance to put the kibosh on that swell idea, she continued, "Or better yet, bring her here. Sandy and I can look out after her, at least for one night. The poor girl sounds like she could use a little mothering."

Smothering sounded more like it.

Sandy Beck was my mother's personal secretary and had been with her for as long as I'd been alive. Sandy had her own suite in the house on Beverly and pretty much supervised operations there, and I knew Cissy would rather die than do without her. As would I, since Sandy was as much a part of my family as any blood relation.

Miranda might benefit from Sandy's homemade pancakes in the morning; if she could keep them down.

"Stephen's just about finished with the rod, and then he's leaving, so anytime you want to come by with Miranda is fine. So long as it's soon. I'll likely make it through the ten o'clock news and then it's lights out."

It was a lovely idea and very generous, and I nearly accepted, just to give her a kick. More often than not her cockamamie schemes had me rolling my eyes. Well, come on now, who would've ever truly thought that cockroach races would be such a hit as a fund-raiser? Okay, besides the Orkin man, waiting at the finish line.

Only I couldn't imagine how I'd get Miranda back into the Jeep, when it had taken every ounce of strength I had to bring her inside.

Oy.

So I weighed Cissy's suggestion, making a decision fairly quickly.

Miranda wasn't going anywhere.

Really, she wasn't.

She was passed out, drooling on the sofa cushion, dead to the world.

Did she truly require adult supervision while she slept?

Because I'd rather bunk with Brian Malone if I had a choice. We didn't spend nearly enough time together as it was, and each moment we could was too precious to squander, particularly on a woman who was more longtime acquaintance than lifelong pal. I didn't feel like I owed Miranda any more than a safe ride home and a few kind words, or was that selfish of me?

"Andrea, dearest, I'm sure Miranda will be perfectly safe in her own home," my mother assured me, echoing my own thoughts.

So that settled it.

"She's definitely out cold," I said, "and I figure she'll stay that way for a good eight hours. I'll make sure the doors are locked then I'm heading to the condo. Oh," I added, "thanks for the nice offer, though."

"You're welcome, sweet pea."

Miranda let loose a few rip-roaring snorts and curled into the fetal position beneath the fuzzy afghan, and I added, "I'll come by and check on her first thing in the morning."

"How did you ever get so soft-hearted, Andrea, really?" But it was said with kindness, uttered gently.

"I must've inherited that from my mother," I quipped, hearing her laughter before I told her "Good-bye" and hung up.

It was nine-thirty, I realized, looking at the time on my cell before I stowed it away inside my purse. I had no reason to linger, did I? Not with Miranda snoring on the sofa, looking peaceful as a baby.

I did a quick tour of the first floor, jiggling all the doorknobs and giving the windows the once-over to make sure the house was secure. I shut off all but the kitchen lights, leaving Miranda a note on the granite counter, telling her I'd be back tomorrow and asking her to call my cell if she woke up alone and wanted someone to talk to (since she likely wouldn't be able to ring her mother in Brazil).

Then I let myself out, making sure the lock on the knob clicked, as I had no key to turn the dead bolt. I gave the duplex once last glance, telling myself Miranda would be just fine. I highly doubted she'd take another potshot at Dr. Sonja that night. She didn't even have her gun, right?

So what could possibly go wrong?

Feeling better at the thought, I started up the Jeep and drove home, to my own bed, and to Malone.

Chapter 3

 It wasn't the sun that woke me, nor an alarm clock, just a heavy sense of obligation knotted in my gut.

After I'd forced my mind awake, I remembered what that obligation was.

Miranda DuBois.

I closed my eyes again, wishing I could forget.

Because, really, did I *want* to get up first thing on a Saturday morning to head back to Miranda DuBois's place, when I could have stayed beneath the covers snuggled up beside my sweetie, listening to the rhythmic sound of his breathing and thinking how earnest he looked with his eyes closed and lips parted, brown hair tousled around his sleeping face?

If I answered "Hell, no," would that sound shocking?

Did that make me suddenly coldhearted and

less the compassionate marshmallow who rescued stray pets and gun-toting beauty queens?

If it did, it was way too early in the day—and I was way too crabby—to worry.

With a grunt, I swung my legs to the side of the bed and deposited my bare feet on the floor, shuffling groggily toward the bathroom.

I hurriedly pulled myself together, nixing a shower and slipping into my sweats. I brushed my hair, scrubbed my face, and put in contacts so I could see a fair piece beyond my nose.

After I'd tracked down my keys and grabbed my cell, I was ready to go. Five minutes in all, and I hadn't woken up Malone.

Not bad.

I thought about writing Brian a note, but figured I'd be back before he cracked a lid. Heck, it was just 7:30 A.M., according to the mantel clock, an ungodly hour for normal folks to get up on a weekend. He'd had a deposition until fairly late last night—which is why I'd gone out with Janet—and needed all the shut-eye he could get.

If I was lucky, I could crawl back in bed with him and catch a few more winks myself after I'd run this morning's errand.

Once in the Jeep, I turned on the radio to wake myself up, yawning all the while. I passed a smattering of other cars on my way south to Miranda's—and my mother's—turf of Highland Park. Correction: they weren't cars so much as those Urban Assault Vehicles, as Malone liked to call them; mammoth SUVs that guzzled gas and usually had only one occupant instead of the armies they could hold.

I missed the good old days, when cars were cars, and my Wrangler could see over all of them.

As the sun teased the treetops, sending dappled light dancing off my windshield, I tried to better my frame of mind, not wanting my trudge down to the Park Cities to muddy the rest of my day.

So I focused on the pleasant things: the colorful mums and petunias planted along the landscape; the plentiful garage sale signs; and the slow turn of leaves from green to reds and umbers. I even cracked my window to allow in the early November air. Crisp enough to warrant a sweatshirt, but not downright chilly. The kind of weather I loved best and didn't get for long in Texas. Even less these days with global warming threatening to drag our Indian summers into winter.

The joggers and dog walkers were out in full force, and all seemed rather ordinary for a typical Saturday morning.

And that was fine with me.

I had enough craziness in my life to appreciate the quiet when I could find it, which was never enough. Maybe it just had to do with getting older, but I dwelled less on grandiose dreams and more on the here and now: on the people I loved who loved me back, on doing what made me happy. The rest was like fat on a T-bone. It might give the meat flavor, but you weren't missing squat when you cut it away.

I was singing along—loudly and out of tune— with Geddy Lee and Rush as I neared the Dallas

Country Club. Miranda's place wasn't far, though it might take a bit longer to get there than I'd imagined.

Spotting congestion ahead, I slowed the Jeep to a crawl. From the look of things, there'd been an accident, as several Highland Park police cars sat cattywampus on the street, bubble lights rolling.

Had a pedestrian been struck? Or had someone's pet run into traffic and gotten clobbered by the grill of a Beemer?

Ugh.

My voice caught in my throat, putting an end to my dreadful rendition of "Fly by Night," and I switched the radio off.

People drove so damned fast these days, and those humongous SUVs plowed through neighborhoods like tanks. It was even worse when the driver from Hell had a cell phone in one hand and an Evian in the other.

Yeesh.

Rolling the window all the way down, I stuck my head out to better see. I didn't spot an ambulance or fire truck, so I hoped whatever had happened wasn't fatal.

Cars approaching from both directions stopped at the bottleneck, though a gesticulating cop did his darnedest to keep traffic moving.

I figured it wouldn't do much good to try to drive any closer to Miranda's. So I aimed for a place on a side street, doing a passable job parallel parking the Jeep. Walking a few blocks would hardly kill me.

My cell and keys squirreled away in the pockets of my zip-up sweatshirt, I headed toward the police cars, noting how neighbors had begun to congregate on the lawn in front of Miranda's duplex.

What the devil was going on? I wondered, picking up my pace.

My stomach pitched as I had a terrible thought: Dr. Sonja had decided to press charges after all, and the police had trotted over bright and early to make an arrest.

And, selfish me, I'd ditched a depressed and boozed-up Miranda, leaving her to fend for herself.

Oy vey.

Talk about guilt.

If I'd felt any more like a heel, I'd have been glued to the sole of one of Mother's Stuart Weitzmans.

I quickened my steps, imagining the cops were about to drag Miranda down to the station to book her for attempted murder, or at least aggravated assault on a Picasso.

I prayed that wasn't it. Miranda DuBois was tough, but she was no Martha Stewart. She'd been raised on Egyptian cotton sheets, weekly mani/pedis, and five course meals. She couldn't survive two weeks in Camp Cupcake, much less a life sentence in maximum security.

Another thought came to mind, and I glanced toward the curb and then the driveway alongside the duplex; but I saw no sign of Miranda's Jaguar.

I almost wished it had been there, maybe backed into a tree. Though I guessed Delaney Armstrong hadn't had the chance to send a lackey over with it yet. Delaney probably didn't awaken at seven-thirty on weekdays much less the weekend.

Rats, I mused, my hopes dashed, as I preferred to think a hung over Miranda had banged up her pricey automobile en route to Starbucks for her morning coffee as opposed to imagining her posing for her mug shot.

When I reached the sidewalk in front of the duplex, I forced my way between a white-haired man holding tight to a wriggling beagle and a woman in black Lycra with an iPod Nano banded to her forearm and tiny earphones looped around her neck.

From there I could see the door of Miranda's duplex standing wide open and uniformed officers moving in and out.

Uh-oh popped into my brain. Something clearly wasn't right.

I wondered where Miranda was and if she was scared out of whatever wits she had left.

"What's with the swarm of blue?" I asked, feeling like I'd wandered into a play where everyone knew the plot but me.

"I dunno," Beagle Man offered. "I was out walking Waldo when I heard the sirens, but I haven't seen anyone come out of the place. I'm betting it's a burglary. We've had a few too many of 'em in these parts the past few weeks."

Burglary?

So all this brouhaha might be because a thief had broken into the duplex and made off with an armload of rhinestone tiaras while Miranda slept off the gin? Was I warped because that sounded

better than picturing Hockaday's "Most Likely
to Shag Johnny Depp"—well, the title was unof-
ficial—in prison stripes?

Call me a fair weather friend.

"Is Miranda okay?" I finally asked the pair on
my either side, having seen no sign of Miranda.

"Who's that?" Beagle Dude looked puzzled.

You mean there was an actual living and breathing male who didn't watch "Five at Five"—the
Channel 5 News at five o'clock—so he could check
out the low-cut blouses that showcased Miranda's
infamous bosom?

God bless the ignorant.

"Miranda DuBois. She lives there." I pointed at
the open doorway, just as a familiar face appeared
and glanced out.

The woman didn't appear to notice me, but I
recognized her quickly enough. She had the same
salt-and-pepper hair cut boyishly short and wore
a blue uniform and badge with a small brass name
tag that read: DEPUTY DEAN.

Anna Dean, to be precise, deputy chief of the
Highland Park police.

My throat closed up and a shiver zipped up my
spine.

The last time I saw Deputy Dean was at my
mother's house, when a woman lay dead on Cissy's
Persian carpet.

Had death brought Deputy Dean to the duplex?

If so, I wished I'd stayed in bed.

Death wasn't one of my favorite things to deal
with, not first thing in the morning, and definitely
not if it meant Miranda had been in jeopardy.

"Excuse me," I said, my heartbeat twanging as I drew away from Beagle Man and Lycra Woman as the latter was explaining to the former, "Miranda DuBois's the gal on the Channel 5 News who looks like that old movie star, only more stacked. . . ."

"Ava Gardner?"

"No, the blonde . . . you know, Grace Kelly."

Their voices trickled off as I carefully picked my way toward the front stoop, where Anna Dean stood talking to a younger woman in uniform. Until I got nearer, I hadn't discerned that both had on latex gloves and plastic booties over their ugly regulation shoes.

That didn't bode well, did it?

"The M.E. should be here any minute," I heard one of them saying as I approached, but my head was too fuzzy to separate the low drawl of one from the other. I knew what M.E. meant—the county medical examiner—and it made my palms go clammy.

If Beagle Man was right about a burglary, maybe Miranda had awakened while the thief was still inside her duplex. Had they tangled? Had one of them been mortally wounded in the struggle?

Were that the case, I only hoped the burglar got the worst of it and not Miranda.

The very idea was far too depressing to dwell on.

Letting my imagination run amok wasn't helping. If I wanted the dope, I'd have to get it from the source.

Which is why I stopped several feet short of the front stoop and the pair of uniformed females and cleared the cotton from my throat before I croaked, "Deputy Dean?"

She turned abruptly, wearing an expression of displeasure at being so rudely interrupted.

I could tell she didn't recognize me at first, probably because I was alone and not with Cissy. Mother and I made such a memorable mismatched set.

"You shouldn't be here, ma'am," the younger cop piped up, and hopped down from the stoop, thumbs hooked in her utility belt. "We'll need you to stand back there on the sidewalk with the rest of the folks. Can't have you contaminating the scene."

The scene?

So it was officially a "crime scene," or some version thereof?

Yowza.

I told myself that could mean many things, like the site of a robbery or a burglary or vandalism. It didn't have to mean *homicide.*

Did it?

I told myself not to panic.

"Is Miranda all right?" I asked, for the second time in the past five minutes, though all it earned me was a pair of disapproving glares.

The younger cop tried again, "Ma'am, if you'd please move to the sidewalk, like I asked—"

"I'm Andrea Kendricks. I'm a friend of Miranda DuBois," I said in a rush, though calling myself Miranda's "friend" was a wee exaggeration. "I was here last night. I dropped her off after a party," I went on, directing my rambling at the deputy chief and ignoring the ponytailed officer who was trying her damnedest to shoo me off like a horsefly.

I was about to explain about a less than sober Miranda crashing Dr. Sonja's collagen-fest at Delaney Armstrong's when Deputy Chief Dean put a hand up and stopped me.

"I know who you are, Ms. Kendricks, and I'd like you to come inside with me, please. I have a few questions to ask you about your final moments with Ms. DuBois."

Well, huh. That didn't sound good.

My stomach clenched. "Questions for me . . . my final moments with Ms. DuBois . . . come inside with you"—I stumbled over my tongue, repeating her words like an autistic parrot. My feet felt frozen to the stoop.

"So you're Andy?" The young ponytailed officer stared at me, her nearly browless eyes assessing, as if I were suddenly far more interesting than I'd been just a moment before.

I didn't like how she said my name. Didn't like it a bit.

I wet my lips and dared to ask again, "Is Miranda all right?" My gaze swung back and forth between both women in blue, though neither did more than give me a purse-lipped look that surely boded ill. "What's going on? Does she need a doctor?" I frantically spun my mental Rolodex. "Or an attorney?"

I could get either for her in a jiff, particularly the latter, since I knew a defense attorney who happened to be sleeping in my bed at that very moment.

"Officer Danforth, would you tell the M.E. to hightail it in as soon as he arrives," the deputy chief said, rather than answer my question.

Her subordinate nodded, giving a crisp, "Yes, ma'am," before heading toward the street to scout for the medical examiner's van.

"You, Ms. Kendricks, follow me," Anna Dean said, in the same tone of voice my mother used when she meant serious business.

Could you blame me for dragging my heels?

"I don't want to contaminate the, um, scene," I told her, because I didn't have plastic booties on over my sneakers . . . and I didn't want to squish through anything that shouldn't be squished.

She almost smiled at me. "You'll be fine. We'll keep our distance," she said, and I wasn't sure yet what we'd be keeping our distance from.

Whatever it was, I felt very uneasy.

I still hadn't glimpsed Miranda.

And no one seemed willing to tell me if she was okay or not.

My daddy had always told me not to jump ahead of myself, so I was trying hard not to; but I couldn't help but wonder.

And worry.

She jerked her chin toward the door. "This way, please."

I took a tentative step behind her, into the tiny pink foyer I'd passed through last night when Miranda had been leaning so heavily on my shoulder I thought she'd take us both down. Instead of leading me forward into the living room where

I'd left Miranda sleeping on the couch, the deputy chief took a hard right, into the kitchen.

She gestured at a bar stool surrounding the granite-topped center island, and I went straight to it and sat down.

Rather than take a seat herself, she rounded the island and stood on its other side.

She picked up something with her latex-gloved fingers, and I swallowed hard when I saw what it was.

The note I'd scribbled to Miranda before I left, the one asking her to call if she awakened and needed something.

"You wrote this?" Deputy Chief Dean asked.

I clasped trembling hands in my lap. "Yes," I said.

"We were just about to dial that cell number when you showed up," she told me. "You may be as close to a witness as we've got."

A witness?

To what? I wondered.

But I had a more important thing to ask. I tried again, "Is Miranda all right? She didn't hurt anyone, did she?"

"Hurt anyone?" Anna Dean's eyebrows peaked, and I bit my lip. "Why would you think that, Ms. Kendricks?"

"Well, um, because—" I wasn't sure what to say. I didn't know what I'd walked into, and no one was filling in any gaps. If there was the slightest chance Miranda had done something horrible after I'd dumped her on the sofa because I preferred spending the night with my boyfriend to babysitting a thirty-one-year-old woman, I would never forgive myself.

Ever.

"Because what?" Deputy Dean prodded.

For a split second I came closer still to blurting out what happened at the Pretty Party, because I figured Anna Dean would find out soon enough, if she didn't know already. And if she didn't yet, heck, when the latest edition of the *Park Cities Press* hit the newsstands and subscribers' mailboxes later in the day, the cat would be so far out of the bag ain't nobody could catch it.

"Andrea, please, whatever you can tell me about Miranda's whereabouts last evening, the more you'll help us all," the older woman said, her voice softening, obviously using my first name to establish a connection with me, to entice me to confide in her; to make me crack.

It worked like a charm.

I couldn't stand the pressure.

Raising my gaze, I looked the gray-haired deputy chief directly in the eye and said, "Miranda was pretty upset last night. She crashed a gathering at Delaney Armstrong's place on Bordeaux." And I wouldn't have been there had Janet not tricked me into accompanying her. "I hadn't seen Miranda all that much since Hockaday. Then, all of a sudden, she came barreling through the door and nearly knocked me over." Which is when I'd smelled the alcohol on her, but I didn't mention that part. "By the time I got to the living room, she was threatening Dr. Sonja."

"Dr. Sonja Madhavi?"

"Yes." I had to swallow hard to get enough spit to continue. "Miranda was sobbing, saying her career was over and that it was all Dr. Madhavi's fault. Then she pointed a gun at the doctor and fired"—ah, hell, I let it all spill, even though doing so made me queasy, like I was betraying Miranda—"but her aim was way off, and she nicked the frame of a Picasso hanging over the fireplace."

My voice wobbled as I finished, "I don't exactly know Miranda well, Deputy Chief, at least not anymore. Our mothers used to set us up for play dates when we were little"—though Miranda used to delight in bulldozing the castles I made in the sandbox—"and we both attended the same prep school, but we hardly stayed in touch. Still, I don't think she intended to kill anyone. She's a pageant girl, you know. If they want to dust someone, they have their mamas hire a hit man." I flashed a shaky grin, so she'd see I was kidding (although it *had* happened once that I knew of).

Only she didn't laugh.

She didn't even grimace.

I swallowed again, my smile gone. "Miranda . . . is she in trouble? Someone from the party pressed charges, is that it?"

"No," Deputy Dean said, solemn as a grave digger.

No? Oh, well, then.

"Did she try to stop a burglar?" I asked, my voice seeming to echo in my skull. "The man outside with the beagle said there've been lots of break-ins in the area lately, so I thought maybe she woke up and found someone here. . . ."

"No." Deputy Dean shook her head and sighed. "No, Andy, Miranda DuBois didn't encounter an intruder, not that we're aware of."

"If there wasn't a burglary, and Dr. Sonja didn't press charges, then why all the fuss—" I started to ask, because it made no sense if this place were a crime scene and no one had even been injured.

So what was going on?

Wait a minute.

The gears finally clicked.

I heard Miranda's voice, soft and slurred, whispering: *That's not how I wan' this to end. How does that go, something about how the truth will set you free? That's what'll happen, you know. Then it'll be all over.*

Her final words to me.

I hadn't thought much about them until now, hadn't dwelled on what they meant.

How I want this to end . . . truth will set you free . . . it'll be all over.

"She didn't hurt herself, did she?" I blurted, and looked at Anna Dean, looked as hard as I could, at the same time scared to death I'd see the truth in her eyes. "She didn't—"

I couldn't finish.

Couldn't bring myself to say *kill herself.*

I didn't need to.

The answer was written all over Deputy Dean's grim face.

"I'm sorry, Ms. Kendricks."

I stared at the note in the Baggie until my eyes blurred, and I wondered, if I hadn't taken off last night, would Miranda still be alive?

Chapter 4

 Miranda DuBois had committed suicide?
No way.
No how.
How could that be?

I was with her, saw her snoring on the sofa, barely ten hours before. I wouldn't exactly have called her "perky" or "exuberant," but I never for a moment thought she might take her own life.

I wouldn't have deserted her if I had, not even for Brian.

"Tell me more about last night," Deputy Anna Dean prodded as I sat on the kitchen stool, wringing my hands the way a cleaning woman with OCD would wring a dirty mop. Over and over and over. "Why did Miranda show up at Delaney Armstrong's house? Did she know Dr. Madhavi would be there?"

I wasn't an expert on the Pretty Party circuit,

by any means, but I did know they operated a lot like the cookware parties, the candle parties, the lingerie parties, the sex toy parties, the whatever-the-latest-fad-was parties, ad nauseam (make that, *nausea*). A hostess sponsored the event at her home, invited a dozen of her closest friends, then the doctor showed up with her assistant and a slew of potions and lotions available for purchase on the spot. Dr. Sonja also gave "sample" injections on the house, sort of like door prizes with the object of getting the women hooked so they'd schedule serial appointments to stay wrinkle-free.

The deputy chief listened intently until I was done, at which point she drew out a notebook, flipped it to a clean page and aimed her ballpoint pen at the first line.

"Can you tell me who was at the party, Andy?"

My throat felt so dry I had to swallow a few times to moisten my mouth enough to continue. I then proceeded to spill the names of the dozen or so who'd attended, including myself, Janet Graham, Delaney Armstrong (since it was her place), Dr. Sonja, and the dermo's buff assistant, a blond dude with trim mustache and unbelievable biceps. I didn't know his full name, but I'd heard him called "Lance," as in, "Pack up my stuff, Lance, and let's get the hell out of here!"

Deputy Dean's pen didn't pause until she'd finished making a list. Then she quizzed me about Miranda's face. "She told you Dr. Sonja gave her injections that had disfigured her?"

Um, she'd told the whole Pretty Party that, basically, with that *you stinking quack, you ruined my face* line.

But I put it more simply to the deputy chief. "I clearly got the message she believed Dr. Sonja's injections had caused her eye to twitch and her mouth to droop. She'd been off the air for three weeks because of it. She assumed her career was over, because the damage didn't appear to be going away."

"She wanted revenge?"

"I guess so." What was it Miranda had said to me? Something about the truth setting her free and bringing them all down with her. I'd *assumed* she had plans for revenge, as any good pageant girl would, but had she meant she'd put a pox on the good doctor's practice by killing herself and smearing Madhavi's name instead?

My mind was too confused—none of it made any sense.

I flashed back to a moment from childhood when Mother had dragged me to the Miss Tiny Texas pageant, or some such nonsensical thing, in order to see a pint-sized Miranda take runner-up in the contest, something she didn't cotton to very well. Instead, she'd let out a plaintive howl and ripped the winner's sash off her wee shoulders, declaring, "It's mine, it's mine, it's mine."

I'd never thought of Miranda DuBois as someone who gave up easily. She'd always had such a fight in her.

"This is crazy," I whispered, and Anna Dean looked up from the notebook she'd been writing in.

"Did you say something, Andy?"

I bit my lip, shaking my head.

She moved on to her next question: "So you ended up driving Ms. DuBois home from the party? She was incapable of driving herself? Why was that?"

"She was drunk," I said, deciding there was no reason to lie. I did leave out the fact that Miranda had reeked like she'd bathed in gin, as if she'd been drinking for hours beforehand. Why slander a dead woman?

"You left her car there?"

"Yes, and her keys," I told Anna Dean. "Delaney swore she'd have someone bring the Jag over today. I hadn't considered that we might not get into Miranda's place. But when we pulled up, the front door was unlocked and the garage door was open. Though I made sure everything was shut tight before I took off."

"What about her gun? Did you see it?"

"Her gun?"

"Did she have it with her when you brought her home? As in, on her person," the deputy chief clarified.

That one I could answer with a good dose of certainty. "No, Miranda was unarmed when I packed her into the Jeep."

Like, I would've given her a lift if she'd been drunkenly waving her .22.

Right.

"Are you sure?" Anna Dean didn't look at all pleased with my response.

"Without a doubt," I told her, because I knew I

was telling the truth. "At the party, someone else picked up the gun after Miranda dropped it."

The policewoman didn't take a breath before pouncing on that one.

"Who picked it up, Andy?"

"One of the other guests, I assume, or maybe Delaney since it was her house. I don't know." I shrugged. "All I know is Miranda didn't take it."

"But you didn't see who retrieved it?"

Um, that was kinda like asking if Dorothy recalled all the bits of debris blown around by the twister.

"It was awfully chaotic at the time," I explained, picturing the crazed crowd of people in Delaney's living room after the shot rang out. "All I remember is trying to help Miranda up and noticing that the gun was gone. Someone else must have grabbed it."

Someone other than Miranda.

"So you're saying unequivocally that Miranda DuBois didn't pocket her own gun?" Anna Dean came at me from a different angle. "You'd be willing to make a formal statement to that effect?"

Man, she was nothing if not persistent.

I was sure, yeah.

But was I *unequivocally* sure?

Enough to swear to it in a police report?

Gulp.

Miranda hadn't exactly been wearing a muumuu, seeing as how she'd had on skintight jeans and a T-shirt with a bright pink blazer. I'd skimmed the blazer off her shoulders before she sprawled out on her couch, and it wasn't like her gun had fallen out of a pocket; because it hadn't.

But was I one hundred percent positive without a reasonable doubt, not even a teensy-weensy ounce of "maybe"?

I sighed. "I guess I can't be certain, no. Not a hundred percent."

Even ninety-nine percent sure left one percent wiggle room.

"Thank you for your honesty, Andy." The deputy chief gleamed approval at me as she squared her shoulders and scribbled down another note.

Why so much interest in Miranda's .22?

It wasn't like she'd done any damage with it except to Delaney's artwork, though Anna Dean seemed to be trying awfully hard to put Miranda's gun back here, at the duplex, after the Pretty Party.

Oh, crud.

Deputy Dean's insinuations smacked me upside the head.

Call me dense, but, by George, I think I finally got it.

"Is that what killed her?" I ventured to ask, my voice meek as a mouse. "She was shot with her own gun?"

"I'll let the M.E. determine cause of death, if that's all right with you, Andy, and then we'll know more," was all the deputy chief would offer. "I don't want any misinformation leaking to the press prematurely."

I'd take that as a yes.

I didn't say it, but I was thinking it.

The instrument of death must've been Miranda's own gun.

"Who found her?" I asked, because it seemed benign enough, and I was wondering whether if I'd arrived any earlier, would it have been me.

The deputy chief blew out her cheeks, obviously mulling over what she wanted to share with me. "The woman who lives in the duplex next door heard noises in the early hours of the morning."

"What kind of noises?"

"A woman's raised voice and then a pop, like a door slamming. She said it wasn't the first time she'd been awakened by sounds coming from next door. Ms. DuBois could apparently throw quite the temper tantrum," the policewoman explained. "So Mrs. Cameron assumed it was nothing and went back to sleep."

Of course she had.

This was Highland Park.

No one woke to noises and assumed something nefarious was going on next door. Any thumps in the night were likely caused by the hired help sneaking leftover tiramisu from the fridge, spoiled teens without curfews slipping in the back door, or a restless ghost.

"Around 6:00 A.M., Mrs. Cameron went outside to retrieve her newspaper," Anna Dean went on, "and she noticed the front door to Ms. DuBois's duplex was ajar . . . "

Ajar?

"But . . . " I'd shut and locked it when I'd taken off. I'd double-checked to make sure, even though I hadn't closed the dead bolt because I didn't have the key. Had Miranda gotten up sometime during the night and wandered out? Or, perhaps, let someone in? She'd been so zonked out when I'd departed that either seemed unlikely.

" . . . Mrs. Cameron knocked at first then let herself in, sensing something was wrong. She discovered Ms. DuBois on the living room sofa."

Right where I'd left her.

So, a nearly comatose Miranda had awakened from a drunken stupor, unlocked and opened the front door, before lying back down on the sofa to kill herself?

"That can't be right—" I started to protest, but Anna Dean didn't seem inclined to listen to my protests.

Maybe she was used to those around the victim saying, *No, that couldn't have happened. She wouldn't have gone there, done that.*

I wet my lips, moving in a different direction, figuring there was surely one thing that would prove one of us right and the other wrong. "Did she leave a note?"

"We haven't found one, no. But we did find this." Deputy Dean produced another plastic bag, sliding it across the counter.

The paper within the bag was crumpled, but not so I couldn't read it.

Due to your current unfortunate circumstances, your membership in the Caviar Club has been revoked. We wish you luck in your recuperation. Should your situation improve, please reapply, and we will give your application our prompt attention.

"Do you know what the Caviar Club is?" she asked, and I shook my head.

"No." I'd never heard of it, though it sounded like any one of innumerable private cliques around the city, part of why I liked staying out of the world of the Dallas glitterati. The games they played made my head hurt. And this one apparently didn't want a member who had an eye tic or a droopy mouth.

"Could be a wine- or food-tasting club," I said, the best guess I could offer. "Those are popular. But why would they kick her out just because she had an eye twitch and a sneer?"

"Whatever it is, rejection can be killer," Anna Dean said soberly, and I silently concurred.

Too many women these days sought acceptance in places they shouldn't; and, when they didn't get it, life seemed hopeless.

Had Miranda's botched injections made her feel like her life was over? Had she made a middle-of-the-night snap decision to forego retaliation and book a stay six feet under?

You *could* be too rich or too thin, I thought. Or too pretty.

I sighed, passing the plastic-encased note back to the deputy chief. I mumbled an apology, wishing I knew more, wanting so much to shed light on what had happened; but I was just as confused as she was about Miranda DuBois's final moments.

"Did you check her computer?" I asked, as it had been sitting right there on the coffee table near the sofa. "Maybe Miranda left some kind of message on it."

Deputy Dean squished up her forehead. "What computer, Andy?"

"Her laptop," I said. "It was in the living room. I turned it to sleep mode before I left because the screen was so bright."

The deputy chief fairly squinted at me. "There was no laptop in there, Andy. Perhaps she put it away after you left. We'll look around."

I suddenly thought of something else. "Did you check her phone for the last number dialed?" I asked. I just couldn't fathom Miranda pulling her own plug without reaching out to someone. Like her mother. They'd always been so tight. "Maybe she tried to call someone."

"We're still looking for her cell phone."

No laptop or cell?

"That's odd," I said, because it was. "And you don't think she was burgled?"

Deputy Dean looked affronted. "The house appears neat and intact, but we're being very thorough, rest assured of that. And if you don't mind"—her voice turned impatient—"how about you leave the questions to me?"

I shut up, my cheeks no doubt a warm shade of pink.

"All right, then"—her calm restored, she continued the grilling—"what time did you leave?"

I squeezed my eyes shut, warding off a vaguely woozy sensation, then forced myself to look directly at the policewoman, wanting desperately to emulate her cool exterior and feeling anything but. In fact, I was feeling downright nauseous.

"It was around nine-thirty." My mouth tasted

funny, as if I'd swallowed old mothballs. "I spoke to Mother on my cell first. Cissy Kendricks of Beverly Drive," I clarified. "I can give you her number if you want to double-check with her. I'm sure she knows exactly how long we talked. She was, um, in the middle of something, and I interrupted her."

"Oh, I've got Cissy's number," she said.

I would've laughed under any other circumstance. Instead, I laced my fingers together to steady them and nodded. "Of course you do." I remembered then that my mother and Anna Dean had cause to connect, beyond the dead body in the living room. Cissy had joined the deputy chief in chairing the most recent Widows and Orphans fund-raiser.

"Go on, Andy," Deputy Dean's firm voice nudged. "What happened after you hung up with your mother?"

"Yeah, after." I cleared my throat. "I took off for home about five minutes later, once I was sure Miranda was fast asleep and locked in." I turned my hands palms up on the granite island. "That was it, really. I didn't hear from Miranda, so I figured she'd slept through the night. I came back this morning to see if she was okay." Despite myself, tears welled, and I sniffled. "I should never have left her alone, should I?"

But Anna Dean obviously didn't have any comforting words to offer. I doubted anyone could say anything that would make me feel better about this.

"When you talked to your mother, did you

mention to her where you were? Who you were with?" she quizzed.

"Yes." My head bobbed. "I'd called to ask for help. Cissy's lifelong friends with Miranda's mother, Debbie Santos, and I thought Cissy might phone Mrs. Santos and let her know how upset Miranda was. I thought she might need someone with her to support her, someone close."

Much closer to her than I ever was.

"Mother suggested I bring Miranda to Beverly Drive, so she and Sandy could keep an eye on her. But Miranda was sound asleep. I hadn't wanted to wake her." My voice cracked as I said it, wishing in hindsight I'd done things differently.

"Did you say Miranda's mom's name is Santos?" Anna Dean's pen stopped moving. "It isn't DuBois?"

"Not anymore. She's been married more times than Elizabeth Taylor," I explained, "and her latest husband was Ernesto Santos, a diamond importer from South America. They're divorced."

"Ah," said the deputy chief, stopping pen again to ask me, "Do you have a number where Mrs. Santos can be reached? That would save us some time digging up the information ourselves."

Speaking of South America.

"She's in Brazil, on a two month vacation," I said, repeating the line provided by my mother. "The, um, spa where she's staying doesn't allow cell phones, and they have no television, radio, Internet, or landlines."

I didn't add that the plastic surgeons who'd be overseeing Mrs. Santos's "vacation" didn't allow distractions to healing . . . well, besides the cabana boys in Speedos, or so I'd heard. "Cissy might know some way to reach her," I offered.

Mother had connections everywhere. She could pull strings like nobody's business, which sometimes came in mighty handy.

"Are there any siblings?"

"No." That was one thing Miranda and I had found in common. We were both only children.

"Where's her father?"

"Dead," I said, and proceeded to recount what I knew about Jack Reynolds DuBois having been killed in a yachting accident; around two years after my father had his fatal heart attack. Miranda had been in college.

Make that two things Miranda and I had shared: losing our daddies.

The deputy chief sighed, and none too happily. "That'll make it hard to contact her next of kin."

"I guess it will."

The knot of responsibility in my belly had turned into an ache, and I tried not to dwell on the fact that Miranda had been alone in the end. She had one of the most famous faces (and cleavage) in all of Dallas, and yet she'd had no hand to hold when she needed it most.

It didn't matter that I hadn't been her bosom buddy.

That I'd barely seen her since prep school graduation had no bearing.

A girl I'd known had died.

And I'd likely been the last person who saw her alive.

The last one who could've helped, who might have made her change her mind . . .

Aw, crap.

That did it, plain and simple, and all my emotions flooded up to the surface.

Sobs rose in my throat, and I put my hands to my face.

Like a blubbering baby, I cried.

I hated the very sound of it, the way my shoulders shook, the helplessness I felt, and still I couldn't stop until I let it all out.

"Here."

At the gentle tap on my arm, I pried my damp palms from my cheeks and looked up as I sniffled.

Anna Dean pressed a paper towel into my hand.

"I couldn't find a tissue," she said. "This was the best I could do."

"Thank you," I murmured through snot and tears, grateful for her small act of kindness.

I blotted eyes and skin then blew my nose. When I was done, I balled the paper towel in my hand, not sure what to do with it. I felt blotchy and awkward, and wished ever so briefly that I was more like my mother, who always seemed so in control of every situation.

I finally stuffed the wadded towel in the pocket of my hoodie, and made a disgusted noise before I blathered on: "If I were Cissy, I'd have a proper hankie, folded and pressed, ready to go. But I can never seem to find a Kleenex when I need one. Sometimes I wonder if I wasn't adopted after being left in a milk crate on the doorstep."

The deputy chief momentarily shed her sto-icism to offer a look of sympathy. "I'm sure even your mother gets rattled, Andrea. Everyone does, though some are better at hiding it than others."

"It's not even like Miranda and I were close, but I feel like I've been hit by a Mack truck," I said wearily, and glanced back at the doorway, hearing voices and movement beyond the kitchen.

"You've gotten a shock, and it'll take some time to sink in. I'll call you again if I have any more questions."

I turned to her, wiping my nose on my sleeve. "You want me to leave?"

If I'd been a normal person, I would've wel-comed the chance to escape, to get out of a place so recently visited by the Grim Reaper. But I wasn't done yet. I still had so many questions.

"If you wouldn't mind, Andrea, I do have work to do." The deputy chief crossed her arms over her chest, and her shiny badge winked beneath the kitchen lights, as if I needed a reminder of who she was and why she was there.

Instead of taking the hint and vamoosing, I flung an ultimatum at her: "Promise me you'll investigate this further. Maybe things aren't as clear cut as they seem on the surface. Miranda just wasn't the kind of girl to give up so easily."

"You said you weren't very close to her, so maybe you didn't know her as well as you think," Deputy Dean said in such a logical way that I felt like nodding.

Only I didn't agree. Or perhaps I didn't want to.

I couldn't believe that Miranda DuBois had woken up after I'd taken off last night and decided to off herself, just like that.

It wasn't possible, was it?

Though what did I know about suicide? I'd never tried it, never even considered it, even when I'd felt the most alone.

Maybe Miranda had felt too damaged—too humiliated—to greet another day. Maybe it hadn't taken much thought at all.

The stoic mask returned to Anna Dean's face, and I wasn't surprised when she said, "We'll see what the medical examiner has to say, but the evidence is looking pretty strong from where I stand. I'm not one to rush to judgment, though, Andrea, and I won't do it here. When the M.E. tells me the cause of death, that's when I'm sure and not a moment before then."

"Thank you." At least she hadn't dismissed my concerns. That had to count for something.

The deputy chief rounded the granite island. "Why don't you stop by your mother's before you go home? It might do you good to have someone to talk to about this."

Oddly enough, the idea of seeing Cissy and telling her about Miranda didn't sound all that atrocious. My mother could be hard on me sometimes, a tad overbearing and overprotective; but beneath the Chanel and pearls beat a truly caring heart. Even if she didn't like to show it, Cissy felt things very deeply. I'd grown up thinking my mother was indomitable, sort of a modern day Joan of Arc who could stand in the fire and not flinch. I'd only begun to see how wrong I was over the past year.

Despite the fact that one would rarely ever glimpse Cissy Blevins Kendricks with a hair out of place, she bled red like everyone else. (Okay, so it was Coco Red by Chanel, but still.)

I slid off the stool, rubbing damp palms on my thighs. "You're right," I told Anna Dean. "I should go."

There was nothing else I could do for Miranda besides.

It was too late for that.

Chapter 5

I shuffled out of Miranda's duplex just as the medical examiner's van pulled up, and I can't say I was unhappy to miss what came after. I didn't want to view Miranda's lifeless corpse encased in a body bag as it was wheeled outside on a stretcher.

Long ago I'd decided it was far, far better to remember people as they were (i.e., alive and breathing). If you got a glimpse of them in death, you could never shake it from your mind.

Trust me on that.

And call me insensitive, but it felt even worse when the deceased was someone young with an interrupted life. It always left you to wonder what they could have become had they stuck around.

Though, most often, dying wasn't a matter of choice.

Sometimes life derailed like a bad day at

Amtrak, and there wasn't much you could do except hang onto the handrails, grit your teeth, and ride it out.

I knew Miranda DuBois and I had never been tight, and maybe it shouldn't have been so difficult for me to accept that she had chosen to check out of the Heartbeat Hotel way earlier than scheduled.

But it was.

I just couldn't reconcile that a woman who'd braved her way through beauty pageants, debutante balls, sorority rush, and television news would end it all because she was no longer the prettiest girl in the room.

Sure, Miranda had been superficial and vain, but she could conjure up tough when tough meant winning instead of losing. Pageant queens were no pansies, despite how they fluttered around in glittery ball gowns and rhinestone tiaras. Miranda might've oozed charm on the surface, but she had the cunning of Donald Trump. She'd used what she had to get where she wanted to be. Was that such a bad thing?

She'd carved herself a place as a bona fide Dallas celebrity with a sandwich named after her at Who's Who Burgers in Highland Park Village, and a cartoon rendering of her bodacious blond self hung on the walls of The Palm on Ross Avenue in the West End.

In the yearbook, Miranda had written her ambition as "To be famous," and she'd achieved that, for sure. Were a droopy lip and an eye tic worth giving up all that?

My answer would have to be, "No."

Was I in denial?

Maybe that was it.

I was suffering from a severe case of guilt.

Most assuredly, I wasn't taking Miranda's alleged suicide well. My insides felt like ill-prepared oatmeal: mushy and full of lumps.

Daddy had always advised that I listen to my gut, and my gut was telling me there was more to what had happened to Miranda than anyone realized.

Until I better understood, I couldn't get her out of my mind.

I nearly called Brian.

For my own peace of mind, I needed someone to hear me out and explain away my doubts, and Brian was one of the best listeners I knew.

But I didn't do it.

I hated the thought of waking him up. He'd been through a lot lately, with his heavy workload at ARGH (aka Abramawitz, Reynolds, Goldberg, and Hunt, the primo defense firm in the city), not to mention a money-laundering case that had nearly done him in. Then his parents had popped into town, and we ended up taking them along to the Birthday Party from Hell at my mother's.

Talk about trying times.

If Brian wasn't such a Steady Eddie and natural-born Eagle Scout (much like my daddy had been), he would've needed to book a room at the funny farm.

Besides, what good would it do to jolt him out of a sound sleep to grouse about Miranda's death?

He hadn't even known her beyond watching her on the news on occasion. I'm sure he'd sympathize, but it wouldn't mean anything to him, not the way it should.

Instead, I followed Anna Dean's suggestion and headed over to Mother's.

My mother had known Miranda. Even better, she knew me. I never thought I'd say this, but if anyone understood how I was feeling at the moment, it would be her.

As I left Miranda's street, I passed a silver VW sedan whose redheaded driver bore a striking resemblance to Janet Graham; but I didn't ease my foot from the gas pedal, not even a little. I wanted out of there. Getting as much distance between myself and Miranda's place was foremost on my mind.

I'd barely begun to breathe again when I turned off Beverly and into the brief circular drive that led up to Cissy's house.

Though I'd grown up within the walls of the 1920s mansion, had spent eighteen years of my life there being followed about by Sandy Beck, who made sure to erase all traces of my grubby fingers from the silk wallpaper and brush my crumbs from the chintz upholstery, the place would forever be Mother's.

Every room had her mark upon it, from the polished marble tiles in the foyer, to the vintage chandeliers, hand-carved moldings, and eclectic mix of antiques and expensive reproductions bought at auction or occasional trips to Europe. The only rooms that didn't bear Cissy's stamp were my

father's study with its dark wood and leather, soft-
ened only by the artwork (including some pieces
of mine), and my bedroom, where I'd been allowed
to paint on the walls and had attempted my own
version of Claude Monet's *Garden in Giverny*.

Sometimes pulling up in front of the heavy
door flanked by the whitewashed pair of terra
cotta lions made me catch my breath, and not
only because the place was something out of
Architectural Digest; it was like taking a step into
the past.

My own past.

When I walked through the halls and up the
gracefully curving stairwell, I relived sensa-
tions I'd felt when I was young and not so sure of
myself. I got a flutter in my belly that had seemed
ever-present when I was a child, a wondering
about if I'd measure up, if I'd be good enough,
pretty enough, and perfect enough to make Cissy
love me.

It didn't matter that I'd come a long way from
being that insecure girl who grew up in the very
tall shadow of a mother who seemed to do everything right.

Maybe that was something I'd never shed, the
reminder of who I'd once been, and that was okay
with me. Because I appreciated the woman I'd
become, and I knew I didn't want to go back, not
for anything.

Though my mother hadn't quite given up on her
dream—make that delusion—of turning me into
a blue-blooded Highland Park princess, a proper
heiress who never dressed off the rack and whose

goal was to chair countless fund-raisers and make the annual best-dressed lists.

I'm sure she'd keep trying to lure me back "into the life" until her dying breath, and I'd keep resisting. It was an endless chess game we played, and it gave me something to constantly complain about.

And complain I did. Mostly to Malone, who'd fast learned just to nod and make sympathetic noises.

As I rang Mother's doorbell, I thought of Miranda and how she'd done all the things—*become* all the things—that I hadn't. Many of those goals my mother wished I'd accomplished for myself; heck, for us both. But how had they benefited the late Ms. DuBois in the end, huh? What had titles and fame and perfect looks gotten her?

A tag on her toe at the county morgue.

Surely no one's aspiration.

Some of my fellow geeks at Hockaday had openly hated Miranda's guts, enough to wish her dead way back then. Would they be happy when they heard the news? Would they feel like they had triumphed?

There were plenty of girls I hadn't exactly liked when I was younger; the kind who'd made me feel less than I was.

Miranda had been one.

She'd never been cruel to me, nothing like that, and I'd never despised her, or even been jealous. I'd just felt a great sense of distance, as if we were from two different planets, speaking languages the other couldn't comprehend.

As kids, we'd been thrown together by our mothers fairly often, but the togetherness never stuck. Miranda had been winning local beauty pageants when I was still finger-painting. She was the only girl I knew who wore lipstick in third grade, and she graduated from knee socks to panty hose by grade five. To this day, I didn't don either lipstick or panty hose except on occasions as rare as alignment of all the planets in the solar system.

As a grown-up, the world I'd chosen to live in hadn't intersected often with my old classmate's, unless I was coerced into doing something for my mother, like attending a charity function or volunteering at a fund-raiser. If, perchance, I bumped into Miranda, we'd exchange pleasantries. But that was about it.

Before the Pretty Party at Delaney's, it had probably been at least a year since I'd last seen her—at the "Shoe-in the New Year" bash at the Jimmy Choo store in Highland Park Village that Cissy had co-chaired to raise funds to shod the homeless—and the always flashy Ms. DuBois had looked on top of the world. I hadn't wanted to go, but the nonprofit that would reap the dough was one whose Web site I had designed and still managed. The party hadn't been all that bad, though I hadn't stayed long. Miranda was just arriving as I was leaving that night, around ten o'clock.

Who could have imagined she'd be dead within twelve months?

Certainly not I.

"Andy? Are you okay?"

I hadn't even heard the door open, and, at the

sound of Sandy Beck's worried voice, I blinked to clear my lashes of unshed tears and brushed aside my dreary thoughts.

"No," I said, and shook my head. "I'm not."

"What is it, honey? Don't tell me it's Brian again?"

We'd all had cause to worry plenty about Malone during the mess involving the Oleksiy case, and I had never been happier than when we put that behind us. But it was over and done, and we'd moved on.

"Brian's fine," I assured her. "He's home, sleeping off a deposition."

"Thank God." She put a hand to her heart, over the pearl buttons of a gray cardigan, and I was tempted to throw my arms around her familiar shoulders and bury my face in her neck, as I'd done often enough when I was little. Sandy always smelled like roses, and usually I found the scent reassuring.

But not this morning.

I stood there like a zombie, saying nothing, my senses numbed around the edges, the shock sinking in.

"Goodness, Andy, don't stand outside in that chilly air. You'll catch pneumonia."

She drew me inside and shut the door behind us. "Your mother's up in her sitting room, finishing her toast and coffee. Go on and talk to her. She's why you're here, isn't she?"

Sandy Beck had always been able to read my thoughts like a psychic. Or maybe I was just that obvious.

"I have some bad news about Miranda DuBois,"
I said.

"What kind of bad news?"

"The worst," was all I could think to muster,
unable to voice the phrase, *She's dead*. I think Sandy
guessed pretty well what the worst was, considering my puffy eyes and hangdog expression.

"I'm so sorry, sweetheart." She tucked a thumb
beneath my chin and gave me a good long look,
before she sighed and took my hand, patting it. "If
there's anything I can do . . . "

"Thank you."

Then she let me go, and I headed up the stairs,
as I had so many times before; treading carefully
on the Oriental runner, my weight causing each
step to gently groan.

I slid my hand up the banister, the carved
length of it polished smooth, glistening with the
Murphy's oil soap that I knew I'd smell on my
palm long afterward.

At the top of the stairs I glanced aside to see my
father's study, and found myself giving a wave at
the door, as if he still sat behind his mammoth
desk and would look up, calling out, "Hey, pump-
kin. How was school?"

Some things you just never forgot.

There was a time when I would have knocked
before entering my mother's sitting room, but on
this particular morning I didn't even pause at the
threshold.

I walked straight in and found her perched on
her settee, the newspaper settled on the cushion
beside her; on the table in front of her sat a coffee-

filled Limoges cup atop its matching saucer. The plate that had once held her toast was bare of all but the smallest crumbs and a smear of strawberry jam.

She glimpsed my approach over the top of her reading glasses and quickly removed them, as I know how she hated to be seen wearing them.

"My God, Andrea," she drawled, the thin curve of her eyebrows arching. "You look like death warmed over."

That good, huh?

"It's Miranda, and it's my fault. I never should have left her alone last night," I got out before I choked up, feeling guilty all over again, and began to hiccup.

My mother swept the newspaper off the settee and plunked me down beside her. "There, there," she said, and rubbed my back until my hiccups stopped.

Then I told her what had happened when I went to Miranda's duplex that morning, how Anna Dean was there, awaiting the arrival of the medical examiner's van.

"Miranda's dead?" she repeated, and the pale slip of her forehead puckered. "Are you sure?"

Well, I hadn't exactly seen her death pose, but I think I trusted the deputy chief of the Highland Park Police Department to know a live person from a dead one.

"Yes, I'm sure."

"I don't believe it." Cissy's blue eyes went wide. "She's as full of life as anyone I know, and far too pretty to die."

I nearly choked, trying to swallow down that one.

Too pretty to die, huh?

I doubted that being pretty could ever stave off death the way garlic and crosses could ward off vampires, but I knew what she meant, despite the overt flippancy of her remark.

Miranda had been one of those women who'd seemed too beautiful to be real, the kind who floated through life without a care in the world. Or, at least, that's how it looked from the outside.

But I knew better.

I had witnessed Miranda's last few hours—well, the last few hours before her *last* few hours—and they'd hardly been a cakewalk.

When I told her Deputy Dean had suggested that Miranda orchestrated her own demise, Mother reared her head, her lips tight, obviously no more convinced than I. In fact, she looked downright mad.

"Anna Dean thinks Miranda DuBois killed herself? Pish posh!" Cissy sniffed, as if catching a whiff of Dollar Store cologne. "I don't believe it for a minute. That young woman took care of herself like an Olympic athlete. You know how pageant girls are."

"I know, I know." Something I'd already told myself a million times over. Anyone who'd ever come up against a Texas beauty queen realized they might look like candy on the outside, but on the inside they were as hardy as a cockroach. "That's exactly what I said to Deputy Dean, but she doesn't agree. A neighbor heard a noise in the wee hours. When she went out for her paper later, she found Miranda's door open and went inside."

"Dear Lord." Mother's hand went to her heart. "I can't imagine anything more awful. It's just not right to lose someone so young and vital," she moaned. "No child should die before her mother."

Miranda might've been youthful and vital, but she was human after all, and lately life had thrown her curves that had her questioning her own worth and doubting that it amounted to much.

Was it so implausible that her anguish over the damage done by Dr. Sonja's botched injections had triggered doubts and insecurities that were too much for her to bear? Not to mention getting booted from a club that sent her a formal "kiss off" on letterhead.

I shared my concerns about Miranda's state of mind with my mother, though she mostly shook her head, repeating, "It would be so unlike her, really, so unlike her."

But Cissy hadn't watched Miranda's emotional collapse in front of a dozen guests at Delaney Armstrong's. If she had, she would've understood that Miranda's pain had been all too real.

"She brought a gun with her, Mother, to shoot Dr. Sonja, or at least frighten her," I reiterated, "which isn't exactly something a rational person would do."

"So Miranda was a smidge melodramatic? That doesn't make her suicidal," Cissy countered, and crossed her arms defensively. She seemed to get angrier the more I attempted to lay groundwork for the notion that Miranda might have indeed ended her own life, and I wasn't sure if she was mad at me or at Miranda.

"Maybe she figured her life wasn't worth living if she wasn't perfect anymore," I said, putting it out there, plain and simple, and Cissy's frown deepened.

Beneath her pale shade of powder, her skin turned a hot shade of pink. "Beauty isn't everything," she announced, her drawl less molasses and more venom, "but for some, it's all they've got. Or so they believe. And it's too bad, isn't it, sweet pea? God gives us all a million different ways to shine, and sometimes we just have to look a little deeper than the glitter."

Great balls of fire.

Had my mother really said that?

I blinked at her, half expecting her to morph into Mother Teresa.

But, nope.

She hadn't changed into anyone else.

Cissy was still Cissy.

Sometimes we just have to look a little deeper than the glitter.

Wowee kazoo.

That was quite a profound statement, coming from the Queen Bee of Dallas Society aka Her Highness of Highland Park, a woman who'd spent most of her life keeping up appearances and doing her damnedest to convince me that being a well-heeled society matron with the perfect house, perfect clothes, perfect marriage, and perfect life was the only dream worth having.

Okay, maybe I'm exaggerating a smidge (but only a smidge).

Just when I thought I had Cissy nearly figured out, she proved me wrong. Then again, grief affected each of us in mysterious ways. It certainly had made her philosophical in this case.

"Miranda was such a strong-willed child, so full of energy," my mother said quietly. "I still can't buy the idea that she'd do something so final"— she flicked a hand across the air—"and without so much as a word to her mother. You said she didn't even leave a note behind?"

"The police didn't find one." So Anna Dean had let drop.

"But Debbie and Miranda were so close, like two peas in a pod." She sighed and stared off into space.

"Are you sure you're all right?" I asked, as she looked awfully glassy-eyed. "Maybe you'd like a little brandy in your coffee?"

She snapped out of her trance, making a noise of disapproval. "Heavens, Andrea, it's barely eight-thirty in the morning. You know that I never drink before noon unless it's mimosas with brunch."

"I'd say all rules go out the window at times like this."

"It's not booze I want," she said, and sighed the most doleful of sighs.

The silk of her robe swished as she rose and stepped around the table that held her breakfast dishes. She went over to her lovely little Louis XV desk and fiddled with the small drawers, removing a slim leather wallet, which she brought over to me. Settling beside me again, she flipped the monogrammed album open to reveal a color photograph from the predigital era.

"Do you remember that picnic?" she asked, and I nodded.

"Yes."

It had been during spring break. Mother and Debbie Santos (then Mrs. DuBois) had taken me and Miranda to Longboat Key, where Miranda's daddy was having a very large house built on the Gulf side of the island. We'd ventured over from our suites at The Colony to see how construction was going, taking our lunch with us, and we ended up picnicking in the middle of a great concrete pipe. Or, at least, Miranda and I had, at our mothers' urging.

In the photo, we had our backs pressed against the curve of the pipe, our legs bent, feet braced on the other side. I looked miserable with my frizzy hair and lobster-red sunburn. I remember ants in my peanut butter and jelly sandwich. Miranda, on the other hand, looked poised and cheerful and brown as a berry.

I handed the wallet back to Mother and smiled sadly. "It's too bad we can't go back, huh? Set Miranda on a different path entirely."

But we couldn't, as we both knew good and well.

If life had a Rewind button, I would have hit it many times before, whenever I'd wanted a chance to do-over. Like before I lost Daddy. If I'd just had another few moments with him, to tell him all the things I never did, to say "I love you" once again.

But there was no instant replay in real life.

Once. That was it. If you screwed up, you screwed up. If you fell under the wheels of a bus, you didn't have a cat's nine lives to try again.

It sucked, however you cut it.

"Do you honestly think Miranda *wanted* to die?" my mother asked me, looking me straight in the eye.

I wanted to tell her no, to reaffirm what she herself was thinking, what I'd been thinking all morning. But I wasn't so sure of anything anymore. I hardly knew Miranda and could only guess what had been going through her head last night. She was upset, for sure, but suicidal?

"I don't know," I finally confessed, sighing loudly, wishing I could reassure her. But I couldn't. I mean, I did have doubts and questions, like about the open door, about the gun, and I remarked as much to my mother. But I hadn't been there when "it" happened, so I would never know for sure. "I'd like to think she didn't, but if it's not true, then it would suggest that she was—" I stopped, swallowed down the word *murdered*, because I didn't want to go there, either.

Cissy nodded, seeming to understand the conundrum. She remained silent for a moment, closing her eyes and pressing the photo album between her palms. After a while she sighed, opened her eyes and glanced at me. "How will I tell Debbie about this godawful mess? How can I tell a mother that her daughter is dead?"

Call me Ms. Redundant, but I said "I don't know" again, because I didn't have a clue, especially with Mrs. Santos in Brazil, probably wrapped in bandages, recuperating from whatever she'd had nipped and tucked so that she could hang onto what was left of her own beauty, her own youth. I thought of how far away she'd feel when she learned about Miranda.

She'd doubtless blame herself for not being there when Miranda had needed her, just as I had blamed myself.

"Deputy Dean said she was going to try to get ahold of Mrs. Santos somehow," I told my mother as she sat beside me, uncommonly silent. "I'm sure she'll find a way to track her down in Brazil and give her the news."

"Not if I tell Debbie first."

"You're going to call the spa?" And force them to put Mrs. Santos on the line, whatever her condition, even if she was swathed in bandages from head to toe and sipping her three squares through a straw.

"Oh, Andrea, I can't let the police do it, can I? It's going to break her heart enough to hear it from me, and we've been friends for so many years."

She sat in profile, as if afraid to meet my eyes, but I could see her chin was trembling.

I had to wonder how hard she must be fighting to maintain her decorum. Would she wait until I was gone, shut her door, and then cry in the shower so no one else could see her tears?

It was hard for her, I knew, to show any kind of weakness. But she'd let me glimpse her vulnerability before, and I hadn't freaked. I wished she'd let me see it now. It felt good sometimes to think I could be the strong one.

Her fingers still clutched the photo album, and I put my hand over hers.

"Do you want me to stay?" I asked her, part of me hoping she'd say yes, that she needed me.

Though I wasn't surprised when she didn't take me up on my offer.

She turned to me, and I noticed the tightness in her face softening. "Thank you, sweetie, but I'd like to do this alone. You go on home and spend time with Mr. Malone. He's probably wide-awake and wondering where you are."

I couldn't help feeling rejected, but I nodded anyway.

She leaned near to embrace me, holding fast for a moment before releasing me. It was as close to a bear hug as I'd ever gotten, and I found myself wishing it had lasted a few seconds longer. Mother wasn't very touchy-feely. Most of the hugs in my growing up had come from Daddy.

Don't get me wrong. I knew how much Cissy loved me. It was just a bit harder for her to show it sometimes. I'd gotten the impression from the rare stories I heard about her own mother—my grandmother, Leona Barrett Blevins, dead before I was born—that their relationship had been rather distant. My daddy, I believe, used the word "strained," whispering to me once that Leona

Blevins had been an old-fashioned and very pig-headed woman.

Hmmm, sounded a lot like someone else I knew.

Though I wouldn't call my relationship with Cissy "strained," we'd never been of like mind where much of anything was concerned: my becoming a debutante, for one, and my attending art school in Chicago rather than a Texas university (namely, SMU), for another. Still, we had managed to close the gap between us, the older we both got, despite being prone to colossal misunderstandings.

So we weren't the Brady Bunch? We could muddle through whatever life threw at us . . . and usually did.

For a long while after she left the sitting room in a flurry of pale blue silk, disappearing into her bedroom and closing the door between us, I remained where I was, hands in my lap, breathing in the scent of her—the soapy clean of her morning bath mixed with an overlay of Joy perfume—and pondering what a powerful force our past had on our present.

Like my bumping into Miranda last night—or, rather, her bumping into me—and how she'd managed to inject herself into my life again, turning my neat little corner of the world topsy-turvy in just the past twelve hours.

Was that fate? Coincidence? Or a fistful of rotten luck?

I leaned toward the latter.

Regardless, my emotions had been on a roller-coaster ride, and I felt drained and exhausted.

I lifted a hand from my lap, touching the photo album Mother had left behind on the cushion of the settee.

But instead of thumbing through it, I picked it up and put it back in Cissy's desk. I didn't need another glimpse at my old memories.

Trying to deal with much more recent ones was proving difficult enough.

Chapter 6

I hugged Sandy Beck and told her good-bye before crossing the foyer and leaving my mother's house. Though I didn't regret coming by to talk about Miranda, I felt no more at peace than when I'd arrived. I kept thinking of Cissy calling Debbie Santos to give her the bad news, and wondered if I should stay awhile despite Mother telling me to go home to Malone.

Ignoring the tug of war inside me, I pulled the front door closed and stood on the stoop for a moment, blinking sunlight from my eyes.

Which is when I heard the voice.

"Hey, Kendricks! Great timing, girlfriend. Now get in the car!"

I would've recognized that bossiness anywhere, even blindfolded.

"C'mon, Andy," Janet shouted at me out the rolled-down window of her silver VW. She had the motor running, and I wasn't sure if she'd pulled into Mother's driveway a minute before or if she'd followed me from Miranda's and had been waiting there since I went in. Or maybe she was psychic.

"What're you doing here?" I asked, a million questions running through my head. Had she spoken to Deputy Dean? Did she know that Miranda was dead and that the police thought it was suicide? Did she have any inkling of my current status as "the last known human to have seen Miranda DuBois alive," or was she still oblivious?

Guess there was only one way to find out.

But it meant taking a ride.

"Please," she begged before I could politely refuse. "I'll bring you back as soon as possible, I promise," she went on as I hesitated, glancing longingly at my Jeep and then back at the VW.

Would she let me off the hook if I told her all I wanted was to get home to Malone and go back to bed for a while? Crawl under the covers and close my eyes, pretending to start the day over when I woke up again?

"I really could use your help, Andy." She even removed her 1940s style cat's-eye sunglasses to look dolefully at me. Saying no would've been like kicking a puppy.

Yeesh.

She needed my help?

Like I was much good at helping anyone, I mused, but shuffled over to the passenger door of her Jetta and climbed in.

"Hang on tight," she said, not even waiting until I'd fastened my seat belt before she shot off, racing down the curve of the drive and zipping onto Beverly Drive at a speed decidedly above the legal limit.

She turned onto Preston Road, but still hadn't indicated what our final destination was, and I had a feeling it wasn't an early lunch at La Madeleine.

"What's going on?" I asked, feverishly hoping it was something silly. "Is there a fire at Jimmy Choo? Did a plague of locusts descend on the Junior League?"

Or did it have to do with you-know-who?

Sigh.

I figured it wouldn't be long before the whole world knew; and Janet was so well plugged in with so many sources, her learning about anything gossipworthy in this town was more a matter of when than if.

"Miranda DuBois is dead," she said, without so much as glancing in my direction. "But you already know that, don't you?"

And from her tone, I knew that she knew that I knew.

If that made sense.

"You saw me pulling out of her street earlier, didn't you?" I asked, and she arched her slim red eyebrows.

"Of course I saw you. And I know you saw me. But did you call and fill me in? Noooo," she said, drawing out the word. "You'd already beat me to Miranda's and talked to Deputy Chief Dean, who was kind enough to inform me you'd headed over to your mother's."

Ah, so her pinning me down at Cissy's wasn't ESP.

"I went to Miranda's to check on her. Because I'd given her a ride home last night, and she wasn't, um, thinking straight." I picked my words carefully, not liking the way Janet had stated things, as if I'd done something intentionally deceptive. "I had no idea she would be . . . that she'd have . . . you know," I finally got out, realizing it was harder to discuss than I'd imagined. I swallowed hard.

"Poor girl," Janet said, sounding as if she meant it. "She might not have been a rocket scientist, but she was all right."

"Did Anna Dean tell you anything . . . about how she died?" I asked, wondering if my friend, the Ace Society Reporter, had gotten more out of the deputy chief than the probable cause of death being suicide.

Janet sighed. "Unfortunately, I got diddly squat. She wouldn't give me anything quotable, just that Miranda was dead and her neighbor discovered her at the crack of dawn. She said the cause of death is pending autopsy, but I got a sense she had it figured out already 'cuz she intimated they weren't exactly combing the neighborhood for suspects."

"I think you're right," I agreed, not saying any more.

If Deputy Dean wasn't ready to inform the press that the police believed Miranda DuBois had shot herself with her own gun, then I wasn't about to fuel the grapevine. So I didn't mention any of the details of my conversation with the police officer, not about my probably being the last person to have seen her alive, nor about how I might have prevented Miranda's dying altogether if I'd just been a little less eager to cuddle with Brian.

Oy.

Janet banged a hand against the steering wheel, and I jumped, knocking my skull against the window.

"Dammit, Andy, I know it sounds cold as hell, but I can't get maudlin about this. I've got a story to write, and the deputy chief barely said a bleeping word. I couldn't even get any of the blue uniforms canvassing the neighborhood to spill off-the-record. All I managed were a few worthless quotes from a woman with an iPod and a dude walking his dog." She moaned, and tears welled on her lashes. "I can't let myself get scooped this time. I just can't."

So that's what this was all about? I thought as I rubbed the sore spot on my head.

Getting a story?

What happened to compassion at the loss of a fellow Hockadaisy? Or at the very least, mourning a woman who'd climbed the ladder at Channel 5 to become one of the city's most recognized talking heads? That meant something, right? It begat a little respect.

"But Janet, you're not the crime reporter for the *PCP*," I reminded her. "You pen features on Pretty Parties and charity balls. You don't write—" I caught myself, having nearly said, *about suicide*, before I finished, "—obituaries."

I saw her bite her lip, gnawing for a good, long minute before she answered with, "Well, it's all connected, right? I mean, Miranda crashing the Pretty Party at Delaney's last night and nearly shooting Dr. Madhavi's head off—"

Nearly?

For Pete's sake, Miranda had missed Sonja Madhavi by more than a foot.

"—and Miranda turning up dead the next morning. It's like crime and fashion coming together with a bang. I'm the only one who could do the story justice. Besides"—she squirmed—"I knew her. Maybe not well, but well enough to make it personal. Don't you think we owe it to Miranda to get as many facts as we can? I'm sure she'd appreciate having the truth out there, right, Andy?"

The truth will set you free.

Miranda's words again came back to haunt me. I only wished I knew what she'd meant beyond the obvious. Because I was sure she'd meant *something*, and I'd wager it had nothing to do with being written up in the *PCP* posthumously.

"So you want to do this story for Miranda's sake?" I said, decidedly skeptical.

Janet sniffled, jerking up her chin. "Yes. I do." Then she added quietly, "And for my own."

Her forehead was creased with worry, and she wouldn't peel her eyes off the road long enough to glance at me. There was way more to this than what I saw on the surface, but Janet obviously wasn't ready to share with me yet.

Like a good friend, I would wait awhile before I pried.

"So where are we going?" I asked, because I knew I wouldn't get far by grilling Janet if she wasn't willing to talk. I had a sense, though, of precisely where we were headed, because the route seemed all too familiar from my days growing up in Highland Park and being dragged on shopping trips with Cissy when I would've rather stayed home with my paints and easel. "Are you taking me to North Park?"

North Park Center aka "the mall," at least that's what I used to call it.

"Yes." She kept her eyes focused ahead with such intensity, I would've guessed she had cataracts and could barely see the road. Only she didn't. Janet's sight was 20/20.

Even when she wore her "smart girl" glasses, it was just for show (or, more likely, to imitate her idol, Katie Couric).

Barely a beat had passed before I spotted the huge fortress of the shopping center and read the Barneys and Neiman Marcus signs looming over the gray of the parking lot.

She jerked the car to a stop in an empty space and turned off the engine, finally looking at me again, her eyes hyperwide with excitement. "Look, Andy, here's the plan. I want to be the first to get Dr. Sonja's reaction to how these tragic events have unfolded, namely, Miranda's attempted plugging of the good doctor and this morning's news that Miranda has passed. Since The Pretty Place opens at nine, it's imperative I be on hand just as soon as the doors open."

Ah, The Pretty Place. Where North Park shoppers could drop in for a quickie Botox injection or glycolic peel before hitting the shops and giving their Platinum AmEx cards a real workout.

The way things were going, pretty soon Taco Bell would start offering customers free liposuction with every bag of chimichangas.

"Do you have an appointment?" I asked her.

Janet blushed. Which was odd.

"Uh-huh," she murmured. "I scheduled online. There were a couple openings for this morning."

"So you're meeting with Dr. Sonja under false pretenses so you can do an ambush interview. Is that it?" I said, not liking how that sounded but knowing I couldn't stop Janet with a bulldozer if she'd set her mind to it. "But I'm not sure what that has to do with me."

If Janet wanted to gild her story with a tawdry lily à la the *National Enquirer* that was her prerogative. But I wasn't quite sure how her interviewing Dr. Sonja Madhavi required a flunky.

Janet unhitched her seat belt and did a half turn toward me, wedging an elbow against the steering wheel. She didn't look comfortable in the least, and the way she flattened her gaze on me as if intending to hypnotize didn't exactly make me feel at ease, either.

"Okay, Tonto," she started in, "here's your part, and don't screw it up, all right? Because one shot is all we've got."

Nice how she emphasized *we* like we were a team. Maybe she forgot I wasn't on the *Press*'s payroll.

Then again, I didn't imagine they came any

more melodramatic than Ms. Janet Rutledge Graham. Colorful was her style—and I didn't just mean her hair—and was part of what kept her from being an Average Josephine.

Still, I could tell she was serious, so I didn't crack a smile. Not that I'd wanted to. I hadn't felt much like smiling since I'd approached Miranda's duplex that morning and encountered the stretch of yellow crime scene tape across the grass.

Janet clasped her hands together. "If you can just keep Dr. Sonja's boyfriend busy while I talk to her alone, I'd be ever so grateful."

Dr. Sonja's boyfriend?

I stared at her blankly.

"Lance Zarimba," Janet said. "He's her aesthetician. He was with her last night at Delaney's. The blond guy with the 'stache?"

The one who'd calmed Dr. Miniskirt down when she'd been near-hysterical after Miranda's potshot over her head at the Picasso?

"Oh, yeah, I remember him."

Janet did a little gaze-aversion again, which made my shoulders stiffen. "Well, I might've made you an appointment with him at nine o'clock, too, so he'll be distracted while I'm in with Dr. Madhavi. You don't mind, Andy, do you? It's just for fifteen minutes tops, and I put it on my business card so it's my treat. You can have him unplug your zits." She cocked her head, squinting at me. "That's not such a bad idea, is it?"

I had an appointment with an aesthetician to get my pores sucked out? Just so Janet could snag a few moments alone to grill Dr. Sonja?

Excuse me?

That's not such a bad idea, is it?

Another dig at my appearance?

Wasn't it just last night that Janet was harping on the wrinkle between my eyebrows, and now she was pointing the finger at my pores?

And she called herself my friend?

Should I mention that her bright orange-red hair looked a wee on the frizzy side this morning? And she still had a chunk of sleep stuck in the corner of her left eye?

Yeesh.

Suddenly self-conscious, I pulled down the visor flap and checked out my skin in the mirror.

"Stop it," Janet said, and slapped the visor back up again. "Let's get going. The Pretty Place should be opening in, like, two more minutes, and I don't want to be late."

Reluctantly, I emerged from the car and followed Janet across the parking lot.

She'd anchored the VW outside Barneys, but the department store didn't open until 10:00 A.M., so we took the mall doors in, bypassing chichi shops like Ferragamo, Michael Kors, and Carolina Herrera to get to the corner nook where The Pretty Place was situated.

A couple of the restaurants were open for the breakfast crowd, and a handful of mall walkers were making the rounds in crushed velvet sweatsuits, pausing now and then to gaze into a window display.

A few had even stopped in front of Dr. Sonja's "Botox in the Box" establishment and were running fingers down a posted menu of services, then glancing at a conveniently hung mirror just beside it and tugging at their faces.

Why did the cynical part of me suspect it was a fun house mirror, which made everyone's reflection distorted?

Janet nudged me forward, toward the entrance to The Pretty Place, which had glass walls and doors so we could see one of Dr. Sonja's underlings doing a fast tidying-up of shelves and counters lined with Dr. Sonja's personal line of cosmetics, powders, and potions before she opened up.

Until she let us in, we were left to stand outside the clear box, staring at the blown-up photos of perfectly sculpted parts of the female anatomy: flat belly, tight thighs, lean arms, unlined eyes, and plump glossy lips.

I wondered if the women who booked appointments for treatments really believed that Dr. Sonja could make cottage cheese vanish or turn a saggy stomach into six-pack abs in one visit.

Janet paused beside me as I studied the enormous photograph of a model's uplifted derriere. "She's selling an illusion, huh?"

"More like a delusion," I said dryly, figuring the percentage of actual females over age twenty who had bodies without cellulite was somewhere in the single digits. "No one looks that perfect unless they're airbrushed."

Janet sighed. "Selling youth and beauty is probably the world's greatest con of all time."

"Way bigger than pet rocks," I agreed.

And far too many people fell for it.

Since Brian had pretty much moved into my condo—though he still kept his apartment in Addison—he'd ordered cable for my television, something I hadn't done in the ten years I'd lived alone since college. Though vowing to never watch reality show drivel, I'd caught a few episodes of *Dr. 90210* and *Extreme Makeover*, enough to know that there was an endless supply of women who wanted tummy tucks post-childbirth, larger breasts than God had given them, or faces pulled so tight that not a wrinkle (or natural expression) was left behind. The worst of it was when a mother pushed a teenage daughter into buying into the bigger-breasts-equals-higher-worth theory.

Obviously, a B-cup didn't cut it in today's society. The age-old battle cry of "We are woman, hear us roar" had become "DDs or bust!"

The very idea made me cringe.

I had to hand it to Cissy.

She may have bemoaned my desire to become an artist. Ditto my refusal to bond with the popular girls at Hockaday or campaign for class president. Okay, okay, yes, she was, shall we say, pretty vocal when I'd dropped out of my debut. But she had never, ever—not once—insinuated I needed bigger boobs.

"You okay?" Janet said, and I blinked, turning toward her.

"I was just experiencing a moment of gratitude for my mother," I admitted.

Janet rubbed my shoulder. "Don't worry," she said. "It'll pass."

As I hoped the next fifteen minutes would.

With a jangle of keys in the locks and a rattle of glass, the front doors to The Pretty Place came open, and Janet grabbed my arm and dragged me in.

Chapter 7

 The receptionist looked very much like a walking advertisement for Dr. Sonja's treatments. Some might say that was a compliment.

I wouldn't.

If she had any wrinkles whatsoever, her tightly drawn ponytail obliterated every one of them. Her skin appeared so fiercely stretched and smooth, I was amazed when she opened her mouth and it actually moved of its own accord, without any strings from above confirming that she was a puppet and not a real girl.

"You're both here for nine o'clock treatments, yes?" Her unlined eyes glanced quickly across her computer monitor as she settled down behind her ultramodern desk (an unblemished white laminate, I noticed). "You're Ms. Janet Graham and Ms. Andrea Kendricks?" she asked.

"Yes, that's right," Janet said, stepping in front of me as if afraid I'd do something to spoil things for her. Like maybe ask the receptionist if she was assembled at the Botox factory. "I'm Ms. Graham, and I'm anxious to see Dr. Madhavi. Is she ready for me yet?"

The Stepford Receptionist checked her flat screen again. "I see Ms. Kendricks is having the rosemary-tangerine pore-tightening botanical facial, and you're having the revitalizing Vitamin E enhanced bee—"

"That's right, yes, uh-huh," Janet cut her off, nodding profusely, and I couldn't help but think she was acting really weird, even for her.

Too many double lattes, perhaps?

Or maybe she was feeling unsettled and anxious for the same reason I was. Maybe she was all worked up about what happened to Miranda.

I started to put my hand on her arm, was about to ask if she wanted to sit down, when I heard the click-clack of high heels on marble floors, and Dr. Miniskirt herself appeared through a rear door.

The muscular guy with the mustache from the Pretty Party—Lance Zarimba—followed not two feet behind her. His posture mimicked Dr. Sonja's, from the tilt of his blond head to the way he crossed his arms.

"Ah, the delightful Ms. Graham from the Park Cities news. I see you brought a friend along to try our services. You were both at the Pretty Party last night, weren't you? Talk about a nightmare," she said, and leaned a hip against the jutting edge of the receptionist's desk. "It's a wonder I'm calm enough today to work."

Her white lab coat barely covered up a shiny gray skirt that revealed plenty of thigh above the knee. Her slim fingers winked with bling that was nearly as shiny as the glistening shadow above kohl-lined eyes that settled narrowly upon Janet and me.

"So that craziness with Miranda DuBois didn't frighten either of you off?" she asked. "How very brave you are."

She didn't wait for either of us to respond, but went right on to say, "Well, let's hope that an unhappy woman's tirade won't scare away any of my clientele. It's just a shame when people can't deal with personal misfortune privately. I hope that poor girl gets the help she so obviously needs."

Personal misfortune?

Miranda's meltdown had been triggered by bad results from injections Dr. Madhavi had given her. Was it Miranda's fault she'd been left with a twitchy eye and droopy mouth? More important, did the celebrity skin doc realize that Miranda would never get any kind of help at this juncture, not unless it was supernatural?

I started to rise from my chair, thinking someone needed to say something in Miranda's defense, perhaps a subtle remark such as, *Hey, don't speak ill of the dead, you plastic pusher!*

But Janet jumped up, practically knocking me down again.

"Can we get started, Dr. Sonja? I'm all ready," she said, practically bounding like a puppy toward the dermatologist.

The cool expression on the doctor's tawny features shifted like a melting icecap in Antarctica as she cracked a smile, rubbing her hands together as if overeager clients were one of her favorite things.

And they probably were, considering the prices The Pretty Place charged for their services.

Cha-ching!

"Come with me, sweetie," Dr. Sonja said, inclining her regal head toward the door where Lance Zarimba lounged. "We'll get our resident society columnist looking like a glamour puss in no time!"

The blond muscleman stepped aside, allowing his boss/paramour to pass by with a strangely exuberant Janet Graham in tow.

Not that I was cynical or anything, but Janet seemed a tad too excited about this particular interview, especially when the subject was Miranda DuBois and her tragic passing. I would've thought a more sober attitude better suited the occasion.

Hmmm.

What kind of treatment did Receptionist Barbie say Janet was having? A revitalizing Vitamin E enhanced something or other?

"Ms. Kendricks?"

I looked up to find the Blond Mustache staring down at me.

So I stared back.

He was a good enough looking guy, with

bright blue eyes and a tight Clorox-white T-shirt that closely hugged all his rippling muscles. But what I found most mesmerizing was the fact that his skin was as gorgeous as a Lancôme ad. No ingrown facial hair or red bumps from shaving. My God, but he had teeny pores!

Life simply wasn't fair.

"Ms. Kendricks, are you ready for your rosemary-tangerine pore-tightening botanical facial?" he asked, not leaving out a single word, when I could hardly remember much beyond the rosemary-tangerine part, 'cuz it made me hungry.

"Yeah, sure. Ready." I nodded and rose from my chair, hoping I wouldn't come out of this with blotchy skin, as I had the one time I'd allowed my mother to drag me to Elizabeth Arden's Red Door.

"I have sensitive skin." I coughed up the excuse as Sir Lancc led me past the reception desk and through the rear hallway with its white walls and serene New Age music piped through the air. "So I'm not sure I should be putting any mystery crud on my face."

"That's okay," he tossed over his shoulder in a soothing, low-pitched voice. "Our mystery crud is safe for all skin types."

"But what about your, um, environmental ethics?" I asked, bound to find some way out of this. "Do you do testing on animals?"

He paused in front of the third door to the left. "Only if they've studied," he said as he grabbed hold of the doorknob to let us in.

"Studied what? Oh, yeah, I get it."

Ha ha.

The guy was a regular comedian.

I walked into a room with celadon walls and a water sculpture burbling gently in the corner. It smelled of antiseptic and herbs and maybe a little like Lance Zarimba's testosterone. A mirror on the far wall caught me wrinkling my nose.

I sure hoped to heck that Janet was managing to get something quotable out of Dr. Sonja, or I would remind her forever of the day I suffered pimple extraction at the hands of an aesthetician with cranked-up pecs.

"Relax," Muscle Man said on cue. "You'll feel exhilarated when I'm through with you. I guarantee it."

He flashed his pearly whites and gestured toward a reclining chair in the room, sort of a fancier version of the one my dentist used. I wondered if I'd get a paper bib to wear or a free toothbrush before he shooed me out the door when he'd finished unplugging me.

"Extend your legs and put your head right here"—he patted a paper-covered pillow at one end—"and I'll cover you up with this nice warm cashmere throw. Then we'll work on turning you into the swan you really are."

Okay, was he implying I was an ugly duckling? Or was I just being too sensitive these days, after Janet's insinuation that my pores needed unclogging and her remark about the wrinkle between my brows?

"Close your eyes, Ms. Kendricks, and listen to the water in the fountain," Zarimba instructed as

I settled onto the reclining bench and he drew the heated throw atop me, covering me from chin to toe.

I pretended to shut my eyes, watching through slits as he washed his hands at the sink before he settled on a stool beside me and drew a swing-armed lamp over my face.

Then he squirted something that reeked of rosemary onto his fingertips and rubbed it over my skin. "I'm cleansing off the toxins," he told me as he wiped the substance off with a tissue. "They settle into our skin from pollution outdoors and even from within with unhealthy eating."

Egads, was I going to get a lecture on clean living from this fellow, too?

Was he going to tell me to cleanse my freezer of the Häagen-Dazs in order to avoid toxic build-up of blackheads? Well, that was something I just wouldn't do, not even if it meant having perfect skin for eternity.

"This will feel cool," he said next. "It's the tangerine botanical pore-tightening mask. I'll leave it on for five minutes."

He plopped slices of chilly cucumber on my eyes, which meant I could no longer peek through my lashes. The soft bristles of a brush flicked across my cheeks and forehead as he covered my face with scented goo. I could even taste it on my lips.

Hmmm.

Not bad. Kinda like orange Jell-O.

Dr. Sonja's boyfriend chuckled, having apparently caught my tongue doing a little exploring.

"If you're going to ask if the mask is edible, it isn't meant to be, not really. But I guess if you were starving, you could eat it. It's all organic."

Hello? Did he think I planned to snack on the face mask?

I snorted and managed to suck a bit of tangerine goo up my nose.

Ugh.

"You have great bone structure, Andy, if I might call you that," he said, retrieving my right hand from beneath the throw. He began massaging my fingers, and I stiffened.

Was a hand massage part of the pore tightening package?

"Wow, you're tense."

And why wouldn't I be?

I was witness to a shooting at a Pretty Party the night before, and, according to Highland Park's deputy chief of police, I was the last person to see Miranda DuBois sucking in oxygen. And now my hand was being, um, manhandled by someone other than Malone?

Though, it did feel awfully good.

So long as he didn't reach beneath the cashmere to manhandle anything else.

"You're not used to being pampered, are you?"

"Who has time?" I murmured.

Besides, I wasn't big on primping. Life was far too short to worry about facials and manicures and pedicures. I'd rather spend my time on things that mattered more, like my painting or Web design or Malone.

"You're one of those earthy women who use lip

balm more often than lipstick, am I right?" he went on. "I'll bet you take five minutes to brush your teeth in the morning and don't put on makeup unless you're going to a funeral, huh?" He chuckled in that oh-so-cool and throaty voice. "But you have one of those faces that could be really beautiful if you just put a little effort into it. We get so many clients who tend to overdo. It's rare to see someone who's actually underdoing."

There he went again: complimenting me with put-downs.

Was there something in the water?

Rather than feeling bolstered by his backward praise, I felt a gush of resentment. Could be a build-up of all those years my mother said practically the same things, which only made me want to "underdo" all the more.

I didn't know if I was supposed to talk or not, but I couldn't help myself. Words flew out unchecked.

"Would you say that someone like, oh, I don't know, Miranda DuBois overdid it?" I asked.

I felt his fingers stiffen, releasing their hold on mine, and he quickly shoved my hand back inside the blanket.

"Miranda DuBois? Why would you even . . . ?" He paused, but I'd caught the tremor in his tone. "Ah, I get it. The Pretty Party. I heard Sonja mention something about you and your friend being there last night."

He obviously didn't recall seeing me there. Probably a result of my underdoing it. The prissy girls got all the attention.

"So you witnessed the big bang, did you?"

"Yes," I said, and wished I could open my eyes to look squarely at him. Only the cucumbers made that impossible. "I was the one who took Miranda home after the"—*how did one put it delicately?*—"incident with the Picasso."

"She was pretty worked up, wasn't she? It's too bad she couldn't have done things more quietly. It would've been better for . . . everyone."

His voice sounded tight, even bitter.

I heard him get off the stool and move around the recliner. Then he picked up my left hand and began kneading it, far less gently than he had the other side.

"Didn't she have a right to be mad?" I dared to inquire, perhaps stupidly, since I was wrapped in a cashmere throw, flat on my back, with goop on my face and cucumber slices holding my eyes closed. "I mean, shouldn't Dr. Madhavi have done something to fix whatever went wrong? Miranda certainly blamed her."

"Miranda brought it on herself," he said, way too quickly.

He unceremoniously dumped my hand against my thigh. He must've pushed his stool away, as I heard it slap against the cabinets.

"Hey," I said in my most soothing voice, not wanting him to desert me while I was still encumbered by cucumbers. "I was just curious. I didn't mean anything by it."

I was beginning to think that mentioning Miranda wasn't such a hot idea.

"Look," he said, after a pause that seemed forever, "I don't know if the girl was your friend or not—"

"She wasn't," I told him—well, told the air, because I wasn't sure where he was standing exactly. "Not really."

"You have to understand something. Miranda was a problem for Sonja. She was desperate for something to make her more perfect. She was just like every other beautiful woman, afraid of getting older. She should have left well enough alone." His sneakers squeaked on the tiled floor, pacing around me. "Sonja did what she had to do."

"So you were there when she injected Miranda?"

"Is that what she told you?" His voice went up a notch. "Did she say something about me?"

About him?

"No, she didn't mention you."

"Oh."

I couldn't tell if he was relieved or crestfallen. He got so quiet that I felt the need to speak.

"Listen, you don't have to explain Miranda DuBois to me. I grew up with her," I told him. "She was always a perfectionist. It must've been hard meeting such high expectations."

"She was so beautiful already," he said. "She shouldn't have gone to Sonja in the first place. She should've just stayed away."

He kept saying *was*, which began to bother me.

Did he know Miranda was dead?

Or had he used the past tense because Miranda had stopped being Dr. Sonja's patient weeks ago, after the blow-up over the botched injections?

Whatever the reason, I felt suddenly uncomfortable discussing a dead woman. Even if I was the only one in the conversation who knew she was dead.

"Let's not talk about Miranda. How about we don't talk about anything, okay?" I pleaded. "I think this mask is starting to harden."

It was like having plaster of paris on my face, making it more difficult to move my lips. Plus, I had the odd sensation of cucumber juice leaking through my eyelids.

I was about to reach up and take off the danged vegetable slices when Lance's fingertips brushed my skin as he removed them for me.

The stool creaked as he settled back onto it, and I felt a warm cloth being rubbed gently across my face, wiping off the tangerine goo.

Thankfully, Lance Zarimba performed the rest of my facial in relative silence, only piping up when he wanted to explain what he was doing; as in, explaining what kind of crud he was smearing on my face.

When my fifteen minutes were up and he was finished, he took the cashmere blanket away and raised the head of my chair so I could look into the hand-held mirror he proffered. My skin looked surprisingly pink and shiny. Not a blotch in sight.

Could be there was something to this rosemary-tangerine pore-tightening botanical facial after all.

I got up from the chair and turned to thank him, but Lance was already halfway out the door, mumbling something about having to prepare a room for his next appointment.

So I found my own way back to the reception desk and hung around for a minute, glancing at the products for sale until Janet appeared a few minutes later.

She looked flushed, her frizzy curls even more frazzled, if that were possible. And she cupped her hand over her mouth as she approached and said, "C'mon, Andy, let's go," which emerged kind of muffled 'cuz she was speaking through her fingers.

"What's wrong with you?" I asked as we passed through the glass doors of The Pretty Place and then crossed to the mall exit, before heading out to the parking lot.

She didn't pause to explain until we'd reached her Jetta, at which point she dropped her hand and looked me right in the face.

I blinked a few times, before I went ahead and stared outright.

"Go ahead," she said. "Say something."

"What did you do?" I asked, still trying to reconcile the "before" Janet with the "after" Janet standing before me.

"It's just a little bee-pollen plumper with a shot of Restylane. It'll go away after three, four months."

Good God, I sure hoped so.

I kept thinking of the Grinch and how his heart was two sizes too small. It was sort of the same with Janet's lips. Only suddenly they were two sizes too big.

"So did you get what you wanted from Dr. Sonja?" I asked, meaning the interview, or possibly the giant fish mouth. I squinted at her, thinking, *Wow*.

"She acted surprised when I told her Miranda was dead, but she didn't exactly seem crushed." Janet paused, glaring at me. "Why are you staring, Andy?"

Like she had to ask.

"Wow," I said aloud this time, because the word was stuck in my head; and because I couldn't believe she'd gone and done something like this. "Are you sure you can fit those suckers in the car with us?" I teased.

"For Pete's sake," Janet snapped. "Just shut up and get in."

Chapter 8

I had rarely been so glad to get home in all my life.

When I crawled out of bed at seven-thirty and dragged myself to Miranda's, I'd only envisioned being gone forty-five minutes at most.

By the time I got back to the condo it was after ten o'clock.

I dropped my keys on the kitchen counter as I passed through my tiny digs, half expecting to find Malone at the breakfast table, munching on cereal and toast. Only I was pleasantly surprised to find him still asleep.

After I stripped off my sweats, I slid back between the sheets. He grunted and his arm snaked around my belly, murmuring in a husky voice, "You smell like salad dressing."

That was probably the nicest thing anyone had said to me all day.

Despite the craziness on my mind, I curled up with him and slept for another two hours. When we finally got up for real around noon, I briefly filled Malone in, and he suggested something to take my mind off things: an afternoon movie.

I hadn't been to the picture show in a long while, so I happily agreed.

I even turned off my cell the whole time we were in the theater. I didn't want anything to intrude on my time with Malone. We didn't get much "us only" moments these days, what with the hours he worked at the firm. So I'd take what I could get, even on a day like this. No, especially on a day like this.

I didn't switch my cell back on until Brian and I were walking out of Valley View Mall after having lunch and seeing the latest Harry Potter flick.

Malone was right about it taking my mind off more serious matters. It had certainly done the trick. It didn't hurt that the theater audience was sparse and we'd pulled our usual "sit in the back row" maneuver so he could put his arm around me and I could sling my legs across his thighs and nestle against his neck.

Between snuggling, we'd watched the big screen, whispering to each other throughout about how the next installment of Harry Potter would have to explain why Harry looked middle-aged if they didn't recruit younger actors for future pics.

Brian had suggested seeing another show and totally blowing our entire day at the theater. Much as I enjoyed holding hands with him in the dark and breathing in the scent of stale popcorn, I realized I couldn't hide from real life forever.

I just hadn't figured reality would intrude so quickly upon stepping from the shadows of the mall into the afternoon sun.

My cell had barely been on for thirty seconds before I heard aborted bursts of Def Leppard's "Pour Some Sugar on Me."

I squinted at the number of messages on my voice mail—twenty-one in a two hour span. Wow, a record for me.

What the heck had been going on while I was in the mall?

I cut off Joe Elliott mid-"Sugar" and flipped it open.

"Yo, Hot Lips, what's up?" I said, knowing who was on the other end, thanks to good old caller ID.

Your mother? Brian mouthed, and I laughed. Like I'd greet Cissy with a "Yo," much less call her "Hot Lips."

I shook my head and mouthed back, *Janet Graham,* just as Janet started tearing into me.

"Good God, Andy, where've you been? I've been ringing your cell for, like, *ever,* and I've left a million messages!"

A million wasn't far off, though it was more like a dozen.

"Sorry," I told her, "but I was at the movies with Brian—"

"You were at the *movies*?" she screeched, her tone suggesting I'd committed a mortal sin. "What's wrong with you? I can't believe you were out of touch when so much has been going on. Surely, you've heard all the dirt by now, yes?"

What dirt? I wondered, until my brain kicked in and I realized whatever it was must have to do with Miranda DuBois.

Terrific.

"First off, why didn't you tell me you were the last one to have seen the late great Second Runner-Up Miss USA alive before she purportedly killed herself?" I listened to her rant as I followed Brian through the parking lot toward his red Acura. "I was with you for, like, an hour this morning. How could you not share that kind of buzz *immediately*? And you call yourself a friend."

The last one to have seen Miranda alive.

Just hearing that phrase made me flinch.

And how had she found out, by the way?

I knew I hadn't told her.

Oh, oh, no, please, it couldn't be.

A wave of panic hit me, and I stopped where I was, smack in the middle of a lane of traffic. A horn honked, and I regained my senses fast enough to move aside as an impatient XTerra rolled past.

I was certain Anna Dean hadn't informed the media about my presence during Miranda's final hours.

I wasn't so sure that my mother hadn't let it slip. And Highland Park was like a small town in so many ways. All Cissy had to do was tell a few of her friends . . . who told a few of their friends . . . and then someone was whispering it in the ear of the society pages editor of the *Park Cities Press*.

Namely, Ms. "I Stick My Nose in Other People's Business for a Living" Janet Graham.

"Are you there, Andy? Hello? Do we have a bad connection?"

Unfortunately, no, we didn't. I'd heard every stinking word.

"Who told you I saw Miranda last?" I asked, my voice rising as Brian turned around to look at me, his car keys dangling from his fingers. He stood near the trunk of his Acura, while I was still five yards back. It would take me two days to reach it at this rate. "Have you been talking to Cissy?"

"Well, um, not directly," came her ambiguous reply.

I scowled into the cell. "What does that mean?"

"Geez, girl, don't bite my head off. I got the dirt through the most public of channels, and you would've already heard about it had you not been hiding in the cinema with your boyfriend for half the damned day."

"Go on," I said through gritted teeth.

"The Highland Park police called a press conference because of pressure from the media," Janet said, talking so fast I could barely keep up with her. "A reporter from Miranda's own station heard the chatter on the police scanner, and they got a camera crew over to the duplex just as the M.E. was wheeling her out the front door."

This all couldn't have happened much after I'd left Cissy's house and gone to The Pretty Place at North Park Center with Janet, not long after my conversation with Deputy Dean about the final night of Miranda's too-short life.

"The HPPD spokeswoman didn't give details, just kept it simple, saying that a local woman was dead, pending notification of next of kin. It's not like they were gonna be able to keep something like this a secret, since Miranda DuBois was a celebrity," Janet went on, acting more like the *PCP*'s ace crime reporter (which they didn't even have) as opposed to their one and only society scribe. "Every major media outlet had a microphone there, and the natives got pretty restless when their questions about the cause of death and whether the police were looking for suspects went unanswered."

I'd kind of been hoping—naïvely—that Miranda could be put to rest peacefully, once her mother returned from Club Suture. I hadn't even considered that her death might turn into a three-ring circus.

It was that *National Enquirer* atmosphere we lived in these days, where news about anyone who registered anywhere on the "fame and fortune" scale became instant front page headlines.

I wondered how long it would take before newsprint about Miranda's passing got buried beneath something more sensational. Like the pastor of an area church getting snagged in a sex scandal—which seemed to happen every other weekend of late—or Ross Perot getting snapped taking out the trash in his BVDs.

Oy.

"So how'd my name come up in all this?" I asked, because Janet hadn't exactly settled that part yet. The only folks who knew I'd gone into the house with the police, other than my mother, were Deputy Dean and that ponytailed officer. Okay, and Beagle Man and Lycra Woman, but I hadn't introduced myself to either, and surely neither one had Janet's number on speed dial.

Toot toot.

Brian had gotten impatient, waiting for me to catch up, and brought the Acura to me instead. The red coupe pulled up, nearly brushing my thigh, and its horn bleated yet again. The passenger door unlocked with a crisp click. I kept the phone to my ear and grasped the door handle with the other, but that's as far as I got.

Janet took a breath before racing forward: "The deputy chief finally took a shot at calming down us nasty reporters, assuring us it didn't look like foul play was involved because there was no sign of an intruder at the duplex, and that the decedent appeared to have died by her own hand, using a weapon registered to her, all nice and legal-like. She went on to say there was preliminary evidence supporting the fact that the decedent had gunshot residue on her skin so no one need worry about a killer running around the neighborhood."

Wow, that was a lot of scoop from the usually tight-lipped Anna Dean.

But Janet still hadn't answered my question.

"And my name came up when precisely?" I prodded.

"Geez, get thy panties out of a twist, you pushy broad," she quipped. "I'm getting to that."

Toot tooot.

Malone laid on the horn a little longer this

time, and I opened the door and, holding onto the window, put one foot on the door frame, poised to climb in but not quite making it.

"So, they're just about to wrap things up, offering a lot of 'no comments' and not making anyone particularly happy, which is when your mother appeared out of the blue, wearing the most gorgeous chocolate wool double-breasted trouser suit—"

"My mother showed up at the police station? In a trouser suit?" I repeated, blinking out of dumbfounded confusion, and I heard Brian grumble, "For God's sake, Andy, get *in*."

But I wasn't listening to him.

"I know, I know," Janet said, "She normally doesn't do the trouser thing, does she? But it was Chanel, of course, and she looked perfect, as usual. You should've seen her shoes. . . ."

Cissy had shown up at Deputy Dean's press conference?

Why?

What was she up to?

"I don't care about what she wore," I said, interrupting Janet's fashion commentary. "What did she *do*?"

"She didn't tell you?"

"Tell me *what*?"

"I can't believe you're so clueless," Janet said, and I nearly told her there was a lot my mother did that I never knew about until after the fact. That was par for the course.

I hadn't spoken to Mother since I'd left her alone to phone Debbie Santos at the spa in Brazil. Lately, it seemed, I couldn't seem to leave anyone alone for even a few hours without disastrous results, could I?

What possible reason would Cissy have for showing up at the police department and interrupting a press conference?

"Janet, spill!" I demanded, because I didn't intend to go around in circles with her on this one.

"Okay, okay." The Park Cities Gossip Queen took a deep breath and slowly released it. "Apparently, Miranda's will leaves her mother in charge of everything, but since Debbie Santos is temporarily stuck on foreign soil, the always dressed-to-kill Cissy Kendricks has been named trustee or custodian or guardian *ad litem* of Miranda's remains and her property until her mother can wing it back from South America. Cissy related the dreadful story about Mrs. Santos receiving treatment from Brazilian specialists for a rare strain of the bird flu brought on by close contact with a toucan during an excursion into the rain forest."

If Mother's tales of Debbie Santos's toucan bird flu and rain forest excursion weren't far-fetched enough, neither compared to the bit about her becoming guardian of a dead woman.

What the heck was going on?

"Cissy's in charge of Miranda's remains and her estate until Mrs. Santos returns?" I squawked. "You've got to be kidding me! You are kidding, right?"

What was next?

Would Mother knock Priscilla and Lisa Marie aside to take charge of Graceland?

"It appears perfectly legal, yes," Janet confirmed. "Your mother even had an attorney from ARGH standing at her side throughout. He presented the paperwork to the deputy chief and nodded as Cissy winged her way through her comments."

"When can Debbie Santos get back?" I wondered aloud, because the sooner she let my mother off the hook, the better it would be for everybody.

"According to your mama, Mrs. Santos won't be fit enough to fly for at least a week, and so all her demands as sole living heir to Miranda DuBois will be executed by the honorable Cissy Blevins Kendricks," Janet said with all the hype of a pro wrestling ringmaster. "Oh, and that's not the best part!"

"There's more?" I leaned against the roof of Brian's car, feeling woozy. I wasn't sure I could take hearing anything else.

But I would get an earful, regardless. Of that, I was positive.

"Your mother, acting on behalf of Mrs. Santos, has hired that Hollywood forensic pathologist, Dr. Larry Woo, to conduct an independent autopsy, as she doesn't believe her daughter committed suicide and wants Dr. Woo to draw his own conclusions, separate and apart from whatever the M.E. finds. She's putting pressure on the county medical examiner's office to get their postmortem done within twenty-four hours. Can you even believe this?" Janet sounded way too excited. "It's like being in an episode of *Law & Order*, only it's real!"

It was real *crazy*, that's what it was, I thought, and wobbled, my knees knocking. With one hand I hung onto Brian's car for fear of sliding to the pavement, with the other I clutched the cell to my ear.

"Your mother was cool as a cucumber, Andy. You should've seen her." Janet's motor mouth ran on, droning around in my head like the buzz of cars in a Nascar race. "She promised Debbie Santos she'd hire a private eye to be sure a thorough investigation is done, as if the police can't be trusted to do their job. Cissy all but wagged a finger at Deputy Chief Dean, noting that she'd be checking in with her and keeping an eye on the proceedings until Mrs. Santos returned. I've never seen Anna Dean turn such an ugly shade of red."

Holy cannoli, but this had quickly gotten out of hand.

I pressed my fingers to my brow, willing away the headache that had so abruptly taken shape there. "This can't be happening, this can't be happening," I said quietly, my own little desperate mantra.

I didn't worry about interrupting Janet. She had yet to stop yammering about Cissy's starring role at the press conference and the imagined consequences.

"It's a good thing her phone is unlisted, or it'd be ringing off the hook! Oh, hey, you've got your landline unlisted, too, don't you? 'Cuz the media's gonna be after you, too, since the deputy chief forgot to turn off her microphone before she took your mother aside and suggested a conflict of interest, considering you—Guardian Cissy's own daughter—were the last known person to have seen Miranda DuBois alive and kicking. That's when your mother suggested the police better get on the stick, because you have some kind of evidence to prove she didn't commit suicide so they shouldn't be so quick to jump to conclusions—"

"*What?*" I screeched.

Oh, God, oh, God.

My stomach lurched.

"I think I'm gonna be sick," I murmured.

"Oh, wait, I'm not done yet," Big D's own Lois Lane said gleefully. "Cissy told Deputy Dean that you didn't believe Miranda pulled a kamikaze with her .22 any more than she or Debbie Santos did. So what proof have you got, Andy?" Janet asked, so eager that it scared me. "You can tell me, can't you? I can do an exclusive and get it out in a special edition, so you won't have to deal with the rest of the press badgering you relentlessly."

Because Janet certainly wasn't badgering me. No siree.

I smacked a hand against my aching head.

Why was this happening to me?

Proof?

What proof?

Was my mother nuts? Completely insane? Off her Valium? (Not that she took it regularly—she preferred to reserve it for special occasions—but I was beginning to think it might be a good idea.)

My brain went fuzzy, rather like the TV screen once did right after they played the National Anthem in the wee hours of the morning.

"Andy? You there? Hello? Did I lose you? I'm head-ing over to Cissy's now to do a little Q and A. Maybe you could join us," I heard Janet saying in my ear, sounding so far away.

I threw back my head, letting out a strangled, "Aaaarrrgh."

Which Brian heard and threw the coupe in Park, hopping out and racing to the passenger side of the Acura.

"Babe, I think it's time to go," he said, and put a hand on my head and another on my shoulder to guide me into the seat—like the police did with suspects—then he took the phone from my hands, telling Janet good-bye before hanging up, drop-ping the cell in my lap, and shutting me in.

I made no noise of protest, not even a whimper.

I was as close to open-mouthed shock as I could get.

Before I could answer, my cell rang again. It was doubtless Janet, calling me back, determined to get the scoop.

Brian gave me a look that said, "Don't do it," but I retrieved the phone from between my thighs and answered anyway, while he put the car in gear and started to drive.

But it wasn't Lois Lane with her nose for news.

It was Cissy.

I felt my blood pressure rise even before I heard the cultured twang of her familiar drawl.

"My word, Andrea!" the Mother of all Mothers started in. "Where in the world have you been? I've left you innumerable messages, yet you never returned a single one."

Which explained the high count on my voice mail.

She and Janet probably accounted for all twenty-one.

"I was incommunicado," I said, and my eye twitched. "Which is more than I can say for you, Ms. Press Conference Buttinski. Janet Graham's already called to fill me in on your latest stunt—"

"My latest stunt?" Cissy sputtered. "You mean the press conference at the police station, don't you?"

Duh.

I got out a strangled, "Uh-huh."

"I'm not sure what information Janet chose to impart to you, but I was merely acting on behalf of a friend," Cissy defended. "Debbie Santos needed someone she trusted to stand up for Miranda, and I agreed. How was I to know that Anna Dean would be speaking to the media just as I showed up at the station with Debbie's attorney? It was pure coincidence—"

"But you're making everything worse," I interrupted. "You're bringing in a forensic pathologist to do an independent autopsy, and you've threatened to hire a P.I. to do his own investigation, then you out and out lied about my having some sort of proof that Miranda didn't kill herself. My God, Mother! What're you trying to do?" My voice rose to a pitch I'm not sure I'd ever reached before, even when I was eleven and sang soprano in the church choir. "You want to get me arrested for withholding evidence? Can't you just leave things alone, just for once in your life? Why don't you let the police do their thing and just watch from the sidelines, like normal people do?"

As if the conversation wasn't stressful enough, Brian hit the brakes hard, stopping the car abruptly as an intersection with a red light loomed ahead. He threw his arm across my chest, like that would've kept me from going through the windshield if that's where I'd been headed.

"Hey!" I yelped. I wagered he'd been paying more attention to my end of the conversation than to the road.

He mumbled, "Sorry."

I brushed his arm away, leaning my brow against the window and closing my eyes, wanting to restore my equilibrium.

I'd hoped that while I was at the cinema watching Harry Potter magically turn the bad guys into snakes, any potential hype or sordid sensationalism surrounding Miranda's untimely death would evaporate, and the poor woman could have a little peace and quiet in the Afterlife.

Was that selfish of me? Was my mother doing what was right by throwing herself in the middle of things, while I just wanted to be left alone?

"Andrea? Andrea, are you there?"

I pushed the cell up to my ear. "Yes"—unfortunately—"I'm still here."

She launched right into her saint routine: "If I'm making things worse by keeping a promise to a lifelong friend, well, then forgive me. And I didn't exactly lie about what you knew. You told me this morning that Miranda didn't have her gun with her when you brought her home last night.

So how could she have used it to shoot herself? If that's not evidence, I don't know what is."

"Maybe she had another gun," I suggested, bumping my head against the window as the Acura took a curve a little too fast.

"No, she didn't," Mother insisted. "Debbie Santos said that Miranda bought the .22 last spring when she got some unsettling e-mails from a fan, even though her stepfather urged her to get something larger. But Miranda wanted a gun she could carry in her purse. *One* gun, Andy, that's all she bought."

"Did you tell that to Deputy Dean?"

"Of course I did." She sniffed. "I was informed the gun Miranda used to do herself in was indeed registered to her. Which proves my point," she finished, as if that meant everything made sense.

"I think you've seen too many reruns of *Matlock*," I mumbled, because Cissy was acting as if Debbie Santos giving her a legal voice in Miranda's postmortem matters suddenly made her Inspector Morse; or, more fittingly, Inspector Clouseau.

"Now you've gotten me off-track," my mother complained. "Did you listen to any of the messages I left?"

"No, I'm sorry, I didn't." I shifted, leaning back against the leather seat, squinting against the daylight as my pulse throbbed at my temples.

Brian eased the car to a stop at another intersection, this one at Belt Line and Preston. He looked over, raised his eyebrows.

The call waiting on my cell beeped.

I sighed, figuring it was the police, wanting to know about this "proof" I was harboring.

"Andrea? Are you listening to me?" my mother cawed in my ear, and I quickly said, "I've got another call. Hold on, okay?"

I flipped over with a perfunctory, "Hello?"

"Andy? It's Delaney Armstrong. I left a message on your voice mail earlier but you never called back."

So there was at least one call of twenty-one that wasn't Janet Graham or my completely off-her-rocker mother.

"Wow, do you believe the news about Miranda? Though I'm not surprised, considering her recent behavior," she started in, before I could get a word in edgewise. "I found out this morning when I sent my driver to drop off Miranda's Jag, only he said the police were all over the street so he pulled over a couple blocks away and called me to ask what to do. I was debating whether to phone the police or you, when I caught your mother on TV. I figured one of you would know how to handle things, so I had him take the car to Cissy's. Just wanted to get it out of my hair. That was all right, Andy, wasn't it? I called first to make sure it was okay, and Cissy said it was fine."

Of course she did, I thought, grinding my teeth.

"Anyway, I've gotta go. So tragic about Miranda, though. I guess all that fast living caught up with her at last. And to think I used to envy her." She sighed. "The grass is always greener on the other side of the fence, isn't it?"

With that, Delaney hung up, and I took a deep breath before I flipped back over to Mother, not giving her a chance to chastise me for making her wait (she thought call waiting was the work of the devil and rude as elbows on the dinner table).

"I'll be there in ten minutes," I told her, my voice grating like gravel. I was so pissed I could pop. I snapped the cell closed, glanced up and realized we were pulling into my condo's parking lot. "Could you turn this baby around and take me to Mother's?" I asked. "I've got a strong hankering to wring her scrawny neck."

"You know, if you offered up tickets for that, you could probably make a few bucks," Brian said, nudging the bridge of his glasses before he made a ring around the parking lot and headed back the way we'd come.

I was too irked to laugh.

If I came with a warning label, at that moment, it would've read: Danger! Combustible Materials Enclosed!

And Cissy had better be wearing a hard hat.

Chapter 9

Usually, approaching Mother's house meant a quiet drive down Beverly, a lovely old street lined with tall trees and stately, well-landscaped facades. The skitter of leaves beneath tires was about as much commotion as you'd encounter on an early day in fall, beyond birds twittering and blowers whooshing as gardeners tidied up.

It was that way this morning, when I drove over to share the bad news about Miranda DuBois with Cissy.

Somewhere between then and now, Mother had turned quiet into insanity with her unscheduled, over-the-top performance at Deputy Chief Anna Dean's press conference regarding Miranda's death.

Well, I didn't know firsthand that it was over-the-top, but I could only imagine, from the carrots of info Janet had dangled before me.

I didn't so much care that Cissy had gotten involved in Miranda's passing, it's just that her role in this tragedy had morphed into something far greater than I'd ever fathomed. Becoming the late Miranda Dubois's guardian or trustee (or whatever the legal term was) until Debbie Santos returned to the States?

Not exactly a move I'd anticipated, but what could I do? I would have loved to lock her in her suite of rooms until she learned to stop meddling, but I'm not sure I'd live that long.

I was surprised but not stunned by her announcement that she'd hired an independent forensic pathologist and taunted the police with talk of bringing in a private eye. Mother never did anything half-assed, so why wouldn't she cover all the bases?

What amazed me most was the fact that she'd dragged my name into the mess, when the last thing on earth I wanted was to get caught up in another gut-wrenching drama. I'd been a willful participant in more than my share in recent months, and I needed some privacy, some time alone with my boyfriend and my paints.

I had no desire to become entangled in Miranda's death, not for all the coffee beans in Starbucks.

I needed my mother to make some kind of public retraction, so I could extricate myself from this evolving scandal and go back to living my own life. Because I was all for leaving the detecting to the Highland Park police.

Somehow, I had to convince Cissy to take a step back and stop antagonizing the cops. Debbie

Santos could take on the boys and girls in blue when she got home, if that's what she wanted.

This wasn't my mother's battle to fight.

At least, I didn't think so.

As Malone steered the car nearer Mother's address, I noticed the increasing crowd of vehicles parked against the curb on either side. I wondered if, maybe, one of the society dames was having a garden club luncheon, or if someone's horde of relatives had arrived weeks early for Thanksgiving.

Until I realized the parked car crunch led right to Cissy's place, with SUVs and vans from local TV stations standing at the mouth of the drive with microphones in hand. Even a patrol car with a pair of HP cops had joined the mix: one of the uniforms monitored access to Mother's driveway, and the other tried to keep the street from becoming a parking lot.

Call me psychic, but I felt sure the throng hadn't gathered for a book club discussion at Cissy's nor to celebrate the glory that was my mother's yard. Her roses might be the envy of the neighborhood when they bloomed in the spring, but the bushes weren't exactly lush with flowers at the moment and were hardly worthy of satellite trucks and camera crews.

I feared for an instant that Brian's car might be swarmed, but I needn't have worried. Though a few of the loitering reporters surely got whiplash turning their heads to see who was arriving in the little red coupe, not a single reporter rushed toward us.

The officer blocking the drive did make Malone

stop and roll down the window, and he even made me show ID when I told him I was the only child of Cissy Blevins Kendricks and this was the house I'd grown up in.

I guess having the "Blevins Kendricks" part on my driver's license allowed me to pass the test, as he let us through without further hassle.

While I wasn't surprised to see Stephen Howard's shiny pickup truck out front when we pulled up, nor Janet Graham's VW, which was parked right beside it, I raised my eyebrows when I spotted another familiar vehicle: a marked car with plates that clearly tagged it as belonging to the deputy chief of the Highland Park P.D.

But that wasn't the only surprise to greet me. There was also a midnight blue Ford Taurus that had seen better days—I had no idea to whom it belonged—and, most conspicuously, Miranda DuBois's shiny gray Jaguar, which was being lifted onto the back of a tow truck. Delaney's driver must've already been by and dropped it off, and Deputy Dean had certainly wasted no time in having the car hauled away.

Speak of the devil.

There stood Anna Dean, across the driveway, her hands on her gun-belted hips, supervising the operation.

At least that meant the cops were investigating, right? Maybe they'd even uncover something telling in Miranda's car, a voice recorder or a notebook or a piece of crucial evidence like they were always finding on *CSI* just before the "Oh, shit" moment (as Brian liked to call it).

"Looks like the circus is in town," Brian said, parking his coupe around the side, near Mother's garage, rather than pulling up behind the tow truck.

"And Mother's the ringleader," I remarked rather dryly.

I seriously contemplated slipping in the back through the kitchen door instead of having to walk past Anna Dean in front, but I knew I had to face her sometime, regardless. So it might as well be now.

Oddly enough, I felt my Excedrin-sized headache blossoming.

Brian must've heard my groan after he cut the engine, as he asked, "Are you okay?"

I felt a little like a lamb headed to the slaughter for some reason, but told him instead, "I could be worse."

Which was true.

I could have had Dengue fever or the West Nile virus or something equally nasty.

Though I was a little queasy, I wasn't sick. I was just caught in the cross hairs of a very awkward situation.

And I owed it all to Mummy Dearest.

Yippee Skippy.

"You want to go through the back?" Brian asked, reading my mind, but I shook my head. Call me a masochist, but I intended to face the consequences of Mother's actions regardless of how much it hurt.

I clung to his hand as we walked around the front, pausing as the tow truck let out a loud screech and clink of chains as it secured the Jag onto its flat bed.

Deputy Dean caught sight of us as we emerged from the flagstone path that wound through the hedges. She wasted no time in confronting us, thumbs tucked in her utility belt, a tight frown on her lips.

"Good afternoon, Ms. Kendricks," she said, sounding stuffy and formal, though I'd been "Andy" that morning.

Oh, how quickly the wind could shift.

"Hey, Deputy Dean," I said before introducing her to Brian. "So you're going to check out Miranda's car?" I asked, stating the obvious, and she nodded an affirmative. "Do you have to tow it? Didn't Delaney's driver leave the keys in the ignition?"

"Yes, we've got the keys, but we're lifting it on the tow to preserve evidence. We're still regarding this as an open case until the M.E.'s ruling, despite what you may have heard." Anna Dean paused to squint at me, and I felt a little like a germ under a microscope. "You don't have something you'd like to add to what you told me this morning, do you, Andy?"

So I was "Andy" again, just like that?

I felt my eyelid twitch.

"Not a thing," I told her, "even if my mother implied otherwise. Which is why I'm here," I added, raising my voice over the lurch of the motor on the tow truck as it started up and began the slow curve around Mother's driveway. "I want Cissy to go on the record stating she'd been mistaken when she suggested I was holding back information relating to Miranda's death, because I'm not keeping things from the police. I told you everything."

"Is that so?" She still didn't look like she trusted me entirely.

"Yes, it is."

She glanced at Brian and then back at me. I was surprised she didn't come around behind me to see if I was crossing my fingers.

Which I wasn't.

"All right." She gave a clipped jerk of her chin. "If you do think of something that may help us, I'd appreciate it if you'd come straight to me instead of running off to Cissy. I'd hate to have to charge you with interfering in an investigation."

I had to bite my tongue to keep from reminding her that she was the one who encouraged me to seek solace at my mother's house that morning, after I learned that Miranda was dead. But I didn't want to piss off a high-ranking member of the Highland Park police, particularly after Cissy had done such a brilliant job of it already.

"Yes, ma'am, I'll come straight to you," I said, in my best Little Miss Manners mode.

"Your mother's making this more difficult than it has to be, what with beating us to the punch calling Mrs. Santos in Brazil and flying in a pathologist from L.A. to independently examine Ms. DuBois's remains. I somehow doubt he's going to find anything to refute the county M.E.'s report, which we should have by tomorrow, by the way."

I knew the forensics lab had cases backed up and was months behind. Malone was forever complaining about the slow rate of return, especially on DNA, for his firm's criminal cases. But I guessed that Miranda's high profile had pushed her case to the front of the line. I wasn't surprised.

"You yourself witnessed Ms. DuBois's devastated state of mind and reckless behavior last night," Deputy Dean went on. "We spoke with Dr. Madhavi not long ago, and she admitted Ms. DuBois had been harassing her and seemed especially distressed since her adverse reaction to the wrinkle filler. It's unfortunate the doctor didn't report Ms. DuBois's menacing behavior early, as we might've intervened." As Anna Dean spoke, her jaw muscle kept contracting, though the bulging vein at her temple was sign enough that she was irritated.

I didn't interrupt her, as it was obvious she had more to say.

"I never like to make pronouncements before all the facts are weighed, but this one smells like suicide to me." She jerked her chin at me. "So, Ms. Kendricks, if you could just go about your own business and get your mother to back off, the whole department would sure appreciate it. It's hard enough doing our job without the public interfering."

"Don't worry about me," I assured her. "Though I'll see what I can do about my mother."

As if I could ever get Cissy to do anything.

Anna Dean seemed satisfied enough with my response and started to head toward her squad car, when I thought of something I'd forgotten to ask her.

"Deputy Dean," I called, and scrambled across the drive after her. "What about Miranda's laptop. Did you recover it? Or her cell phone?"

She answered, tight-lipped, "We did find her cell in the sewer in front of her house. Ms. DuBois must've dropped it, and it's got heavy water damage from being down there overnight. We're still trying to salvage data from the chip. But, Andy, there was no laptop in the duplex, so I'm sure you were mistaken. It was late, and you were preoccupied."

I was mistaken?

Oh, really.

I stood there, blinking at her, not sure what to say without insulting her. As if I would hallucinate seeing a computer on a coffee table. Was the photo on the screen a figment of my imagination? Had I dreamt I'd put the laptop in sleep mode so it would go dark?

Yeesh.

Brian came up beside me and slung an arm around my shoulders. "You hanging in there?" he asked.

"By my fingernails," I said, frowning.

I watched Anna Dean take off in her marked vehicle without even turning on her bubble lights, much to Brian's muttered disappointment.

Well, if the deputy chief didn't believe me about the laptop, I guess I couldn't blame her, considering my parentage. Cissy was nothing if not a colorful figure in the Park Cities, and my own life was routinely bizarre, though I could pin that as well on the nuts stuck on my family tree.

No use fretting over something I couldn't change.

Brian and I shuffled over to the front stoop, and I patted the heads of the whitewashed terra cotta lions standing guard on either side of the front door. I'd named them Bert and Ernie when I was a kid, though that wasn't exactly public knowledge.

Hey, everyone had secrets they took to the grave, didn't they? Mine were probably meek compared to most. I wondered if Miranda had died with deep, dark secrets she'd tried to keep.

I'd barely touched my finger to the doorbell when the portal was pulled wide and Sandy Beck let out a "Thank goodness it's you, Andy!"

Then she hustled me and Brian inside.

I could hear voices beyond the foyer, and before she shepherded us in their direction, Sandy worried the pearl buttons on her dove gray cardigan and whispered, "Cissy appears to have whacked a hornet's nest, hasn't she? The deputy chief was just here—"

"I know," I butted in. "I ran into her outside."

"And Janet Graham's in the den." Sandy put a hand to her heart. "Good Lord, what happened to that poor girl's lips? Was she in an accident?"

"Not exactly," I said, knowing as I did that Janet's newly enlarged lips were no accident. "I believe it was, um, an allergic reaction to something she ate."

Don't ask why I lied. It just came out that way.

Sandy looked satisfied. "Well, Janet has planted herself on the sofa and I doubt she'll leave until she gets something extremely gossipworthy out of your mother, though I daresay Cissy should be nearly tapped out after the show she put on this morning at the police station."

Whoa.

My eyes went wide with shock. Sandy rarely ever criticized Mother, even sideways, so I could tell she was upset.

She sighed and tapped her chin. "I wonder if Janet will be staying for dinner. Should I set extra plates for y'all, too? Oh, dear, but I've no idea what that dear girl's allergic to. Perhaps I should ask in case she's here too much longer?"

"I have a feeling we'll all be gone before supper, Sandy, so I wouldn't worry about Janet or anyone else if I were you."

Heck, if I had my druthers, Malone and I would be out of Mother's house in ten minutes flat, after I set the record straight.

I thought of something else and asked Sandy, "Is Stephen here? I saw his car out front."

She cocked her head toward the kitchen. "He's interviewing the private investigator your mother is thinking of hiring."

So the dinged-up old Ford belonged to a P.I.?

I exhaled, the air lifting my bangs from my forehead.

Either the dude didn't like to spend extravagantly on cars or he wasn't very good at what he did. Perhaps he was someone Mother was using simply to keep the local police on their toes. As if they needed prodding.

"Oh, he appears to be a very nice man," Sandy

said, though I hadn't asked. "I'm heading back to the kitchen myself, to see if they need more coffee, then I'm ducking into my room and locking the door for a while. It's been a rather hectic day, as you can imagine."

Sandy did look frazzled. Her normally placid face—warmly etched with lines from a life well lived—had the glazed look of someone who needed Calgon to take her far, far away.

"You go on," I told her. "I've got a few words to say to Mother, as you can imagine."

"Bad words?" she asked, raising fuzzy gray eyebrows.

"If they are, it'll be the bare minimum, I promise. Not enough to send me to hell in a hand basket," I assured her, and she patted my hand before she headed off.

Locking herself into her room, huh?

Sounded like a smart choice to me.

I'd always said that Sandy was a genius.

Tempted as I was to grab Malone and leave so we could play hermit at the condo until this latest debacle blew over, I knew I had to straighten out my mother. I felt like she'd used me to get a point across, when this situation involving Miranda DuBois had zip to do with me. If Cissy's intention was to support Debbie Santos in her quest to find out exactly why her daughter had died, I had nothing against that. She just had to leave me out of it.

"You can do this, Andy," Brian said, giving me a gentle nudge. "You can stand up to your mother. I've seen you do it before, and without use of deadly force. Don't let her intimidate you."

"If she'd only just mind her own business, I'd never have to argue with her again," I said, and he laughed, shaking his head.

"Like that's ever going to happen in our lifetime."

I wanted to say something like, *I'm sorry my mom's such a nut ball* or *Maybe this'll be the last time she makes a mess I have to clean up*, but he clearly already knew how things stood after nearly five months of dating *moi*.

"If you need me to throw a block for you, just give me the high sign," he offered, hardly looking very tough with his button-down shirt and crew neck Polo, with that cowlick of brown curled upon his forehead. Imagining him throwing a body block was cause enough to soften my hard heart the tiniest bit.

"Thanks," I said, and laced my fingers with his, gripping as I pulled him forward. "Now, for your viewing pleasure, come watch me ever so gracefully kick my mother's derriere. Figuratively speaking."

Without hesitation, he followed me down the hallway toward the den where the lions congregated, and I squared my far-from-broad shoulders, gearing up to face them.

When I stepped through the transom, a floorboard creaked underfoot. The jabber of voices quieted and all eyes turned to me.

Then, as quickly as they shut up, they started yapping again, throwing out questions with the intensity of ticked-off tribesmen spitting blow darts.

"Andy, how *could* you keep such a huge secret from me? Not telling me you were with Miranda before she died? Or about the fact that she didn't off herself like the police believe? My gosh, how long have we been friends? Since before puberty?" Janet rattled all this off without a breath between. She sounded wounded—heck, she *looked* wounded, with those fattened chops of hers.

My mother simultaneously kicked in a pink-cheeked apology: "Sweet pea, I *tried* to explain what I meant when I said you had proof that Miranda didn't kill herself, but I think Janet needs to hear it from the horse's mouth, as she obviously doesn't believe me. . . ."

Where were the plagues of locust when you needed them?

If I could've blinked and had them swarm the room, I would've done it.

Instead, I took in a deep breath, let go of Malone's hand and rounded the overstuffed sofa, to stand in front of the great marbled fireplace that centered the room.

I cleared my throat, which had no effect whatsoever, and then I said—very loudly—"Would the two of you, please, just shut up for a second and listen to me?"

My mother and Janet fell silent, and I was finally able to have my say without having to resort to covering their pie holes with duct tape.

Chapter 10

Malone shot a *Do you need me?* look from across the room, but I shook my head. I might be a soft-hearted marshmallow when it came to my emotions, but there were times when I simply had to stand up for myself.

This was one of them.

I turned my attention to Cissy and Janet, my mother in a brown suede skirt and taupe silk turtleneck, Janet in a blinding magenta suit (with matching magenta lips); both of them glared at me, and I sighed, the frustration I'd felt only seconds ago seeping away, sadness in its stead.

"I don't know what you want from me," I told them, my voice strained. "All I tried to do was help out Miranda, and now I'm under suspicion for—" I hesitated, having no idea exactly. "—all sorts of things."

When no one uttered a rebuttal, I continued,

"The only thing I'm sure of about Miranda's death is that I wasn't there when she breathed her last. So I can't say what happened. If you want to figure it out, I'd suggest you call a medium who can channel the nearly departed and get Miranda's perspective." I tossed my hands in the air, letting go of my angst and my guilt, because I was through feeling responsible. "I have no clue whether or not she killed herself, though I'd like to think she didn't. Except the alternative is . . . well, it's not any better, is it?"

There, I'd said it.

I felt relieved and unsettled at once.

"But, Andy," Janet piped up, "Cissy said you had proof that Miranda didn't take her own life. So 'fess up. What is it?"

"Astoundingly, Mother was exaggerating," I told her, fixing my gaze on Cissy, who in turn glanced up at the ceiling, as if spotting a damp spot where none existed. "I don't have any kind of tangible evidence, just a strong gut feeling."

My mother lost interest in the ceiling and chimed in, "We should listen to our intuition more often. It's what God gave us women to make up for not installing an inner compass. Though the automobile industry's taken care of that one, haven't they, with On-Star and talking maps?" She plucked at invisible lint on her suede skirt. "I do so love that little voice that tells me when to turn right and left. It sounds so much like Meryl Streep. Do you think it's her, perchance?"

"I don't know, Mother," I said, fighting hard the temptation to roll my eyes. Cissy came up with the darnedest things sometimes.

"I guess it could be Lauren Bacall," Mother went on inanely. "Sometimes it does sound like the old Tuesday Morning commercials."

Brian coughed behind his hand and pretended to study the signed Ansel Adams photographs hung on the wall above Mother's cherrywood desk. He must've decided I didn't need his protection, as he excused himself, giving me an *I'll be waiting outside* glance before he beat it.

I ached to follow him, but stayed put.

"So your evidence is just instinct?" Janet prodded. She had a pad of paper balanced on her knees, and a pen in her hand, and I knew that anything I said might very well end up on the Society pages of the *Park Cities Press* in an expose about Dr. Sonja, the shooting at the Pretty Party, and the suspicious death of a local debutante slash beauty queen turned news anchorwoman. "You don't have anything tangible?"

My God, she was as bad as Anna Dean, who'd wanted me to swear to God and the world in a police report.

"If there was any tangible proof that Miranda didn't kill herself, I would've turned it over to the cops already, Janet," I said, sounding huffy. Heck, feeling huffy. "It's just that Miranda didn't seem like she wanted to chuck it all after what happened at Delaney's. I got the feeling she was mad as hell." I went ahead and told her, "Miranda sounded like she wanted revenge, not a way out."

"Andrea?" my mother piped up. "While I'm thinking of it, if you wouldn't mind, there's something I need to talk to you about. It's most urgent—"

"You're darned right there is," I replied, but I held up my hand. "When I'm done with Janet, it's your turn," I said, and she frowned, tight-lipped, but let it drop.

Thank heavens.

"But the police seem to think Miranda killed herself with her own gun, isn't that right?" Janet said. "So *they* must have proof that's what happened."

Perhaps I should've just shut up then and there.

But I didn't exactly have a reputation for being the strong, silent type. Could be I was more like Cissy than I wanted to admit.

"If it went down that way, someone from Delaney's party must've stopped by and dropped off Miranda's gun after I left her duplex," I said, wrestling aloud with the only scenario that made sense, "because I could swear that someone else snatched up the .22 when Miranda dropped it on Delaney's living room floor, and I'm pretty danged certain she didn't have it on her when I took her home."

"Cissy wasn't lying, then?" Janet nearly gasped, and my mother sat up ramrod straight, her smile smug. "Not full throttle anyway. You *saw* something. That's some kind of proof. You're a witness."

"I didn't witness Miranda's death," I reminded her, "only how things played out beforehand. As for whether or not my mother lied, she stretched the truth a smidge by implying I had something concrete," I said, then added more quietly, "so, I guess, it wasn't a total fabrication, if you put it that way."

My heart pounded a mile a minute after I was finished, because I'd admitted flat-out what I'd told Anna Dean about Miranda's gun, and it was the truth as I knew it. Even though I realized Janet might use it in an article questioning the police spin on Miranda's death being a suicide.

"I would never flat-out lie. I was raised better than that," my mother drawled, "though there's nothing wrong with an occasional truth stretching, particularly when one's intentions are good. Such as that time when Bunny Beeler asked how her Versace gown looked at the Cattle Baron's Ball, and I didn't want to tell her the lime-green sequins made her appear rather like a large stalk of celery, so I tweaked my honest opinion into a whispered, 'Bunny, you look good enough to eat,' since I was rather hungry and a stalk of celery with a little cream cheese would've been a lifesaver."

My mother is a loony tune, I thought, and blotted out Cissy's voice as she meandered into another story about some little white lies she'd told.

Apparently Janet did likewise, as she sought to reclaim my attention, doing weird things with her eyebrows, pursing her newly engorged lips and waving the hand that held her pen so that I was a little afraid it might become a projectile.

"Excuse me if I'm more confused now than ever, Andy," she said. "So we've got the police claiming there was gun powder residue on Miranda's hand, and my sources indicate the weapon *was* indeed registered to Miranda DuBois. I know they haven't done the autopsy yet and run all their forensic tests, but doesn't that prove she pulled the trigger of her own .22?"

I squirmed, tempted to say, *I guess it could*, because it all sounded so neat and tidy when she put it that way. Still, all the pieces didn't fit.

And there *was* an explanation for part of Janet's—and the police department's—initial theory anyway.

"You were at the Pretty Party when she shot the Picasso," I reminded her. "So far as I'm aware, Miranda didn't retire to the loo and wash her hands afterward, which would account for the residue, right?"

At least, Miranda hadn't washed her hands in the time I'd been with her, which was considerable, including after the gunfire at Delaney's, in my Jeep on the way to the duplex, and until she'd fallen asleep on her sofa. Though that didn't mean she hadn't fired a gun—or even *her* gun—again. Only I still had doubts that she'd smuggled the .22 back home without my ever catching sight of it.

"So that would point back to your idea that someone else returned the gun to her last night"— Janet picked up the thread I was weaving and took it home—"and either dropped it off or used it to . . . you know . . . " She hesitated.

"Yes, I know."

To kill her.

"Andrea, darlin', I have a feeling you're going to want to see what I have to show you," my mother tried again, waggling a finger in my direction. "Do you think we might have that moment to chat right about now? I have, um, a handbag I want you to take a look at."

A handbag?

We were discussing whether Miranda DuBois committed suicide and she wanted to show me a purse?

She had the oddest expression on her face, almost like the Christmas when I was nine and had asked for a boa. She'd wrapped up this awful rabbit fur thing that made me burst into tears when I opened the box (did I mention I'd joined PETA when I was a very computer literate six?). I'd wanted a boa *constrictor*, not a stole made from dead bunnies.

"Later, Mother," I said, because Janet wasn't done with her questions, and I had something to add as well. Janet cleared her throat loudly, and I whispered, "Later," again to Cissy.

"So what about the note, Andy?" Janet asked, her silver pen poised above her notepad. "When I asked Anna Dean, she mentioned a letter they'd taken into evidence, but she wouldn't clarify what it was about."

If they'd found a suicide note, it was after I left the duplex.

"I'm not sure what you mean," I said, because I wasn't.

"The *letter*," Janet verbally nudged at my blank look. "The one that purportedly gave Miranda the heave-ho from a club she belonged to. Anna Dean indicated it might've pushed Miranda over the edge."

"Oh, *that* letter," I said, realizing what exactly she was yammering about.

The missive from the Caviar Club.

"I saw it," I told her, and she cocked her head attentively. "Deputy Dean showed me the stationery, to see if I'd heard of the group. It was from the Caviar Club," I explained, and I saw Janet's eyes go round as pennies. "It said something to the effect that she'd been dropped from membership because of her current unfortunate circumstances. It was all crumpled, like she'd wadded it into a ball."

Janet scooched to the edge of her seat. "The Caviar Club, you said? Miranda DuBois was a member? Are you sure that's what it was?"

"Yes, I'm sure," I said, and noticed Janet's cheeks turn all pink and shiny. "You've heard of it?"

Well, of course she had. Janet knew about every club in the city. That was part of her gig.

"I'll say I've heard of it." She put her pad and pen on the coffee table—well, dumped them with a clatter, really—and gave a jerk of her head toward Cissy. My mother kept glancing at her watch, like her handbag revelation couldn't wait another minute.

"Do you mind if we talk alone?" Janet hissed in my direction, though my bat-eared mother obviously heard her, as she fairly jumped out of her chair.

"My goodness, but I should see how Stephen's doing with Milton Fletcher in the kitchen. Janet, dear, do you need anything? Coffee, tea, or lip balm?" Mother offered, cocking her head to one side as she gazed at my friend.

"Uh-uh." Janet shook her head, self-consciously touching her mouth.

"All right, then." Cissy turned toward me. "Andrea, you come find me before you leave, you hear?"

"I will," I promised.

"You'd better," she threatened before disappearing faster than a quarter up the sleeve of a magician.

The private eye's name was Milton Fletcher?

I thought that sounded like a relative of Jessica's from Cabot Cove. I imagined him a gray-haired and grizzled older man with patches at the elbows of his corduroy jacket.

"Andy, yo, are you listening to me?" Janet said, her impatience making her prickly. Or maybe it was the bee pollen and Restylane.

"I'm listening."

Yeesh.

"Please, Andy, *focus*. This is important," she said, and gestured toward the sofa, patting the cushion beside her.

I dutifully went over and plunked down. She made no move to scoop up notebook and pen, so I guess whatever we said henceforth was truly off the books.

"The Caviar Club," she whispered, though there was no one else in the den. "Do you know for sure that Miranda DuBois had been admitted? Are you positive?"

"Yes, positive," I said, because I'd seen with my own eyes the "Dear Miranda" letter telling her she'd been unadmitted. "Anna Dean bagged the letter telling Miranda she'd been booted. It's as good as a suicide note as far as she's concerned.

She figures Miranda getting rejected was related to her death."

"As in, she killed herself because the Caviar Club gave her the heave-ho?"

"Deputy Dean seemed to believe it was a contributing factor, yeah."

Janet looked like someone had lit a fire under her, and it wasn't just because her bright red hair had been spiked out in all directions, which seemed a little at odds with her magenta Joan Crawford suit, which fit her like a shoebox. She quivered like a rattlesnake's tail, hardly able to sit still.

"What an interesting coincidence," she murmured, drumming her chin with her fingertips. Then the drumming abruptly ceased. "Did the deputy chief know what the Caviar Club was, by any chance?" she asked.

"No, she didn't have a clue, and neither do I," I admitted, though it didn't take a genius to realize Janet had one up on me. "I'm guessing it really doesn't have to do with wine tasting, does it?"

Janet merely smiled; a quirky grin that assured me she knew better. "No, it's not a wine-tasting club, although they do go for pricey champagne," she said, and scooted closer, though there was less than a hairbreadth between us. "It's about something more old-fashioned than apple pie."

"I thought it wasn't about food."

"It's not." Red-tinged eyebrows went up. "It's about good old-fashioned S-E-X."

Oh, *that* kind of club.

Well, hello.

Chapter 11

"Remember when I told you I was working on a feature story for the paper?"

The one about superficiality and appearances and Dr. Sonja Madhavi that had inspired her to blow up her lips like an Angelina wannabe?

"Yep, I remember," I said.

Janet opened her mouth, glanced at the open door, and reconsidered. She popped up from the sofa and crossed the room to shut us in. I heard a click and realized she'd locked the door.

Geez, Louise.

What was going on with her? She'd been acting odd all day.

She dropped back down beside me, leaned her knees toward mine, and said in a most hush-hush tone, "All right, here's the Cliffs Notes version, so stick with me."

I nodded.

"I was working on the piece about Pretty Parties and the Park Cities' obsession with looking perfect, and I decided to do a sidebar on the Caviar Club, after I started hearing buzz about it on the social scene. The kind of buzz that's whispered behind hands, if you get my drift." She picked up her pen again and fiddled with it, her eyes on the Mont Blanc as she said: "If you weren't so out of the loop, Andy, you'd probably have gotten wind of it, too." She gave me a quick glance.

"Whatever." I shrugged.

If she'd intended to hurt my feelings, she hadn't. I *was* out of the loop with regard to where the moneyed set partied these days, and I didn't mind a bit.

"So what is the Caviar Club?" I asked, seeing as how Deputy Chief Dean thought Miranda might have wanted to die after being ejected from it.

"It's all about the pretty people, you see. The beautiful ones . . . " Janet paused. " . . . at least on paper. *Photo* paper," she clarified. "They pick and choose their members based on looks, or looks that they find appealing. They don't want any average folks at their secret parties messing up the ambience. And I guess that means me, because they wouldn't let me in, not to any of the real parties. They just invited me, as the *PCP* society editor, to something specially arranged." She gave her spiky red hair a toss, her fat lips pouting.

"Who's doing the picking and choosing?" I asked.

It sounded awfully narrow-minded and snobbish. What intelligent, well-rounded person only wanted to meet others solely based on looks? It was like buying a gift wrapped in a Tiffany's box and not having a clue what was inside. It could well be a multicarat diamond ring; but then again, perhaps it was a big fat CZ worth *nada*.

"I'm not exactly sure who's playing judge and jury, deciding who the Caviar Club lets in," Janet admitted. "That's one part of the story I still need to find out. I can't get the skinny from anyone I've interviewed. The members I've been able to track down say as little as possible. It's like they're bound to secrecy or something."

"So who did you talk to?" I asked, convinced at this point that the Caviar Club mentality was what had started her obsession with meaty lips.

"They set up a special cocktail party so I could meet some of the club's players and supposedly get what I needed for my story. But it was just a bunch of token nobodies." She sniffed. "Okay, sure, they were good-looking enough, though the women more so than the men. Big surprise, huh? The guys could be bald, so long as they had power and money."

"Power and money are the male equivalent of pretty faces and big breasts," I said.

"Speaking of faces," Janet kicked in, "I could tell Dr. Sonja had worked on quite a few of them." She touched her chin. "All their lips were like fat strawberries. And their cheeks . . . they had that supertight, shiny look. You know what I mean?"

"The Sandra Bullock Apple Cheeks," I said, because I'd heard several of the women at the Pretty

Party request them specifically, as if it were a name brand.

Janet pursed her own fat strawberry lips, and I gawked.

If she'd been self-conscious of her mouth before, I figured she was doubly conscious now. I found myself wondering what would happen if she pricked those babies with a pin. Would they pop like balloons?

Janet ignored my staring and went on: "I didn't meet anyone worth quoting, just your typical Park Cities wannabes who'd only spout the party line about the club." She cleared her throat then mimicked an East Texas drawl that sounded a lot like my mother's. "Oh, hon, it's such a wonderful way to meet like-minded people who are success-ful in their fields and oh-so-philanthropic, always giving, giving, giving."

I guffawed. "You have got to be kidding? Phi-lanthropists who belong to a private club that caters to narcissists. What a bunch of hypocrites."

"And that's not the half of it, Andy," Janet went on, this time in her own voice. "I spoke to a woman named Theresa Hurley, the mouth-piece for the owners, and she gave me a general password to get into the Caviar Club's Web site. There's not much there, mostly a submission form for interested parties. But there is a mission state-ment." She laid a hand on her heart. "'Our goal is bring together those of the same level of aesthetics so as to avoid intermingling with those of lesser aesthetics.'"

"Are you kidding me?" I snorted.

She laughed. "I swear. God, Andy, you'd die if you read it. It's like the Pretty People's Nazi Party credo. If you're not deemed physically attractive enough to get in, go piss on yourself."

"Lovely," I remarked, once again happy to not be a joiner. I would've rather mixed with the apes at the zoo than with a bunch of jerks who judged each other on something as artificial as size and shape and placement of features.

Janet pursed her lips, making them appear almost normal for a moment. Until she opened her mouth again. "Of course, I decided, what better way to get the inside scoop than to join up, see how things really worked? They don't give you the members-only password that grants access to where the secret parties will be held unless you've gotten your manicured toe in the door. But I couldn't apply as myself, not after having met some of the anointed ones. So I lifted the photo of a model from a New York modeling agency. Slam-dunk, I figured."

She sucked in a breath, only to slowly release it. "Boy, was I wrong. They sent an immediate e-mail rejection. 'Not what we're searching for,' was the line they used. Good Lord"—Janet cackled—"if I couldn't get in with a photo of a Tyra Banks look-alike, I give up. Now I'll never really know what's really going on." Her eyes met mine, and they were hard as steel. "The whole thing smells fishier than the Gorton's factory, Andy."

"I'd say let it go," I suggested. "I mean, what's the big deal? It sounds like a club full of mirror-obsessed ninnies who pick and choose fresh meat that appeals to them. It's not like being superficial in Dallas isn't a citywide pastime. I'm not sure it's even worth a story. Why don't you let it drop, huh?"

"I can't," she said, adamant.

"You're seriously compelled to write another piece about Beemer-driving snots who only want to mix with other Barbies and Kens?"

It was redundant, really.

Weren't we just at a Pretty Party last night, where women lined up for free injections of gunk into their creases? Didn't she just drag me to Dr. Sonja's boutique in the mall this morning so I could get a salad-dressing facial and she could get her Angelina Jolie kisser?

How many articles could she write about the beauty-obsessed in the Park Cities?

Maybe if the whole world stopped worshipping shiny objects, the shiny people would cease parading around in butt-baring jeans and too-tight T-shirts, showing off bodies carved by scalpels and hair glued into place with more gel than the cranberry mold at Thanksgiving.

"You don't get it," Janet said, sniffing. "It's much more than a dating service for the plastic set. *Waaay* more. I've heard the rumors, Andy. I just have to find another way to prove the whispers are true."

I swear I saw the sheen of sweat on her upper lip. Her eyes kept straying toward the door, as though afraid someone could overhear our conversation through solid wood and walls thick as cinder block.

It was like she was about to confess that she had the paperwork proving Tom Cruise was an alien life form, and she was afraid the Scientologists had her oversized lapels tapped.

She ran a tongue across her lips before she hissed, "Here's what I need to confirm, because speculating isn't enough for a front-page feature. Once the club owners decide you're gorgeous enough to get you in the door, that's just step one. When you're there and you pass some kind of loyalty test, they move you up in the ranks. Then it's Sodom and Gomorrah. I've heard what goes on in the back room at their secret gatherings makes *Caligula* seem like a Disney flick."

"*Caligula*?" Wasn't that, like, a million years old? Heck, I hadn't even seen the *Rocky Horror Picture Show* yet. I was way behind on watching cult films, particularly the X-rated kind. "Isn't that, like, from the seventies or something?"

"My God, girlfriend, it's been called the Ben-Hur of Porn." She paused to fan herself with her notepad. "Has a bit of something for everyone, shall we say."

"Um, okay." Was I the only grown woman in the world who'd never seen porn before, even old stuff? "So you're saying the Caviar Club is a sex club," I deciphered. "Like for big-time swingers."

"*Very* prominent swingers with a lot to lose if they're outed," she clarified, and her cheeks turned a shade of pink that nearly matched the magenta of her outfit. "I don't have names, not on the record. But the buzz is there are some biggies involved." Her eyes had a freaky kind of gleam.

"I tried to get Theresa Hurley to cough up something incriminating, but she wouldn't bite. She's like a very thin bulldog, guarding the door."

All very interesting, I mused, but I wasn't sure why she was telling me this.

"Um, Janet, I hope you don't mind my asking," I said, "but what does your Caviar Club story have to do with me?"

It's not like I was a member, or even cared about the secret society.

On a good day over lunch at Patrizio's, I may have been in the mood for sordid stories about Orgies of the Rich and Famous. But it had been a stinky past twenty-four hours, I was dying to fetch Brian and head home for some alone time, and I still needed to chat with my mother.

"First off, oh, pal of mine," Janet said, leaning nearer, "I'm going to need your help again." I started to protest, because I'd already done her a huge favor that morning, and I didn't want to have anything to do with the Caviar Club besides.

"Look, Jan, didn't I help you out at North Park already? So I don't really think—" I tried to gracefully decline, but she talked right over me.

"Consider that I'm calling in a few markers. Because you owe me more than one, lest you've forgotten all the things I've done for you."

Markers.

Oh, boy.

She would have to bring that up.

Yeah, yeah, Janet had come to my rescue more than once, like when she'd filled me in on the background of folks in a chichi retirement home

that I thought might be involved in a couple mur-
ders, or when she'd informed me that a boy-toy
who'd been dating a lifelong friend of Mother's
had a well-recorded history as a gold digger.

"Okay, okay"—I relented, because I was in-
debted to her, and she clearly knew it—"but make
it a small favor, would you? I don't want to do
anything illegal. I'm already no favorite of Anna
Dean as it is."

She flashed a brief, fish-lipped smile. "We'll
talk about specifics later, okay? I've got to figure
out logistics."

"Whatever." Maybe I'd be locked inside my
condo later, not answering my telephone.

Then she seemed suddenly nervous again, clear-
ing her throat and glancing over at the door. "I've
got something else on my mind at the moment,
and, not coincidentally, it concerns Ms. Miranda
DuBois."

"What about her?"

What else was there to discuss? Hadn't we done
that topic to death already (no pun intended)?

"I'm not a hundred percent, but I firmly believe
Miranda sent me an e-mail last night," Janet said
out of the blue, and I nearly fell off the couch.

Last night?

"But that's impossible. She—" I started, unable
to finish, as Janet jumped in.

"She died last night, I know. So it must've been
sometime shortly before that. The e-mail wasn't
signed, not with a name, but it was sent from the
news department of KXAS. Sometimes I get tips
from the anchors or the news writers, so I wasn't

sure it was from Miranda specifically until I knew about her connection to the Caviar Club. Unless there's someone else on the Channel 5 staff who had a bone to pick with the club, it's gotta be her."

I sat up straighter.

So Miranda *had* arisen after I left her alone, at least long enough to shoot Janet an electronic message . . . and maybe open the front door to someone?

Likely someone she knew, too.

Geez, Louise, but this was getting crazier by the minute.

"Why would Miranda e-mail you?" I asked. "Was it about her behavior at the Pretty Party? Did she want you to kill the story?"

"No, it wasn't that at all. In fact, her note didn't make sense until a few minutes ago," Janet answered, keeping her voice low. "She said she belonged to a hush-hush club that wasn't what it seemed on the outside . . . that she had names and pictures . . . revealing stuff from secret parties where everyone got drunk and down and dirty. She was willing to hand over the owners on a silver platter, and she promised to forward the special password to get me into the members-only part of the Web site where they post the surprise location of the next gathering a mere hour before it starts. That's how they keep out the riffraff, you see. She was ready to deal dirt, Andy. If I'd just had the chance to talk to her before—" Janet expelled a slow breath. "If I'd only reached out to her sooner, maybe I . . . "

"Maybe you what?" She sounded like me after I learned that Miranda had died. I was wracked with guilt, thinking I could've done something to change what had happened. "You think she'd still be alive?"

"I don't know." Janet tugged on a dangly earring. "But I'm sure now that her tirade at Delaney's was the beginning of the end for her." Her eyes flickered. "What if punishing Sonja for her messed-up face was only part of the reason she showed up at the Pretty Party?"

If I go down, I'm taking them with me. Then it'll be all over, Andy. And I mean, all over. You'll see.

"Oh, shit," I said.

Janet looked equally grim. "My thoughts exactly. What if there were Caviar Clubbers there, too, and they felt as much a target as the good dermo?"

Yipes, yipes, yipes.

My arm hairs prickled.

If Janet's guess was on the money—if there were really high-profile Dallasites merrily swinging at the Caviar Club's hush-hush orgies—and if Miranda could blow the lid on it all, it screamed MOTIVE like a big, black headline.

It meant Miranda's death was hardly as clear-cut as the police seemed to think.

I wondered about Miranda's missing laptop—because it *was* missing if the cops couldn't find it—and I imagined the possibility of any of those lurid pictures having been stored in her Dell notebook. The thing was right in plain sight when I'd left her duplex. I'd even glimpsed a photo on her screen saver. Miranda clinging to some dark-haired guy. What if someone *had* been there after I left, and swiped the thing after making sure Miranda would never rat on anybody?

My throat felt about to close in on me, not liking what that implied.

What if the owners of the Caviar Club knew she was about to blow the whistle?

Like Janet suggested, it might have been someone at the Pretty Party who'd witnessed Miranda going postal . . . and feared what her fury might further unleash.

So that someone had made sure Miranda wouldn't talk.

Ever again.

"What if your gut's on target, the cops are on the wrong path entirely, and she really and truly didn't commit suicide?" Janet said. "You don't believe she killed herself, Andy, and now I'm thinking you may very well be right. Someone else could have shot Miranda with her own .22. Someone who wanted to keep her quiet about the Caviar Club, very probably someone she knew."

I wanted to agree with her.

But my mouth was too dry to respond.

Chapter 12

"We have to tell the police," I said as soon as I could find the spit to speak, because there didn't seem any way around it.

Anna Dean already suspected I was keeping things from the authorities, and I hadn't been . . . I knew I wasn't . . . until this very moment.

But I felt better, somehow, realizing I was no longer the only soul in town who had a reason to suspect there could be foul play involved in Miranda's death.

Well, except for my mother. Though Cissy tended to see conspiracies everywhere she looked. She thought global warming was an evil plot by the folks at PETA to keep her from wearing mink.

"You have to call the deputy chief and explain about the Caviar Club and Miranda's e-mail," I insisted. "That could be important evidence in their investigation. It could change the course of things entirely—"

"Hold your horses, kemosabe." Janet grabbed my arm and squeezed hard. "No, no, no. We're not calling Anna Dean. We're not blabbing about this to anybody, not your mother and not your boyfriend. You hear me? Not before I've had a chance to get my story. I've spent years penning cutesy prose about debutantes and society matrons and their teas and rodeos for charity, and I've finally got my claws into real juicy scoop, the kind that'll get me on the front page, and I don't mean the Society pages. Don't blow it for me, Andy. I won't let you do it."

She definitely had her claws into *me*, and it hurt.

Her magenta fingernails dug into my skin, and I grimaced.

What the devil was up?

I'd never seen Janet go so bananas over a story before. She wrote and edited the Society pages for the *Park Cities Press*, not the *New York Times*. But the rag gave her clout in this town, entrée into the lives of the powerful and provocative. It was no secret how much she enjoyed the gig and the social perks it gave her. So the only thing I could imagine that would get her so worked up was if her job was threatened.

Jiminy Cricket.

Could that be it?

"Um, ouch," I said, and wrested my arm from her grasp. As I rubbed the spot where her pink finger marks lingered, Janet gathered up her pad and pen and shoved them into her purse. "What is going on?" I asked her point-blank. "I've never seen you so obsessed over a feature."

Or over *her* features, for that matter.

"Don't ruin this for me, Andy," she begged, her chin quivering. She had the most pitiful look in her eyes, and I knew then that something more was involved. "This is my shot to prove myself, and I need it." She wet her lips—no small feat—adding, "Badly."

"Why?" I said, feeling sure now that something precious hung in the balance. If it wasn't her life, it had to be her position at the paper. "Is something going on at the *PCP*?"

Her shoulders stiffened. "Why would you say that? Have you heard anything?"

"No, no, nothing like that." I nudged her with my knee. "C'mon, you can talk to me."

She paused a long while, as if unsure how much to spill, then gave in with a sigh. "I'm not supposed to discuss this with anyone, all these SEC rules and what not. But the newspaper's being bought out by a twenty-five-year-old trust fund baby who's decided to become a media mogul, and he thinks that anyone over thirty is *ancient*." She stopped to gnaw on her upper lip, chewing off most of her magenta lipstick. "He's threatened to replace me with a younger model if I don't start writing flashier, bigger pieces and skewing to a broader audience beyond the Slipper Club crowd."

"A younger model?" I repeated. Janet was only in her early thirties. It wasn't like she was ancient

by any standards, except maybe some twenty-
five-year-old guy's.

"Younger, as in baby." She snagged a compact
from her bag and nervously powdered her nose.
"His girlfriend is twenty-one, if she's a day," she
said so bitterly that I winced. "And, yes, she's a
model, at least for the moment. She walks the
runway for Kim Dawson. I've seen her. She weighs
about eight ounces and wears at least two tons of
makeup. I'm surprised her cheekbones don't collapse under the weight of all the Bobbi Brown
blush."

"Wow, I had no clue all this was going on," I
said, because this was the first I'd heard about it.
"I'm so sorry."

Janet usually kept her work problems to herself, and I hadn't seen this one coming.

I was so out of the loop with the Park Cities
scene that I had no earthly idea some junior Mark
Cuban was buying out the *Press* and threatening
to ax my friend just because Janet was no anorexic
model barely out of her teens.

"That's why I need your cooperation, Andy.
Keep mum about Miranda's connection to the
Caviar Club and the e-mail she sent me, please.
Don't even tell your mother," she said, imploring.
"Give me a couple days, that's all I ask, then we
can go to Anna Dean and tell her everything. But
I *have* to have this story. I need to be the first reporter in town to break it." She tucked her purse
beneath her arm and stood, towering over me in
all her magenta glory. "I'll call you later, and we
can talk strategy, okay? Tell your mom thanks for

the invite to dinner, but I can't stay. Too much to do and too little time. Ta-ta for now."

She swooped down to air-kiss my cheeks before she hurried off, unlocking the door to the den and sweeping out in a rush of deep pink suit and red hair.

I sat a moment, my head still reeling from Janet's confession, before I got to my feet and walked toward the door like a zombie.

I nearly ran smack into Malone, strolling in from the hallway.

He had a bottle of beer in hand—Moosehead, I knew at first glance, if the green of the glass and big moose mug on the label weren't enough indication; and that's what Mother had begun stocking in the fridge for Stephen. I reached for it and took a long hard swig before handing it back a good deal lighter.

But Malone being Malone, he didn't even flinch. He was good at sharing, much better than I could ever be.

"I saw Janet leave," he said. "What's with her lips? Did she super-size 'em at the drive-through? Whew."

"Don't ask." That was the least of my worries.

"You okay?"

I nodded, though I felt a little queasy, probably from trying to so quickly digest everything I'd learned in the past fifteen minutes. "My head is kinda reeling. This has been one long day."

And it wasn't over yet.

"Did you square things with Janet?"

"I guess I did."

If agreeing to keep important information from the police regarding Miranda was squaring things.

I'd come to Mother's to get myself *out* of a big mess, and I felt like I'd stepped in even deeper doo-doo in the process.

Poo.

"Well, I'm glad that's settled, then. You need to relax, babe." Malone gave me a soft smile.

"I still have to deal with Mummy Dearest," I reminded him, though I didn't have the spark to ream her out about her press conference antics, not anymore. Janet's news had knocked the wind out of me.

Lucky for Mother.

"Cissy's the one who sent me after you," Brian said. "She mentioned something about a purse she wants you to see."

I rolled my eyes.

"Don't sweat it, sweet cakes. You'll survive, you always do," he assured me, catching my fingers up with his free hand and lacing them snugly into his. "Hey, I'll bet your stomach's on empty." He gave a tug. "C'mon to the kitchen. Sandy set out a spread before she disappeared into her quarters."

He uttered "quarters" with a hammy British accent, clearly mocking the term my mother used for Sandy Beck's suite at the back of the house.

He thought it sounded proprietary, despite my telling him that's what the rooms had been labeled when Mother and Daddy bought the house eons ago. I'd seen the copy of the typed-up listing Cissy kept in a carved cigar box in Daddy's study. Heck, nearly everyone I'd grown up with in the Park Cities had homes with quarters, whether they used them for the live-in staff or turned them into gigantic closets.

"And you'll get to meet Milton Fletcher," Brian said, finishing off his beer as we headed toward the kitchen. "He seems like an interesting guy. Did you know he was a Navy SEAL like Stephen?"

"No, I didn't."

My mental file on Milton Fletcher was meager, save for the fact he was the private eye Cissy was apparently interviewing for the job of snooping into Miranda DuBois's life and death. Oh, and that he owned the beat-up Ford parked in Mother's driveway.

Hearing that he had a connection to Stephen made sense and had me figuring that my mother's boyfriend was more responsible for his presence than Cissy.

I wondered if the former SEAL was in his late sixties, like Stephen, and if he was losing his hair or wore a toupee, or if he had artificial joints that got him wanded by Security at the airport.

As I had an image in my mind of a gray-haired gent whose knees creaked when he skulked around, searching for clues or stalking cheating spouses, it didn't register at first that the man sitting at the kitchen table—across an almost empty platter of crustless sandwiches—chatting with Cissy and Stephen was, in fact, Milton Fletcher.

I mean, the dude wasn't even wearing a tweed jacket with elbow patches, for Pete's sake. He had on a black turtleneck and a distressed leather jacket, and he was thirty-five, if he was a day, with the thickest head of ink-black hair I'd ever seen outside the Tibetan llamas at the petting zoo.

Stephen must've caught me standing there, gawking, as he rose from his seat, gestured toward the fellow and said, "Andrea, I'd like you to meet Milton Fletcher, a former naval officer and a superb investigator."

On cue, the leather-jacketed dude stood and said, "Call me Fletch."

Like that movie with Chevy Chase?

Well, heck, I guess it was better than calling him "Miltie."

I'd kind of imagined that "Milton" and all its variations had become extinct, as least when it came to men under age fifty.

Maybe it was a vague beer buzz—hey, when you rarely drink, any alcohol imbibed tends to go to your head—but instead of keeping my Milton jokes to myself, I opened up my big, fat mouth and stuck my foot—nay, both my feet—right between my completely natural, un-super-sized lips.

"So you're Milton Fletcher, huh? Did your mother have a thing for *Murder, She Wrote*? Or Milton Berle? You know, that comedian who liked to cross-dress? And what's with the old Ford? Does the rust make it invisible so people can't see when you're tailing them?"

When I finished my sarcastic tirade, I snorted, one of those awkward, totally unfeminine pig-in-the-mud snorts that escaped after I thought I was being particularly funny or clever—often coming off as neither.

Cherchez la pork!

"Andrea!"

Cissy stared at me, horrified, surely assuming that every moment of my Little Miss Manners classes had dropped out of my sievelike brain. Stephen crossed his arms, settling back in his chair, a stifled grin on his face, surely afraid to laugh or risk incurring the wrath of Her Highness.

Thank goodness, Milton Fletcher smiled, too.

I was about to apologize, but I figured Miltie's reaction was the next best thing to outright approval. Hence, no apology required.

See: Chapter Fifteen, *Little Miss Manners Politically Incorrect Edition*, Volume 66, "When It's Okay to be Rude."

"So you're Andy, huh?" he asked, eyeballing me, despite the fact that Malone stood at my elbow. "Hmm, you're not quite what I expected, either. Kind of odd for a chick to have a boy's name, isn't it? I'd imagined you as more of a linebacker, but you look all girl to me."

Even with my two feet in it, my mouth fell wide open.

Malone stiffened, and I prayed he wouldn't sling the beer bottle at Milton's head; though he had better manners than I did, so I didn't figure the smart-ass private eye was in any real danger.

"As for the old car," good ol' Miltie went on, as if he hadn't said enough already, "it beats driving my Porsche Boxer on the job and having to park it in places where I'd be afraid to leave a bike."

"You own a Porsche Boxer? I'll bet it's red, too," I got out, gums flapping, and—God help me—

snorted again just as loudly as before. "Is that symbolic of anything?"

Somehow, that only made Milton Fletcher's smile all the more wicked. "I don't know," he said. "If you want to play doctor—Dr. Freud, that is— perhaps you can interpret the meaning of my needing to drive an incredibly slick, fast machine."

I could only stare at him and blink.

"My heavens," my mother expelled, and Stephen coughed back his laughter.

Malone brushed my arm, and I heard a low growl in the back of his throat. At least, it sounded like a growl.

Fortunately, Milton Fletcher didn't wait for an encore.

He came out of his seat, patted Stephen on the back and said, "I hate to interview and run, but I have work to do." He glanced at my mother and tapped his jacket pocket. "Thanks for the retainer, Mrs. Kendricks. I'll do my best to get to the heart of the matter, I promise, and I'll keep you posted on anything I learn about Ms. DuBois."

"Yes, yes, thank you, Mr. Fletcher—uh, Fletch— and I'm so sorry about my daughter," Cissy apologized, scrambling to escort the P.I. from the room.

But not before he gave me a wink and said, "I'm not sorry about Andy at all. I like fire in a woman. It shows brain activity."

He nodded at Brian before Mother whisked him off, with Stephen following on their heels.

"Did you get a load of that?" I plopped into a kitchen chair and made a face. "I can't believe

Mother's hiring Miltie boy to investigate Miranda's death. He probably spends half the day staring at himself in the mirror. Have you ever met anyone so cocky, right off the bat? 'Fire in a woman? Brain activity?' I think he needs someone to write him new lines, geez!"

Brian set his empty bottle on the table with a clank, straddled the chair and sat down, looking sulky. "He was flirting with you, Andy." He raised his eyes to mine. "And you were flirting right back."

Excuse me?

"I was flirting with *him*?" I'm not sure I'd ever sputtered before, but I was sputtering now. "I was doing no such thing."

"I think you were."

"Was not."

"Were, too."

If he'd stuck out his tongue, I wouldn't have been surprised. He was acting like a big baby in size thirteen shoes.

Anyone who thought that people ever grew up were nuts. The only thing that separated the so-called real world from high school was a locker combination.

I started to reply with something equally juvenile, in the vein of "stop being such a big poo," when it dawned on me that Brian was jealous with a capital J, the way I'd been jealous of his relationship with Allie Price, his ex-chick and colleague at the firm (though I wasn't anymore, not after spending some time with her and understanding that she was no threat to me).

An attractive guy had just paid way too much attention to me in the span of a few minutes—in front of my mom, my dude, God and Stephen—and Malone didn't like it the least little bit.

"Awww," I said, feeling all warm and mushy. I got up from my chair and rounded the table, arranging myself in his lap, catching my arms around his neck. "You're so sweet to get all worked up over nothing."

"Huh?" He blinked, dumbfounded, and I gave him a decidedly appreciative kiss, the kind the French copyrighted (and for good reason).

My mother took that moment to reappear, standing at the mouth of the kitchen, hands on her hips. "Andrea, darlin', would you please get off your boyfriend and come take a look at this bag I've, ah, acquired. It's important, truly. You can make out with Mr. Malone later, somewhere other than my kitchen."

Malone pushed his face into my shoulder, and I felt him shaking with laughter (though he smothered it beautifully).

"Well, Mother," I said, "if you put it that way."

I peeled myself from my boyfriend's lap under my mother's disapproving eye.

Malone's cheeks were pink, like a naughty child, and I was tempted to kiss him again, despite having a chaperone.

Instead, I gave his arm a pat and told him not to wander, as I wouldn't be long. I planned on us leaving just as soon as I finished playing fashion consultant to Mother, which was a laugh riot when you thought about it. Unlike Cissy, I was hardly into couture, considering my favorite shopping digs were low-rent vintage stores and Goodwill for broken-in jeans. My mother would prefer bathing in boiling oil to going Goodwill hunting.

Whatever the mystery behind the bag she'd mentioned, I figured it would only take a few minutes to ooh and aah over it before I could bail.

Cissy led me up the stairs to her bedroom, where the afternoon light filtered in through silky sheers, between creamy drapes pulled to the sides and anchored around upholstered buttons.

I spotted a small black leather handbag sitting in the middle of her bed, atop the soft pink duvet.

I waited until my mother had seated herself on one side of the bed, and then I settled across from her, the purse in between us. An invisible cloud of her Joy perfume filled the space around me, and I knew that if I closed my eyes, I could always, always find Cissy by following her scent.

"Well, there it is," she said, doing a Vanna White and gesturing toward the slim black leather bag, which had a tiny Coach tag dangling from the zipper and looked vaguely beat-up with a generous assortment of stains and scratches across the side.

"Um, this is it?" I asked, not sure what she wanted from me. "This is the bag you wanted my opinion on?" Egads. It was *so* not her style. How to be diplomatic? "Er, well, Mother, to be honest, it's not something I would've imagined you'd carry. It doesn't even look new."

And, if I knew anything about Cissy, it was that

she liked things shiny and polished, never borrowed, never broken-in.

"Oh, did I say this was *my* purse, Andrea? No, no, I don't believe I did." She cocked her head, and her blond chin-length bob caught the light from the ceiling chandelier, giving her a temporary halo. Though when I blinked, it went away.

"Then whose is it?" I asked, and poked the bag in question. "Is it Sandy's?"

"No, it's not Sandy's." Mother reached across the duvet and nudged the bag toward me. "As a matter of fact, it belonged to Miranda DuBois. I removed it from her car before Anna Dean showed up to have it towed. It was in the glove compartment. I'd hoped to find the missing laptop you mentioned, but it wasn't anywhere.

Um, excuse me?

"And you were snooping in Miranda's Jag because . . . ?" I hardly knew what to say, and I certainly didn't want to *touch* the thing. "How could you—" I stopped myself, realizing that an accusatory tone would get me nowhere. So I tried again. "Why didn't you leave it for Anna Dean to find?"

Cissy looked at me like I'd asked the dumbest question on the planet. "I thought there might be something there that would shed some light on what happened. After all, the police don't seem to be listening to *you*, do they, Andrea? And you were with Miranda last night before she passed away, so I figured that it was my duty to do everything I could to assist Debbie Santos in learning the truth about her daughter's death . . . "

She kept talking, but I hardly heard what she said, as her voice faded to fuzzy somewhere after she'd uttered the words, *It belonged to Miranda DuBois. I removed it from her car.*

I had a sudden urge to pick up the purse, sling it against the wall and scream at the top of my lungs.

But I didn't.

Instead, I looked at my calm and collected mother and whispered, "Please, please, please, tell me you didn't really take this from Miranda's Jag without saying anything to Deputy Dean."

"Okay, I won't tell you that," she replied, cool as the proverbial cucumber. "But I did, and I'm not sorry."

Was this another one of her "do as I say, not as I do" examples? It's a good thing I was all grown up (relatively speaking), or I'd figure there was open season on the cookie jar, despite the "no cookies before mealtime" rule she'd instigated.

"Have you unzipped it yet?" I asked tentatively. "Did you see what was inside?"

I winced, awaiting her response.

"Of course I didn't pry inside," she snipped, affronted. "What kind of person do you think I am?"

Did she really want my honest opinion on that?

Oh, boy.

I sighed, thinking, *Mother, Mother, Mother, what have you done this time?* She'd set plenty of precedence for doing the outrageous, if not the unlawful. Like when she'd stolen the mail from the box of a murdered woman who'd once been her friend and bridge partner.

Cissy's blue eyes gazed back at me so innocently. As if poaching a purse from the car of a dead woman—and one whose death had become increasingly suspicious—was de rigueur, humdrum, everyday, no big deal.

And she'd told Anna Dean that *I'd* been the one withholding evidence?

If this wasn't such a serious situation, I would've laughed in her perfectly powdered face. But instead I picked up the purse and unzipped it.

I mean, as long as Mother had done the deed and pilfered the bag from the Jag, I might as well see what was inside it, right?

So I gently spilled the contents atop the duvet cover, and Mother and I bent our heads over the smattering of items, taking everything in and saying nothing.

If there was a clue amidst Miranda's belongings as to what actually transpired before she died, I knew Cissy was as anxious as I was to find it.

Chapter 13

Needless to say, it felt a bit creepy, touching things that had belonged to Miranda, considering she would never handle any of them again.

What would my mother do with the purse and its contents when we were done with them? Give everything to Debbie Santos when she got back in town? And Mrs. Santos would then, what, keep the cosmetics and credit cards as mementoes? Toss them into the garbage?

Sometimes when I dwelled on the morbid, I mulled over the things I'd accumulated through the years—the odds and ends from flea markets, the art work I'd painted or had picked up at consignment shops just because I was drawn to it, and the hand-me-down furniture and gifts from people I loved—and I wondered what would happen to all of it when I was gone. Would anyone want it? Would those who survived me divvy up my stuff? Or would they call for the Goodwill truck and wash their hands of it, without feeling an iota of regret.

I contemplated what I had right now in my purse: my wallet with a few credit cards, checkbook (yes, I was still a paper-writing dinosaur), and a photo of Brian and me, a notepad, a pack of gum, a tiny bottle of contact lens solution, a tape measure, business cards, a couple of Band-Aids for emergencies, pens, and assorted paper clips and rubber bands.

What did that say about me?

Except that I was a fairly boring individual.

If I were gone tomorrow, would someone pitch everything? Toss it all out like used litter from a cat box?

What I found most precious, someone else might deem junk.

It was one of those jokes the universe played on us (one of way too many, so far as I was concerned).

I palmed the green Clinique compact and tube of lipstick, imagining a less than sober Miranda powdering her nose and swiping color on her lips before heading to the Pretty Party last night to scare the *cojones* out of Dr. Sonja (and everyone else, for that matter).

There was a small tube of Retinol, which I thought was used on acne, but Cissy informed me was a prescription wrinkle treatment.

"It peels the layers right off, after it turns your skin a bright red, almost like a bad sunburn," she explained, and I stuck out my tongue and went, "Ewww."

These days, it seemed like "no pain, no gain" applied to beauty instead of muscles.

Blech.

It boggled my brain to consider that an attractive woman like Miranda, barely past thirty, would be so consumed with having a crease here or there.

There was so much else to worry about, considering the state of the world, that being preoccupied with appearance seemed very silly.

Still, Miranda's vanity aside, I didn't imagine her Retinol harbored any dark secrets. Her wallet didn't exactly scream BIG CLUE HERE! either. So far as I could tell, it held little more than twenty bucks cash, a driver's license, and a Gold Visa card.

Oh, wait. I take that back. There was a torn piece of paper stuffed behind the bills, on which she'd written:

Sevruga (Caspian)
Beluga (Malossol)

Fish eggs. Yuck.

I glanced at my mother and held out the note. "Does this mean anything to you?" I asked her.

She squinted at the words for a moment. "Looks like part of a shopping list. Caspian Sevruga and Malossol Beluga caviar. Wonderful stuff. Miranda had expensive taste." Fleetingly, she smiled. "Just like her mama."

I was sure Debbie Santos would be proud, but I doubted Miranda's choice of gourmet caviars had much of an impact on her cause of death. So I stuck the list back in the zipper clutch.

I figured Miranda had to have a bigger everyday purse back at the duplex, the one that held oodles of girl stuff and a billfold filled with plastic; something substantial enough so the police would never realize this little purse was missing.

Besides, it's not like our scavenging had yielded anything worth passing on to the Highland Park P.D.

Nothing from the handbag told us any more than we already knew, and I'd nearly given up entirely when I tried the tiny zipped pocket inside the fabric lining, only to find it stuck. Well, that big ol' zipper end was gone, so there wasn't much left to grab onto.

I left Mother upstairs in her room and headed down to the kitchen to find a pair of pinchers, the kind that Sandy Beck kept in the utility drawer.

Malone and Stephen were finishing up the last of the crustless sandwiches and swapping golf tales when I entered the room.

"Is everything all right?" Malone asked, for probably the tenth time that day.

Really, did I need that much checking up on?

"Sure, sure, fine," I replied as I scrounged in the drawer for the pinchers.

Yep, yep, everything was fine and dandy.

"Did you see the bag?" my boyfriend tried next, and I assured him that I had.

I made no mention of Mother's sticky fingers

and my concern that, should Anna Dean learn what she'd done, Cissy would be locked up for interfering in a police investigation. Then Mother would have to make an urgent call to Vera Wang to have swanky jail togs designed so she wasn't wearing the same ugly orange jumpsuit as everyone else in the Dallas County pen.

I nearly hollered, "Eureka!" when I located the pinchers, then I hightailed it out of the kitchen, racing up the Oriental runner over creaky stairs, back to Mother's room.

Cissy had plumped silk shammed pillows behind her back and removed her shoes. She had arms slung over bent knees, her stocking feet pale as pearls against the pink of the duvet.

"I hope Mr. Fletcher has more luck finding out about Miranda's final hours than we're having," she commented, and I bit the inside of my cheek to stay quiet. "I just feel terrible for Debbie, being out of the country when all of this happened. It's a good thing her Brazilian surgeon has her on tranquilizers. I know I'd be a basket case if I were in her position. The poor dear is wrapped up like a mummy after all the, ah, adjustments, and she can't even get on a plane to come home and bury her daughter. Not for at least a week. Her doctor won't let her fly until she's less swollen."

While my mother continued her gloomy monologue, I delicately worked on pulling the broken zipper with the tiny pliers, so I could see what was in the pocket.

When I finally yanked it open, I gave a little yelp, setting down the pinchers to shove my fingers into the gap and encountering something solid and compact.

"What is it?" my mother asked, unfurling arms from her knees and scooting forward to get a better view as I withdrew the object in question.

It was a slender digital camera.

The model was Pentax, and it wasn't much bigger than a credit card; smaller even than a box of Sucrets.

Janet's description of the "anonymous" e-mail from Miranda ran through my brain again, and I felt a tickle at the back of my throat, which I knew had nothing to do with allergies.

She said she belonged to a private club that wasn't what it seemed on the outside . . . that she had names and pictures . . . revealing stuff from secret parties where everyone got drunk and down and dirty with everyone else. She knew who the owners of the club were, too, and she knew all the dish about their member selection process. And she was ready to spill the beans about everything.

My mother's drawl cut through my mental digression.

"A camera? Well, phooey." She looked terribly disappointed. "Is there anything interesting on it?"

Funny, but I was wondering the very same thing.

"Let's see." I touched the button on top, and the Pentax made a little noise.

The screen on the back turned bright blue and then shifted to a live shot, so I could see my mother through the lens, watching me with her head tipped. I didn't want to play with the thing there in Cissy's bedroom. I wanted to take the camera home, hook it up to my computer and sift through any photographs that might be saved on the memory disk.

So I shut it off.

"I don't want to mess with this here, maybe press the wrong button and delete something I shouldn't," I told her. "I want to be careful, just in case."

"Just in case what?" she asked.

In case there are photographs on the Pentax detailing some of the Caviar Club's private orgies I wanted to blurt out, but didn't.

If the pictures Miranda had mentioned in the e-mail to Janet were contained on the Pentax, I wasn't about to risk screwing them up by playing around with the buttons on a camera I'd never used before.

"I'd hate to destroy evidence," I replied ultimately, the safest explanation, and not untrue besides.

The last thing I wanted was for Cissy to get wind of Miranda's ties to the Caviar Club and start kicking up dust in that direction. Janet would skin me alive, and I was rather quite fond of my epidermis, despite the freckles and occasional zits.

Which is all to say, I kept mum on the subject.

"So that's all we've got?" My mother frowned. "I figured there'd be something, I don't know, more helpful."

"Like a note detailing what happened to Miranda after I left her at the duplex snoring soundly on the sofa and before six o'clock this morning when her neighbor walked through her open door and found her dead?" I offered, because it was the most absurd thing I could come up with, and it avoided answering her question altogether. I'd always been good at deflection.

"Yes, just like that," Cissy said in all seriousness. "Things always turn out so neatly on *CSI*. It's a shame real life is so much—"

"Messier?" I finished for her. "Less cut and dry?"

"Exactly." She sighed and swung her legs gracefully over the side of the bed, slipping her shoes back on. "I have to check with Sandy about when the forensic pathologist is flying in from L.A., and I need to call Sparkman-Hillcrest about Miranda's burial. Oh, sweet pea, I still can't believe this isn't a bad dream," she said, and paused to stare at the pile of Miranda's things scattered across her bed. "But I can't dwell on that, can I? There's so much work to do and so little time."

"Mother, why?" I called out to her as she began to exit toward her sitting room. "Why are you doing this?"

She stopped and ever so slowly turned around. "Why?" she repeated, as if she hadn't heard me right.

I scooted toward the end of the bed, slinging my legs over the footboard and dangling them, like I did when I was a kid and my feet didn't touch the floor.

I rubbed my palms over my knees and said, "You're near-obsessed with proving Miranda didn't kill herself. I know you've been friends with Mrs. Santos a long time, but I don't understand exactly why this seems so all-fire urgent. Can't you let the police do their job and see what they'll turn up? I'm sure they'll be finished with their investigation by the time Mrs. Santos gets home. Then she can deal with them, not you."

Her eyebrows went up and she crossed her arms, one hand reaching up to fiddle with her necklace, an Edwardian locket my father had given to her not long before he died. "I can't even believe you're second-guessing me, Andrea."

She couldn't? Since when?

Though the tone of her voice made me feel awful, and I lowered my eyes, cheeks warming, hating when she looked at me like that, as if I didn't trust her (which I did, for the most part, a good deal of the time anyway).

"Never mind," I said quietly.

She took another few steps toward me. "But I do mind," she insisted. "Because I would hope my own daughter would see why I can't simply stay out of this, have the police rubber-stamp Miranda's passing as suicide, and let Debbie clean up the mess when she gets home from Brazil, full of bruises and stitches."

Well, hell.

If I hadn't before, now I felt like a total schmuck.

I squirmed, kicking my feet against the silk rug.

I didn't even hear her approach me, merely felt her light touch on my chin as she tucked her fingers beneath it and raised my gaze to hers.

"Perhaps this is one of those times when emotions can't be explained, my dear," she told me, her drawl slow and soft, her eyes not accusing in the least. "Do you ever do things because you feel you have to? Even if they make no sense to others?"

Of course I did, and she knew it.

I bit my lip and nodded.

"Well, it's one of those cases. You don't have to get involved any more than you already are, Andrea. You just have to let me be, and I'll do what needs to be done."

That sounded like a line I may have used on her a time or two. *Don't question me, just support me.*

Mother wasn't done yet. "Somehow, sweet pea, I have a feeling you want to see justice done in this case, too. If someone did hurt Miranda, he can't get away with it. We can't let him."

"I know," I said, kicking the toe of my sneaker against the floor. It wasn't like I didn't feel a stake in Miranda's passing, too.

"Darling, remember, this isn't about you or me," she said, and brushed her hand over my cheek. "It's about a little girl who doesn't have a voice anymore. She needs someone to see this through, to make sure she isn't remembered by a lie."

With that, she strode from the bedroom, leaving me alone with the Coach purse and my own insecurities.

Wow.

I shivered and rubbed my arms up and down until the goose bumps disappeared.

I'd seen my mother intense before, and I know

how wrapped up she got when she lost anyone she loved, or even liked the least little bit.

But this time her intensity was so quiet, it left me shaken.

It was hard to fathom that Miranda had been alive last night and dead this morning. It had all happened so fast, the way this thing had caught us all in its net: me, Mother, and Janet, even Stephen, who had helped Mother find a private investigator.

It was freaky, too, how none of us could let things lie.

Was it because we were so dad-gummed inspired to find the truth, or was there something more attached to all our motives?

I knew Janet's was the need to write a story that would save her career, and mine was pure guilt.

Mother's reasons were something else entirely, and I tapped my fingers, trying to sort them all out: a combination of loyalty to an old pal, for sure; the need to set things right for a young woman who seemed to have had it all and suddenly had nothing.

But there was something else.

Mother had definitely made up her mind that Miranda hadn't died by her own hand, without even hearing the county medical examiner's preliminary report or waiting on the findings of the police investigation, which had barely gotten off the ground that morning. It was like *I* had died, the police were calling it suicide, and she refused to believe it for an instant.

It's not that I didn't agree with her about Mi-

randa, because I did, considering the mystery surrounding Miranda's gun and the missing laptop,
and particularly after my conversation with Janet
Graham.

But Debbie Santos's request that my mother
become Miranda's "mommy *ad litem*" had turned
Cissy into a lioness, fur ruffled and claws bared,
ready to do whatever was absolutely necessary to
protect her cub.

Only Miranda wasn't hers.

Call me selfish and insensitive, but this all had
me pondering a single question that had nothing to do with Miranda: had Cissy ever fought so
hard for me?

Had she ever pushed like mad to make sure I
came out on top?

And I don't mean putting all the pieces in place
for my debut.

Oh, sure, she was 110 percent behind that,
but it had all been her doing, her dreams, not
mine. When I informed her that I wasn't going
to SMU—or any other Texas college—but had
instead enrolled at an art school, Columbia College in Chicago, my mother hadn't exactly been
waving her pom-poms, cheering me on. She'd
been sorely disappointed, like I'd struck her with
a double whammy after ditching my cotillion,
even though it's what I wanted.

Every guy I'd dated until Brian Malone had
been on her hit list; and even though she'd been
the one who pushed Malone and me together ini-
tially, he hadn't exactly endeared himself to her
when she realized we'd been "keeping company"

without so much as a promise ring on my third left finger.

Sure, I understood that she loved me, deep down, beneath everything.

Okay, yes, she'd actually ended up helping me out a few times when I needed help out of a jam (even if not a jam of my own making).

But I was her only child, so giving me an emotional boost now and then was to be expected, right?

As I'd grown up, I became accustomed to Mother throwing herself into her volunteer work, which I realized—as I grew out of the house—gave her less time to comment on my life and how I lived it, or to interfere.

Until the past year or so, when she'd gotten restless in a way that I'm sure many mavens of society did once their children left the nest, their husbands croaked or dumped them for shinier trophy wives, and charity work didn't quite hold the sparkle it had once.

I'd begun to wonder if Cissy wasn't at a point in her life where chairing galas and fund-raisers didn't quite fill her up the way it used to.

I had a sense, too, that part of it stemmed from her getting tired of waiting for me to get engaged so she could plan my destination wedding. Instead of holding her breath till the day I would bear a (legitimate) grandchild for her to dote on, she'd decided to take on another kind of maternal "volunteer" gig entirely, though this one was quite a bit more serious than candy-striping at Presbyterian Hospital.

Or, perhaps, I was overanalyzing and overdramatizing things, as usual, because I was knocked off-kilter by the tragedy that had dropped into our laps. It wasn't every day that someone I knew was found dead, and it made it worse that I was at the top of the local police department's list of "last known person to see the victim alive."

I didn't want to be jealous of Miranda.

I mean, Miranda was dead.

So whatever baggage I carried regarding my mother, whatever resentment or jealousy I was feeling because of her recent actions . . . well, at least, I still had time to deal with it—and deal with her—while we were both alive and kicking.

And I would do that.

Really I would.

Just as soon as this ordeal was behind us and we could sit down and have a "heart-to-heart chat," as my daddy used to say.

He also had another favorite saying, usually relating to making peace between me and my mother: "When pigs fly."

I didn't like that one near as much.

Chapter 14

Malone offered to take me out for a quiet dinner after we left Mother's house, but I wasn't exactly in the mood to sit in a restaurant full of unquiet people and make idle chatter while we chewed our way through a couple of courses, no matter how good the food or the company.

Besides, I was too curious about the photos on Miranda's camera and wanted to get home, upload them onto my computer, and check them out. They could all be shots from her summer vacations or a trip to the zoo, but I had to hope there was something more . . . something tying in to the e-mail sent to Janet about exposing the secret lives of the Caviar Club members . . . something that would shed more light on Miranda's sudden death.

Part of it was helping Janet get her story—and keep her job—and part was definitely a curiosity about why exactly Miranda's life had been snuffed out so prematurely.

The rest wasn't so altruistic.

It had more to do with wanting a little peace in my life, which meant getting Janet Graham off my back and getting Mother back to doing her event chairing thing instead of taking over the microphone at police press conferences.

It could happen soon, too, particularly if the Dallas County medical examiner found cause to believe Miranda hadn't killed herself. But Deputy Chief Dean's remark to me about "this one looks and smells like suicide" had me wondering if that would happen.

And why wouldn't I have doubts?

According to Anna Dean, there was no sign of forced entry, the gun used to end Miranda's life belonged to Miranda, and she'd been upset enough to have a nervous breakdown in front of a dozen people at Delaney Armstrong's house only hours before she died.

If it looked like a duck, walked like a duck, and quacked like a duck, then, by God, it was a duck, right?

You betcha.

Unless it wasn't.

On the drive back to my place, I asked Malone if his firm had ever handled a case involving a suicide that wasn't.

He said yes, that Abramawitz, Reynolds, Goldberg, and Hunt had represented a few clients whose loved ones had purportedly killed themselves, resulting in nonpayment of death benefits, only for the deaths to be proven accidental after private investigators, exhumations, and independent autopsies were done.

Then again, they'd also had a few cases where challenges were lost.

Since he knew the legal ramifications of Mother becoming the late Miranda DuBois's legal guardian until Debbie returned to the States, he suggested—okay, advised—that I be careful where I stepped. "Stay out of it," was his point, and I assured him I had no desire to spend Thanksgiving behind bars.

He'd overheard Anna Dean's remarks about not interfering in the police investigation, and I promised him, as I'd promised the deputy chief, that I would not cause trouble.

No lie.

I had no intentions of shaking things up with the authorities. I'd leave that to Cissy. But I couldn't see getting out of helping Janet with her mission to expose the Caviar Club. I couldn't imagine how that would entail anything illegal.

Surely it wasn't against the law to aid and abet a society columnist afraid of losing her job?

When we arrived at the condo, my next door neighbor, a true Texas good ol' boy named Charlie Tompkins, was out walking his old pooch. He hollered a greeting, along the lines of, "Well, howdy there, pretty lady. Hey, there, counselor. Was that your mama on the news this afternoon, Andy?"

Oh, geez.

I gave Charlie a halfhearted wave then turned

my back on him, allowing Malone to do the talking for me, as I was in no mood for chatter.

"Hey, Charlie," he said, while I stabbed my key in the lock. "I wouldn't pursue that line of questioning unless you want to see a live human spontaneously combust."

"Then we'll just zip our lips, eh, pup? No good comes of poking a stick at a cranky woman." The older man laughed and tugged the leash, drawing his dog in the other direction.

"*Men*," I said under my breath as I pushed open the door and Malone and I headed inside. My shoulders didn't sag until I'd turned the dead bolt and locked the big, bad world outside.

"You mind taking care of dinner?" I asked my sweetie as I held on tight to him for a long minute. "I've got something I need to do."

"You want onion and green peppers on a thin crust, right?" he asked, hitting it dead-on.

"Yummy. No wonder I love you." I kissed him full on the mouth, giving him a pat on the tush before I hightailed it into my office, Miranda's tiny camera burning a hole in my purse.

While Brian assumed the weighty task of calling Domino's to place our order, I settled down in front of my computer and set the Pentax on my desk.

I woke Mr. Dell with a tap of my mouse and plopped into my nonergonomic chair—a pretty French style almost-antique with a pillow flush behind my back—and then I got to work, sorting through the rubber bands, binder clips, iPod Nano cords, and flash drives in my junk drawer until I recovered the memory card reader I was seeking.

My heartbeat hastened its tempo as I removed the secure digital card from Miranda's camera, stuck it into the reader, and then slid the reader into a free port.

"Come to mama, baby," I cajoled as I drummed fingertips atop my desk and waited the few seconds it took for the files to load before the slide show began, flashing photos, one after the other, across my flat screen.

I kept one hand on the mouse, in case I needed to pause and study a photo, and I tapped my palm against the thigh of my jeans with the other. I had so much nervous energy, and I was so anxious to find something incriminating, something real, that I could barely breathe.

The first dozen photos seemed pretty innocuous: shots of Miranda at various functions, wearing pastel-hued suits and grinning as she posed with giant scissors about to cut the ribbon on a new PetsMart; standing alongside the mayor and chief of police at the Guns and Buns breakfast fund-raiser, and on and on, until I was afraid there would be nothing.

"Whatcha looking at?"

I jumped at the sound of Malone's voice, and realized he was crouching beside me, squinting at the monitor.

Instinctively, I clicked the mouse and stopped the slide show of Miranda's digital photographs. The image that stuck on the screen was of her at what appeared to be an office birthday party, everyone in silly pointed paper hats, the craggy-faced co-anchor of the evening news staring at

Miranda from the sidelines as she blew out an army of candles on a snow white cake.

"It's nothing," I said, thinking fast, as Janet had sworn me to secrecy. I didn't like keeping things from Malone, but I figured in this case it was only temporary. I'd fill him in on the whole shebang when this mess was all cleaned up.

"Isn't that Miranda DuBois?" he asked, his hand planted on the arm of my chair as he leaned forward to gaze at the screen. "And that's the dude she did the news with. Dick Uttley, right?"

"Uh-huh," I quietly agreed, then chirped, "Was that the doorbell? I think the pizza man's here."

"No doorbell." He shook his head. "You're hearing things. So why've you got this on your computer? Looks like a party. Were you there?"

"No." Well, I wasn't going to lie to him about that. "It's a photograph of Miranda's."

He went, "Hmmm," before asking, "How'd you get it? From her Web site?"

Man, but he was nosy. Must've been all that law school training in badgering the witness.

"Mother had it," I replied, still not lying.

"Are there more?" He crooked a finger at the screen.

Egads.

I bit my lip and said, "A few."

"Well, I know Cissy feels responsible for Miranda. Stephen told me she's going nuts, thinking the police aren't going to look beyond the suicide angle." Brian let out a pithy sigh. "She's really taking this whole thing hard, isn't she? Almost like it's her own kid who died."

"Yeah, just like that," I agreed, and hoped he didn't pick up on the resentment in my tone. I didn't like the sound of it myself.

"So why'd Cissy give you pictures of Miranda? I know you weren't all that friendly with the woman." He glanced sideways at me. "Does Her Highness have an ulterior motive?"

"Ulterior motive?" I laughed. I couldn't help myself. "When doesn't she?"

He snapped his fingers. "Oh, I get it. I know what you're up to."

"You do?"

Gulp.

He arose from his crouch so he towered over me. "Yes, I do." His hands came down on my shoulders, and I tensed, holding my breath until he spoke. "Your mom wants you to put something together, doesn't she? Like some kind of Web site tribute to Miranda. Is that it?"

Web site tribute?

I nearly crowed with relief.

"Well, I guess you could call it a tribute." If trying to fulfill Miranda's vengeful wish of "outing" high profile members of the Caviar Club was paying homage to her. "But it's not Mother who's asked me to help with the project. It's Janet," I said, not fibbing about that part, anyway.

"Janet Graham?" He looked confused. "What's she got you doing? Investigating the levels of ozone killed by the gallons of hair spray used on the heads of local evening news anchors?"

I smiled. Nice to have a boyfriend with a sense of humor.

"Now, *that* would be a good story," I said, wondering the best way to fudge around how I was assisting Janet in her cause, when I wasn't even completely sure what my job entailed. "Um, well, I don't even know exactly what's required of me"—why did I have to be dating a lawyer?—"it's more like doing her a favor."

"What kind of favor? Like going with Janet to get a facial this morning?"

"Um, sort of," I replied evasively.

If I'd said *getting the dirt on who's attending the Caviar Club orgies*, would that have satisfied him, you think?

The doorbell rang.

For real.

"Pizza's here!" I cried, and shut off my computer screen, which quickly zapped to black, never so eager to see the Domino's guy as I was at that moment.

Brian's hands came off my shoulders, and I followed him into the living room, diverting into the kitchen to get out plates and napkins while he paid off the pizza guy.

We settled in front of the TV, and Brian found a hockey game on: the Dallas Stars vs. his hometown St. Louis Blues.

It was like being saved by the bell twice in one evening.

I knew I wouldn't be able to peel him away from the boob tube until the game was over. And since he always complained that the Blues were penalty magnets, dragging things out even longer, I guessed I'd have a couple hours of computer time before he even realized I wasn't sitting right there beside him.

I spirited away my plate heaped with pizza slices and my bottle of Sprite Zero, sneaking out of the room in time to hear Brian swearing at the ref.

"Slashing? Are you effing kidding me? Did you leave your glasses at home, Mr. Magoo? Damn zebras!"

I grinned, the sound of his protests music to my ears.

The world could come to an end; and, as long as there was a hockey game on, Malone would never know it. He would arise from the sofa after the third period was over, find the condo crumbled around him, and go, "My God, what the heck happened?"

I did not begrudge sports for the way they made most men oblivious to everything that went on around them.

It gave us womenfolk time to get our own stuff done.

Though I realized the clock was ticking in more ways than one.

This time, I closed the door to my office before I plunked myself down at my desk.

I turned the monitor back on and resumed the slide show of Miranda's pictures, chewing on a slice of pizza as I watched each frame click slowly by.

The computer shuffled through a good two dozen photos before I saw one than made me reach greasy fingers for the mouse to stop the visual parade.

I squinted and leaned nearer, hovering over

my keyboard so my nose was a mere eight inches from the screen.

It was different from the ones before, darker, kind of hard to make out unless I used the "brighten" feature on my photo software.

I had nothing that assured me these were tableaus from secret Caviar Club gatherings; but I had a knot in my gut as I stared at the monitor, something inside me saying, *This is it.*

There was Miranda, in a dress cut so low her boobs half spilled out, her blond hair tousled on her shoulders, seated on a sofa between two men. They had their arms around her, and she had her arms around them. There was a smorgasbord of drinks and ashtrays spread on the low-set table in front of them, but that's about all I *could* see.

Whoever had used Miranda's camera to take the shot must've had unsteady hands—or else she did the pics with a timer without adjusting the focus—as the quality of the photo was grainy; too blurred for me to make out either man's features. They could've both resembled Mr. Potato Head, for all I knew.

I forwarded to the next photograph, which was darker still, clicking further to the one beyond that and the one after.

At about the fourth such image in the series, I paused. This was fuzzy, too, but I could discern that it was Miranda with those two men on the sofa, only she was locking lips with one, while the other seemed to be kissing her neck. Someone's hands were on her breasts. I couldn't exactly make out whose.

Didn't look like they were naked, not yet anyway, but the nature of the scene implied there was more to come, and I hoped to God whatever Miranda had done beyond what I *could* see wasn't something she had chronicled on her digital camera by a third party—or was that a fourth party?

I swallowed down my distaste and went ahead several additional pictures, finding another sequence of images that appeared to take place in a hot tub. If Miranda had a bathing suit on, I couldn't see it. She held a drink above the foamy waters, and two men and another woman crowded around her.

The lighting was no better than before, and I zoomed in on the faces of Miranda's fellow partiers. They were so crowded together, faces turned toward Miranda, the two dudes on her either side nuzzling her neck, that I wasn't sure if I would've recognized any of the three if they stood in a lineup.

Though there was something about one of the men that jiggled a nerve in me.

He was blond and his shoulders well-muscled, but that's about all I could discern definitively.

A name hovered at the back of my mind. *Lance Zarimba.*

Could it be? But he was Sonja Madhavi's boyfriend, right? So why would he be messing with Miranda at a Caviar Club party?

The woman who was not Miranda was leaning in toward the blond man—kissing him on the cheek, from the looks of things—so I couldn't see much of her beyond a fuzzy ear and throat.

Still, I thought I'd seen enough.

I froze the slide show and slumped back in my chair, not sure I wanted to go through any more of Miranda's digital film.

Could be these pics had zip to do with the Caviar Club and were just from Miranda's attempts at looking for Mr. Goodbar, but my gut told me better.

Geez, Miranda, why?

I couldn't help asking.

Why couldn't a beautiful woman with enough class to have been a symphony debutante and enough chutzpah to be named runner-up Miss America find true love without having to get pawed by a pair of sleazy horn dogs in the process?

Call me a prude, but it flipped my stomach to think that Miranda DuBois had been going to these Caviar Club maul-fests, getting drunk and hooking up with guys—two at a time from the looks of things—when she could've had anyone.

Or so it had seemed, looking at her life from the outside in.

It was hard to believe that the baton-spinning, pageant-winning girl I'd known most of my life—and who I'd imagined had more self-esteem than anyone on the planet—would have wanted to debase herself by participating in these alleged sex parties.

But apparently she had.

The "you're dumped" letter from the Caviar Club proved that she'd been involved.

So did the e-mail tip to Janet.

I could hear my inner feminist railing, *But women should be able to enjoy the same kind of uninhibited, uncommitted, meaningless intimacy that men have for centuries. What's wrong with being sexually liberated? This is a free country, isn't it?*

Just because some men were dogs didn't mean women had to lie down with fleas to be their equals.

God help us all if it did.

Weren't we supposed to be the smarter sex? (Excluding rogue fembots like Jessica Simpson and Paris Hilton, of course.)

My cell phone rang, and I dug it out of my bag before the Def Leppard ring tone had played more than twice. I recognized the number off the bat.

It was Janet.

"What's up?" I asked.

"I think I've got it," she said in a rush. "I've figured out a way to get a ringer into the Caviar Club. I've been studying the Web site, or at least the part I can get into with the basic password, and it looks like there are two ways for someone to become a member. You know the first."

"Submitting your picture," I replied dutifully.

"Well, it seems that there are two layers of Caviar Club membership," Janet dashed on. "The first level is for newbies, the Sevrugas, who don't have control over much of anything. But the second tier, the Belugas, they can invite someone to a party without that invitee having to go through the whole photo evaluation process. I think Miranda was a Beluga. She must've been, or else she wouldn't have tempted me with the secondary password. She couldn't have known it. Only the Belugas can get to the message board with the party information. The Sevrugas have to get it through the grapevine."

Ding-ding-ding.

A bell went off in my brain, and it wasn't the Domino's man at the door.

Janet continued to yap, but I cut her off before the thought slipped away.

"Did you say Sevruga and Beluga?" I asked, and my tone was no-nonsense.

"Yeah, so what?"

I didn't exactly tell her that Mother had swiped Miranda's bag out of her Jag before the police got it, but I did mention finding what I'd thought was a partial shopping list of Miranda's, a torn bit of paper with Sevruga and Beluga written on it, both expensive caviars, though Sevruga was not quite as pricey as Beluga. I noted, too, the other words that appeared beside each: Caspian and Malossol, respectively.

At which point Janet uttered, "No way. Are you sure?"

"Yes." What, she didn't believe me all of a sudden? "Sevruga Caspian and Beluga Malossol."

"Andy," she said, lowering her voice to a whisper. "The password to the general area of the Caviar Club's Web site is 'Caspian.'"

My ears perked up and I pressed the cell closer to my face, as if that would make her voice louder, make everything crystal clear.

"Hold on a sec."

I heard a *tap-tap-tap*, like she was typing on her

keyboard. Then she paused, and all was quiet for a bit until I caught her breathy, "Oh, my God."

"What?"

"It's the secondary password, Andy. 'Malossol.' It gets you into the next level of the Web site, into the private board where they post where each party will be held a mere hour before it starts." She sounded out of her mind giddy. "I'm in, don't you get it? I can find out where to go, get my ringer in, and snag my story. Are you at your computer?"

"Yes."

"Go to the Caviar Club's Web site, Andy. You've gotta check this out."

So I did as I was told, prompted by Janet with appropriate passwords all the way, until I could glimpse the mission statement of the C.C., namely that the purpose of the so-called social club was for beautiful people to mix and mingle with other beautiful people, with invitations extended either by certain anointed Belugas or by submission of photographs through the Web site to be evaluated by the Caviar Club's owners.

It went from bad to worse.

There was a page of professional photographs of a selected cast of members, all of the men in tight T-shirts with puttied hair and all-weather tans, and the women with shirts unbuttoned to the navel, jeans slung as low as they could go, often posed with each other in suggestive situations.

Social club, my aunt Henrietta.

Janet was right. It was all about sex.

Cissy belonged to more social clubs than I could name—garden clubs, bridge clubs, the Junior

League, the AAUW—none of which involved being photographed straddling a slicked-up dude licking her throat.

Ugh.

"You recognize any of the faces in those photos?" Janet asked when I made a remark about how sleazy the poses were.

I told her no and was about to segue into Miranda's camera and what I'd found so far—namely, the photos I felt sure were taken when the Caviar Club parties were really swinging, so to speak— but Janet didn't let me get another word out.

She nearly pierced my eardrum when she shrieked, "It just went up, oh, God, it went up!"

Here we went again.

It was like talking to my mother, or playing twenty questions.

"What's up, for Pete's sake?"

It was as though I'd pricked a balloon and all the air was whooshing out.

"There's a party tonight in a rented-out club in Deep Ellum, and it starts in an hour. So we'd better get moving, huh, Andy? There's so much to do and so little time! Can you get over to my place pronto? I'll call the stylist for the paper and have her bring over all her tools and makeup, plus a few outfits from the latest fashion shoot, since I've seen what's in your closet and it ain't pretty. We have to get you looking good enough to eat, or no one will believe that a Beluga would've tapped you for membership . . . "

Get me looking good enough to eat?

Hello? Did she just insult my wardrobe?

Tap me for membership?

Janet expected *me* to be her ringer inside the Caviar Club?

How much crack had she been smoking?

"No way," I said, but she headed me off like a verbal bumper car.

"See you in ten," she chirped, quickly adding, "Oh, and leave the boyfriend at home."

"Janet!" I screamed into my cell, but it was too late.

She'd hung up.

Chapter 15

It wasn't hard getting out of the condo without raising Malone's suspicion about what I was up to, since I took off while the hockey game was still late in the second period (with the Blues down 2 to 1).

Ipso facto, he barely took note of the fact that I'd grabbed my sweat jacket and purse before toddling out the door, though I'd done the whole "'Bye, sweetie, have to run to Janet's for a while, but I'll be back later. Don't wait up."

I had grave doubts he'd even registered where I'd said I was going. If anyone gave him a pop quiz after the Stars had finished pummeling the Blues (which I assumed they would, since Malone constantly complained about the slump his hometown boys were in this season), he'd probably squint up at the ceiling, scratch his chin and murmur, "Hmm, did she go to her mother's? No? Am I warm?"

That's why God invented cell phones—so distracted boyfriends watching sports could hunt down missing wives and girlfriends once the final whistle blew. It was then, and only then, that the levels of testosterone came way down, the dudes popped out of their beer-induced comas, looked around, and realized their women had disappeared.

If I were an alien set to conquer Earth, I'd do it during the Super Bowl or the Stanley Cup finals. Less resistance.

I only left the condo under duress, of course, as I would've rather stayed at home with Malone and the hockey game, especially after having had such a lousy day.

Reluctantly, I ventured outdoors, dragging my feet as I headed toward my Jeep, and let myself in. I climbed up behind the wheel, slinging my purse to the passenger seat, where it landed with a gentle thud. It didn't contain much besides my wallet, a tube of lip balm, and my cell phone.

Oh, yeah, and Miranda's memory card.

I'd already decided to let Janet copy the photos before I turned the tiny disk over to the police in the morning.

Why not? I'd asked myself.

So long as Ms. Society Snoop promised not to print them in the paper. What else was I going to do with them besides hand them over to Anna Dean, who'd probably discount them anyway, seeing as how the cops were so intent on labeling Miranda's death a suicide? And I would never show them to my mother, considering how much she wanted to believe the Miranda DuBois she'd watched grow up was practically a saint. I couldn't imagine Debbie Santos seeing them, either. She'd surely rather remember her daughter in pigtails and pinafores than with two men kissing her in a hot tub.

Though I knew the shots would give Janet goose bumps, as they'd further substantiate her theory that Miranda had sent her that e-mail threatening to bring down the snooty membership of the entire Caviar Club.

I had a pipe dream that maybe such a gift would absolve me of any debts I owed La Graham, so I wouldn't have to go through with infiltrating the Caviar Club party that started at ten, which might as well have been midnight as far as I was concerned.

Seriously, ten o'clock was my bedtime.

Malone and I could barely keep our eyes open once the evening news came on. It was a struggle for us to stay awake long enough to find out the weather forecast.

Sad but true.

Though if Janet had a mind to make me do this thing for her, I didn't think pleading an early bird curfew was going to have any effect.

Janet Rutledge Graham had been reared in the Park Cities by a mother as tough as mine, and she wasn't one to suffer wimps gladly.

So I had no choice but to suck it up and be the kind of friend who'd offer support in her time of need, just as she'd done for me plenty of times.

If I had to endure a glamour puss makeover so

I could fake my way through drinks with a bunch of Big D's sex-starved pretty boys and girls, surely I would survive. I'd had to wear hot pants and stuff my bra to help a prep school chum in trouble, so vamping it up to pump information out of so-called Sevrugas and Belugas at the Caviar Club couldn't be much worse, could it? Give me an hour and I'd get enough for Janet to write her danged story. Then I'd get the hell out of there, before anyone could say "Louis Vuitton."

Janet certainly wouldn't have a problem with that, eh?

Well, I'd find out soon enough, since traffic was light heading south on Central Expressway, and it was just another ten minutes to her place.

Her apartment was well south of my Prestonwood digs. The 1940s-era complex in Knox-Henderson had been renovated and relandscaped, so it was truly sitting pretty. Her hardwood floors and working fireplace were drop-dead cool, though I figured there was just about a two-week window in January when burning wood seemed feasible. The gentrified area where Janet lived bordered my mother's beloved Highland Park and was a hop, skip, and a jump from Deep Ellum, where there were plenty of clubs and restaurants, one of which was playing host to the Caviar Club's hush-hush party this evening.

I wondered if Janet lived close enough to walk.

Or, rather, *run*, since that's likely how fast I'd be moving once I decided to hightail it out of the desperate singles soiree.

The power of positive thinking.

Uh-huh.

I hung onto that tendril of optimism, thin though it was, as I parked the Jeep, locked it tight, and dragged myself toward Janet's apartment. She flung open the door before I had even reached the Welcome mat, reaching out to yank me inside.

"Where've you been? We've been waiting on you *forever*," she said, as if it had taken two days for me to get there and not twenty minutes.

I barely had a chance to dig the Baggie with the memory card from my purse and hand it over to Ms. J, explaining what it was and suggesting she upload the party pics before I gave the mini-disk and all its files to Deputy Chief Dean come tomorrow.

"Photos from club bashes? Are you sure?" she'd practically squealed at me, and I admitted that I wasn't a hundred percent sure, but I had a strong feeling.

"Your intuition is working overtime lately, Andy, but then I'm a lot like Oprah. I say we should listen closely to that voice inside us," she remarked, then reconsidered and added, "only not the one that tells us we're fat. That one sucks."

What about the one that told you to get your lips inflated? I wanted to ask. But I didn't.

"Can't wait to take a look at these babies!"

After she'd gleefully snatched the Baggie from my hands—and before she disappeared into her bedroom, where she kept her computer—she quickly introduced me to an ultrathin woman with fluffy blond hair and perfectly outlined eyes and lips named Suzy Bee, the stylist from the *Park*

Cities Press, who set me down on a chair in Janet's living room where track lighting rained down on my un-made-up skin.

"You're not going to cover up my freckles, are you?" I asked, because I liked my freckles. They're the only things that kept me from being so ghostly white that I appeared as though I spent my daylight hours in a coffin.

"Just relax," Suzy told me, while she whipped open a multitiered makeup case and began slapping foundation and powder on my face as I closed my eyes and winced.

I hated makeup with a passion. The most I wore on average days was mascara and lip gloss, never base, which had always felt like a face mask. If I'd aspired to be a clown, I would've joined the circus. If Mary Kay Ash were alive, I know she'd put a pox on me for saying so, but I just liked my skin to breathe.

"Sit still, Andrea, and don't scrunch up your forehead, please," Suzy commanded, and I tried to relax beneath the bath towel she'd draped around me. Like she was afraid she'd splatter her sparkly pink eye shadow on my sweatshirt and ruin it forever.

Every now and then Suzy would instruct me to open my eyes and look up or look down as she lined my lashes with a pencil, then layered on the mascara. My nose started to itch, but I was afraid to reach up and scratch; so I crinkled it, feeling like Elizabeth Montgomery in *Bewitched*. Only if I'd really been Samantha, I could've wrinkled my nose and zapped myself out of that chair and into my living room, next to Malone on the sofa in front of the hockey game.

Man, but witches had it made.

"We're almost done," Suzy said after what seemed an eternity, though I kept my eyes open at this point, my attention directed on the door to Janet's bedroom where she was silently—way too silently—checking out the images from Miranda's digital camera.

I'd expected to hear a few oohs or aahs, kind of similar to the noises one made when watching Fourth of July fireworks.

Instead, *nada*.

"I did Miranda DuBois's makeup once," Suzy Bee remarked out of the blue, and my focus instantly diverted.

"You knew Miranda?" I said, realizing then that she must've overheard my conversation with Janet about the photos.

It was hard to be quiet when Ms. Megaphone was anywhere in the vicinity. Janet's pipes operated at a decibel level more akin to a jet airplane engine, twice that when she was on her cell phone.

Suzy Bee tossed her head, flipping light blond hair from her eyes and screwing her mouth up in concentration as she lined my lips. "It was for a photo shoot," she said, talking while she worked. "She was having new head shots done by Esther Gorman, you heard of her?"

I nodded, knowing full well that Esther Gorman was one of the hottest photogs in Big D. "She shot my mother for the *PCP*'s 'Best Dressed' issue," I

said, adding, "ten years in a row." Until they'd re-
tired Cissy to their Hall of Fame.

After Suzy Bee advised me not to move my
head or risk the outline of my lips stretching up
to my nose, she finished what she'd started to say.
"Anyway, I did Ms. Dubois's hair and makeup for
her shoot for *D Magazine*, and she was as sweet as
pie. Didn't say a bad word about anyone, except
that horn dog Dick Uttley." Suzy pressed her
glossy lips into a sour-looking moue. "That man
wears more pancake than anyone I've ever worked
on, and he still thinks he's God's gift to women.
He pinched my ass while I was doing his face for
a PSA for PBS."

"Eww," I said in sympathy.

I pictured the fatherly dude with the wrinkles
and shellacked hair who so earnestly delivered
the evening news, and I wondered if he'd tried
to play footsies with Miranda while they were
on-air. Then my crazy brain went beyond that
thought to another: Would it have been possible
for Dick to buy his way into the Caviar Club to
take a nibble? Or did he get enough action on his
own, utilizing his anchorman persona to reel in
the piranhas? Because I knew there were plenty of
piranhas swimming around this city's fish pond
to make for ample male bait.

"Ms. DuBois had such pretty skin," Suzy went
on, though I'd only been half listening. "It was
like porcelain, really, not an enlarged pore to be
seen. She was worried about her eyelids sagging
and her lips being too small. She said she'd gotten
some e-mails about how old she looked on high

definition, and she was thinking of having some work done. I told her she was nuts. She looked beautiful just the way she was."

Oh, Miranda had some work done, all right, I mused, thinking Suzy was right. Ms. DuBois should've left well enough alone. If she had, she might still be around.

Instead, she'd gone to Dr. Sonja, who'd truly fixed her clock, as my daddy used to say. It wasn't a good thing.

I wouldn't have been surprised if Debbie Santos decided to slap a big ol' lawsuit on the Dermatologist-to-the-Deluded right quick after her plane landed from Brazil, and I wouldn't blame her a bit.

While she was at it, maybe she'd sue the Caviar Club, too, for rejecting her daughter and pushing Miranda into such a state that she'd put her life at risk by threatening to expose people who had everything to lose if she ratted them out.

At least that was my take on it.

Though I knew the Highland Park P.D. felt differently. About how Miranda's life had ended, I mean. No one could refute that both Dr. Sonja's botched injections and the "you're fired" letter from the Caviar Club had been mitigating factors in Miranda's death. Where my conclusion differed from Anna Dean and her merry band of Highland Park detectives wasn't in *how* Miranda had died, but in who'd done it.

" . . . she talked about how attracted she was to some guy she'd met at a party, but she wasn't sure it would work out because he wasn't altogether available," Suzy Bee was saying.

Again I snapped to attention.

"Miranda was seeing an unavailable guy?" I asked, not an easy trick while Suzy applied two thousand layers of lipstick. "As in, he was married?"

"I didn't pry." Suzy shrugged her skinny shoulders. "That's all she said and then she changed the subject real quick."

Unavailable, huh?

Like her co-anchor Dick Uttley, I thought, except that didn't make sense. Suzy had just mentioned Miranda trashing him. Unless Miranda realized she'd slipped when she blabbed about wanting someone she couldn't have—if that someone was her married co-anchor—and covered up by talking smack about Dick.

I shuddered at the very thought of Miranda shagging Richard Uttley.

Did I say "Eww" already?

Then again, I couldn't imagine anyone wanting to do the horizontal mambo with Larry King, and he'd been married, like, four million times.

"A little flat ironing to smooth out your hair, and we're done, hon," Suzy Bee promised, and I breathed a sigh of relief that this torture was nearly over.

How long had I been sitting in that chair?

Half an hour? Forty-five minutes?

Was the hockey game over yet, and was Malone wondering if I'd run away from home?

And where the heck was Janet?

I still hadn't heard a peep from the bedroom. She must've been going through every one of Miranda's photographs with a fine-tooth comb, or at least with the zoom feature.

"Jan?" I called out as Suzy tugged on my hair with a flat iron and I felt the heat against my neck. "Are you alive in there?"

"Give me five," my long lost friend hollered back while Suzy mussed my hair with her fingers.

I glanced at my purse, planted on Janet's dining room table, not quite within an arm's length, and I willed my cell to ring, figuring it was about time Malone surfaced from the Stars-Blues game and started looking for me. Unless the Blues had caught up and they were headed for overtime, even a shootout. Tack the postgame onto things and it could be close to midnight before Brian realized I wasn't sitting at my computer and started looking for me.

Nice to know I was so sorely missed.

"Your face is done," Suzy said, whipping the towel from around my neck and tugging me out of the chair. "Now it's time to dress you properly."

Since when were jeans and a sweatshirt not *proper*?

"We'll have you looking chic in two minutes flat!" Suzy promised, dragging me over to where she had clothing on hangers neatly laid over the back of Janet's sofa. She picked up a bright red jersey dress, shook her head and muttered, "Too flashy." Then she held up a pearl gray jewel-necked sweater and tweedy A-line skirt, squinted at me, and declared, "Too prim and proper. Janet said you need to look bedable."

Bedable?

Seriously, was that a word?

Without further ado, she grabbed up a creamy cable knit dress with pearl buttons up the back and a Peter Pan collar that had a Ralph Lauren label.

"You wear size seven shoes, right? That's what Janet told me." She pushed a pair of black spiky-heeled leather boots at me as I stood there, gawking. "It's the naughty prep school girl look," she explained. "Men love it."

I suddenly felt the urge to sing Britney Spears's "Oops! . . .I Did It Again," which surely should be punishable by an afternoon in detention, bare minimum.

Oy vey.

Despite my better judgment, I took the clothes in my arms and started to head toward the bathroom.

But Suzy zipped around in front of me and cut me off.

"You can change right here," she said. "I don't want you catching sight of yourself in the mirror, not just yet, and you might mess up your hair besides. You'll need me for the back buttons, too."

I'd been dressing myself since I was five, but I guess that didn't matter much. The skeptical side of my brain imagined this as part of Janet's evil plan to ensure I didn't run screaming out the door.

"Fine," I said.

But I did turn around modestly while I changed in the middle of Janet's living room. Suzy Bee fussed and fluttered every step of the way until I was done, the pointy-toed boots pinching my feet and the Peter Pan collar fairly strangling me.

"*Violà!*" Suzy the Stylist cried, and stepped back to admire her handiwork. Then she shuffled me around Janet's furniture until I came face-to-face with a full-length mirror. "So?" she asked, peering at me over the top of my right shoulder. "What do you think?"

I stared at the girl in the mirror, feeling like I should introduce myself, because she wasn't someone I knew.

Certainly, she wasn't me.

Chapter 16

The woman gazing back at me from the silvered glass had eyes that were almond-shaped and smoky, twice as big as they ordinarily were; her cheeks looked smoothed and defined by a subtle blush of bronzy pink. Her mouth was luscious as dewy strawberries, parted lips an earthy pink against white teeth. And her hair . . . good God, where had the unruly mess of wavy brown gone? And it wasn't bundled in a hasty ponytail, no siree, Bob. Against all odds, it actually appeared chic, smooth yet messy, sexy and tousled and framing a heart-shaped face in a way I'd only seen on airbrushed women pouting from the covers of fashion magazines.

As for the Girl in the Mirror's attire, it was as far removed from sweatshirts and jeans as one could get. The clingy knit dress actually showed off curves instead of hiding them, and the four-inch spike heels on the boots suggested tall and slinky rather than petite.

"What have you done to me?" I wailed, and Suzy blinked, obviously taken aback. "I look freaking *gorgeous*!"

I was groaning instead of raving, but it wasn't out of disrespect for Suzy's handiwork. It was because the woman in the mirror wasn't Andrea Blevins Kendricks. Not the one I recognized, and I should know best.

It was the chichi countenance of someone else entirely. Someone who'd obliterated every tiny brown freckle with makeup and had fussed with her hair until each strand did as it was told; someone who'd spent forty-five minutes getting groomed to death by a stylist from the Fashion section of the newspaper and had turned into a complete and total stranger in the process (at least on the surface).

God help me if my mother ever caught me looking like this.

She'd start expecting way too much from me, and I wasn't about to waste half my life prettying myself up just to go grocery shopping, as was the Dallas way (unless one had servants to hit the Tom Thumb for them, which was most definitely the Beverly Drive society matron's way).

"So do you like it? Or don't you?" Suzy was asking, though any attempt at a response on my part was interrupted by a very loud wolf whistle.

Odd, since there was no construction site in Janet's apartment that I was aware of.

I turned my head with its carefully tousled 'do

to see that Janet had emerged from her bedroom, big mouth agog.

"Well, butter my biscuit!" she said, apparently as shocked as I was by the transformation. "I can't even believe it's you, Kendricks. You look like a . . . "

"Fraud," I finished for her, because it was the truth.

"Not what I was about to say at all"—she wagged a finger at me—"no, no, you look like a high-class babe that the Caviar Club would be itching to add to its roster." She gave Suzy a thumbs-up. "You done good, Ms. Bee. I wasn't sure the transformation could be accomplished, but I knew if anyone could turn the Goodwill Girl into Beluga Barbie, it was you."

Goodwill Girl? Beluga Barbie?

Geez.

"You promised a private meeting with Manolo when he's in town, don't forget," Suzy chattered as Janet urged the reed-thin blond and her bait box full of makeup toward the door. "And back-stage passes at the Tom Ford show—"

"Yeah, yeah, I'm good for it, Ms. Bee, no worries," Janet said as she hustled the stylist out of the apartment and shut the door. Dramatically, she leaned against it, letting out a big sigh. "I thought she'd never leave." She took a few giant steps in my direction then stood before me, wringing her hands. "Oh, God, Andy, this whole thing's getting crazier than I imagined. Did you look at *all* the pictures on Miranda's camera from the parties?"

I thought I'd already told her that I hadn't, but I shook my head anyway.

She exhaled slowly then said, "Girl, we need to talk before I send you out to the barracudas."

"Don't you mean the Belugas?" I tried to joke, but she obviously wasn't in a joking mood.

"Sure, that's what I meant," she replied, and reached for my arm. "C'mere and chat a sec before you go." She tugged me toward the sofa but changed her mind and waved me up again. "Wait, you'll wrinkle, and we can't have that. Can you just lean against the wall or something? I'll be quick."

"I'll stand," I said, not inclined toward wall-leaning. "Well, go on."

I was ready to get my Mata Hari act over with, though I had nothing against a good briefing before I infiltrated enemy turf.

Janet didn't sit for long, either. She bounced off the couch, doing a bit of pacing as she talked about the photographs on Miranda's memory card, starting off with the fact that she was as sure as I was that the pictures were taken at Caviar Club parties. But Janet had some evidence to back up her instincts.

"I zoomed in on half a dozen shots, and the Caviar Club's watchdog, Theresa Hurley, was in the background of several of them. She's holding a clipboard in one," Janet told me. "Like she was doing her bulldog routine, checking off names from a list."

Speaking of clipboards, how could I ever slip in without the Bulldog knowing right off the bat that I didn't belong?

I posed the question to Janet, but she waved it off like it wasn't important.

"Unfortunately, I really didn't see anything much more than vaguely blackmailworthy. It takes an awful lot to shock these days," she said, and sniffed. "Let's see, we've got a couple of city councilmen in semicompromising positions, and several party girl heiresses going at it with each other." She shrugged. "Nothing for anyone to get whipped into a frenzy about, much less drive them to commit a murder."

I had a feeling I knew why the big bombshells were missing.

"The really incriminating stuff must be on Miranda's laptop," I said, voicing my thoughts aloud. "And whoever went over to her house last night and shot her realized that. They could have even glimpsed something on the screen"—as I had—"while the laptop was out on the coffee table."

"Well, *that* we'll never be able to prove, any more than we can prove Miranda didn't shoot herself," Janet said, and I glumly agreed. "Still, we've got something, Andy." She sat up straighter. "Did you recognize anyone when you took a gander at the jpegs?" she asked, and there was a gleam in her eye that told me *she* had.

"I thought the blond guy in the hot tub with Miranda looked a little familiar," I said. "It was hard to tell, but he reminded me of Dr. Sonja's beau. I'm not sure about anyone else. It was kinda hard to see."

"The blond dude with his tongue in her ear looked familiar? I'll bet he did." Janet laughed. "Yeah, my eagle eyes spotted Lance Zarimba, too. I wonder how Dr. Botox feels about her dude messing around with other women. Miranda DuBois in particular, considering she and Dr. Sonja were hardly pals."

"Oh, Lordy," I breathed, considering all the implications.

Could Lance have been the "unavailable" man that Miranda had babbled about while Suzy Bee did her make up for *D Magazine*?

"There's definitely a story there," Janet remarked, and, boy, did she look pleased with herself. Her overinflated lips had curled up into a Cheshire cat grin. "It makes you wonder, doesn't it? I mean, if Dr. Madhavi's boyfriend belonged to the Caviar Club, did she know about it? Or is she a part of things, too?"

"Whoa."

"Whoa, indeed."

Take about a tangled web. I don't think they get any more complicated than a love triangle, particularly when one of those involved has a medical degree.

So, let's say that Miranda and Lance had gone at it, and Dr. Sonja found out about the affair.

Could she have given Miranda bad Botox on purpose? To mess her up? To make Lance dump her?

All right, maybe that was a stretch—a big stretch—but my mind was open to anything, like Dr. Sonja having been the one who'd retrieved Miranda's gun from the floor. It was certainly a possibility. And if she had, there's nothing to say she couldn't have dropped by the duplex later on and used Miranda's own .22 to kill her.

"Andy? You're not listening, are you?"

"What?"

Janet had crossed her arms and stamped her foot impatiently on the floor. "I was saying that I also spotted a dear friend of ours in the background of Miranda's photos. A woman we all know and loathe."

I shrugged, because that could be just about anybody.

"Cinda Lou Mitchell," she enunciated, ever so clearly, and my jaw dropped.

Now *that* went beyond a mere "No way."

Cinda Lou had gone to Hockaday, as had Janet and I. Ms. Mitchell had been in my class, and I knew her well (unfortunately). She'd ended up as a reporter for Channel 11, never quite making the top anchor spot as Miranda had at Channel 5. Though Cinda had beat out Miranda in one department: wedding bells. Cinda Lou was on her fourth husband—or was it her fifth?—a geriatric fellow who spent most of his time napping and funding Cinda Lou's shopping excursions, from what I'd heard from my mother.

"Cinda's in the Caviar Club? What if her geezer of a husband found out?" I asked.

"He'd toss her to the streets, wouldn't he?"

"His money-grubbing son would, anyway," Janet corrected. "Which is how we've got an in, or how you've got an in, rather. I made a quick phone call and took care of things," she said smugly. "Cinda Lou has 'tagged' you for tonight. That's the term for inviting a new member, apparently. She'll go along with anything, so long as I don't breathe a word about her wild ways. She swore this is her last fling, and she'll be a good wife to the Honorable Wallingford Matterhorn from this point forward. So if anyone asks, you're there because of your old prep school pal. Got it?"

"I'm there because of your story," I said, "so you'll remain gainfully employed at the *PCP*."

"Oh, *contraire*." Janet raised a neatly drawn eyebrow at me. "You will not mention the story, much less my name, got that? Not only could it be dangerous for you if you did, because we don't know who you might bump into—for goodness' sake, look what happened to Miranda—but they'd toss you out on your ass before you took a sip of bubbly." She tapped a finger in the air as she instructed, "Play it like this, okay? You're joining because you're bored with your boyfriend, and if you're curious about what happened to Miranda DuBois, what's the big deal? You went to school with her, after all. No harm, no foul."

What did she just say?

I pretty much blocked out everything after the "bored with your boyfriend" part.

"I'm cheating on Brian? That's the story you came up with?" It hurt even to repeat it aloud. "Can't you think of something else less tacky?"

Dear God, she hadn't told Cinda Lou *that*, had she? The bimbo would probably lap up every word and have it spread across the grapevine by morning that I was a swinger. Forget about where Cinda had gleaned such information. No one would care. They'd just gobble up the news that

Cissy Kendricks's daughter, the one who'd bailed on her deb ball, was being naughty.

"Nothing else will work as well in this situation," Janet insisted. "And it's just pretend. Try to cozy up to Dr. Sonja's he-man, too, and see if he talks at all about Miranda. If we can tie them together, wouldn't that be juicy?"

She was practically rubbing her hands together and salivating.

My reaction was far less enthusiastic.

"Oh, God." I groaned. "I don't want people to believe I'm cheating on Malone. What if something gets back to him?"

"Please, Andy, it's just for tonight, and it's only pretend. Brian won't ever find out, if you don't tell him. And even if Cinda Lou flaps her trap, it'll only make you seem more interesting and less like the geek you are."

"Gee, thanks."

Why was I starting to feel like it was Kick Andy in the Teeth Weekend?

"I'll keep going at the pics on my PhotoShop while you're gone," Janet said, gradually shooshing me toward the door. "If I see anything else interesting, I'll let you know."

Terrific.

"Oh, oh, the clock is ticking. Let's get a move on." She checked her wristwatch. "You're only twenty minutes late for the party, which isn't a bad thing. Gives everyone else a chance to have arrived already."

Whoopee to that.

I couldn't wait to see which local heathens showed up.

I tried not to dwell on the fact that one of them could very well be a killer.

If I had a choice between spying for Janet at the Caviar Club to-do or having to get a set of rabies shots, I think I would've picked the latter.

"Don't take notes or anything," Janet was saying. "Just remember names and what they're doing. Here, take my cell"—she shoved her fancy phone into my sweaty palm—"it has a camera built in. Snap away if you can do it without rousing suspicion. I'll keep your phone here," she went on, "in case Malone calls. I can tell him you're picking up take-out or something, and I'll have you call him later."

"Ten-four," I shot back.

I felt like Maxwell Smart-ass.

No sense asking how I'd gotten myself into this. Every time I found myself doing something idiotic or inane, I could trace it back to the sucker aspect of my personality. I would call it a defect, except for those times when I was bamboozled into doing something for a truly good cause. Such as when I manned a booth at the Nitty-Gritty Girls Club's bazaar selling pink and blue bracelets to raise money for the neonatal unit at Medical City.

Though I couldn't exactly put tonight's escapade in the same category as volunteering for the sake of saving premature babies.

Helping Janet hang onto her job by getting dirt on the Caviar Club and on Miranda DuBois's connection to it wasn't a charitable act that I could write off on my income tax.

But I owed her one more, and I aimed to pay off all my debts, even if it meant dressing up like Bimbo Barbie. Never let it be said that Andrea Kendricks didn't keep her promises, no matter how shameful or humiliating.

Honk! Honk!

Somebody blasted a car horn just outside, and I saw Janet's neck crane toward the front windows. "That's your ride," she said, "because you certainly cannot arrive at the club in your Jeep."

Oh, right, heaven forbid.

"I could walk," I said.

"In those boots?" Janet sniffed, glancing down at the shiny leather with the four-inch heels. "Puh-leeze."

She had me there.

Yeesh.

Janet wouldn't let me leave with my beat-up shoulder bag, either. She foisted a sparkly Judith Leiber bag into my hands. It was the size of a glove box and smothered in crystals. If I had to guess, I'd say it was worth a couple thousand dollars.

Scared me to think of carrying it around Deep Ellum.

Besides, I could only fit my ChapStick, my borrowed cell, and some cash inside the tiny purse, but Janet assured me that would do.

"Have the Town Car pick you up in an hour and bring you back here for a debriefing. And, puh-leeze, call me on the cell if you need bailing out. Godspeed and good luck," she said as she shooed me out the front door.

I half expected her to salute.

"Oh, and be careful. Keep your head down, whatever that means."

Lord, but it sounded like she was sending me off to battle.

And maybe she was, in a way, which didn't make me feel any more at ease about my mission.

"I'll see you soon," I said, as much a promise as a farewell, and I headed toward the waiting Lincoln, staring down at my feet to avoid cracks in the sidewalk.

I narrowly escaped a tumble off my stiletto boots when my right heel caught itself in the bordering grass; though at least I hadn't stepped on a crack. Didn't want to break my mother's back, or mine, either.

Graceful, I wasn't.

As I tottered toward the black sedan, I ignored all the warning bells that were going off inside my head, reminding myself I was doing this for Janet and maybe even for Miranda; and I wondered, at the same time, if I'd completely lost my mind, and pegged the answer as a firm, "Hell, yes."

Perhaps I was my mother's daughter after all.

Insanity obviously ran in the family.

Chapter 17

The club's French name, Bébé Gâté, flashed across the second-story windows of the façade in bright pink neon.

How appropriate, I mused, considering the English translation was something like "spoiled brat." Seemed to me that it pretty well summed up the crowd I'd be playing poseur amidst this evening.

It was a beautiful old brick building, obviously rehabbed, smack on Elm Street (from which the "Ellum" in Deep Ellum had been corrupted through the years). The club was situated above a sushi restaurant. I didn't see an entrance in the front, which might've been why my driver headed around back.

There, a white awning covered a doorway fiercely guarded by a bouncer who looked like a real-life Buddha, only wearing slouch jeans and a black T-shirt overlaid by enough gold chains and winking bling to make Mr. T proud. At that precise moment, he was opening the brass-handled door to a woman deposited smack in front by a shiny black Mercedes. Apropos for November (*not*), she wore a miniskirt and fur boa.

I stared, and not exactly in awe.

"You said you need me to pick you up?" my driver—whose name was Siddarth—asked, as I sat in the backseat, my breath condensing on the window, making no move to get out.

"Yes, please, in an hour," I told him, and we synchronized our watches. It was nearly ten-thirty, so that would make pickup time eleven-thirty. Way past my bedtime. I hoped I could stay alert enough to keep track of everyone and relay any scoop in a coherent fashion to Ms. Janet later.

The dude waved me off when I tried to pay him from the cash in my borrowed purse, as he let me know "Miss Graham has taken care of things."

Oh, she'd taken care of things, all right, I mused, wishing Janet was in my loaner pinch-toed boots right then instead of me.

I gathered my wits and my courage, and I pushed my way out the door. The bouncer eyed me suspiciously, and I wondered if it was abnormal for Sevrugas or Belugas to arrive at Caviar Club parties in a Lincoln Town Car. Would an Escalade have been more proper? Knowing Janet, she'd bill the fare to the newspaper, and they'd probably gawk at a receipt for, oh, say, a stretch limo Hummer.

Whatever.

It was time to get motivated. I had a role to play.

So I raised my chin to haughty heights as I carefully picked my way toward the club entrance. My goal was to channel Cissy Blevins Kendricks so long as I was acting like a Beluga ingénue, as no one dared question a Highland Park heiress who behaved like, well, a Highland Park heiress. It was all about the attitude.

Okay, that and the Manolo Blahnik boots and Judith Leiber bag. The hair and makeup didn't hurt, either.

"You new here, babe?" the dude with the muscles and the bling asked, checking me out from head to toe as I approached. Guess his suspicion had faded in favor of ogling.

"I'd of remembered if I'd seen you before, fine-looking thing that you are."

"Is that so?"

"Oh, yeah, baby, it's so."

As he leered, I took a personal moment of silence, realizing this guy wouldn't have given me a second glance had I been dressed in my usual attire of jeans, T-shirt, and sneakers, sans makeup, with my hair pulled back in a scrunchie. And if I'd been too lazy to put in my contacts and worn my glasses, I doubtless wouldn't have even garnered a first glance.

I had to remind myself that I wasn't there to judge the superficial, merely to spy on them. I was incognito, playing the role of Andrea Blevins Kendricks, blue-blooded trust fund baby on the prowl for a boy-toy.

Which meant I could hardly lecture each shallow soul I came up against on the virtue of loving what was on the inside of a person, as it would surely blow my cover . . . and I'd be here all night lecturing besides.

So I just smiled at the Buddha-man who'd pulled wide the door for me, and I said in an exaggerated drawl, "Why, thank you, darlin'."

If he'd made any attempt to pinch me as I'd passed, I would've reverted to my normal self and kicked him in the groin with my lethal boots.

But he didn't.

So I grabbed the railing and hauled myself up the steps to the second floor, hearing music blaring—it sounded like Shakira—the closer I got to the top.

Before taking the last few steps, I stopped, steadied myself, and quieted my nervous jitters. I'd never been much of an actress, having avoided following in my dramatic mother's footsteps. She'd done a little theater while a student at SMU, and she thrived on being in the spotlight, even if that spotlight came from the glow of a ballroom chandelier at a charity event.

You can do this, Andy, I told myself, thinking I never gave myself enough credit for my own accomplishments, as off the wall as they may have been.

There was another thing I knew for sure: I had never let a friend down, and I wasn't about to start now.

I carried my head high, summoned up all the inner diva I could muster, and completed my climb up the stairwell, to where a set of French doors awaited. I let myself through those, entering a dimly lit foyer with sheet metal flooring and wall niches filled with bronze nudes.

Music pounded from an adjacent room, the archway between draped in silk. I detected shadows and movement beyond the flimsy fabric, the cacophony of laughter and raised voices competing with the Latin beat throbbing through the air.

I didn't even see the woman standing to my left until she startled me by asking, "Name, please?"

My head swiveled in her direction, and I realized the petite brunette with the clipboard had to be the one Janet had labeled the "skinny bulldog" aka the Caviar Club's mouthpiece.

Theresa Hurley.

Though she looked anything but ferocious. She was positively tiny.

I doubt she stood more than five feet tall in her stocking feet, hardly threatening by any standards. Indeed, I felt Amazonian as I approached her and towered above, teetering on heels that elevated me to a skyscraping five-nine.

"Your name?" she said again, as if I hadn't heard her the first time.

"Andrea Kendricks," I told her, doing my best to look bored in the way that most socialites did, as in, *Ho-hum, one pompous and exclusive party simply blurred into the next*. "Cinda Lou Mitchell tagged me," I said in a blasé tone, recalling the term Janet had used. I added for effect, "She and I go way back to Hockaday. Oh, the times we had." I let out a nervous laugh that surely gave me away.

The efficacious Ms. Hurley strained over that clipboard, scrolling a pen down the list of names, making me nervous the nearer she got to the bottom without apparently finding mine listed.

I held my breath until she flipped the page and tapped the paper with her pen. "Here you are, Ms. Kendricks." She smiled, looking eons friendlier as she said, "You're one of two new Sevrugas here tonight. Please, go on in and enjoy yourself. There's plenty of champagne and, of course, caviar."

"Of course," I murmured, nonplussed.

But inside I was thinking, *Whew.*

I smiled back, hoping mine appeared appropriately haughty; while beneath the tiny pearl buttons on my Ralph Lauren jersey dress, sweat trickled down my spine.

Lucky Break Number One, I decided.

"Oh, and Ms. Kendricks," the Keeper of the Names piped up before I'd taken a single step toward the silk sheer that separated me from the party, "if you'd just sign this confidentiality form, you can go on in and enjoy yourself."

Confidentiality form?

"What's that?" The words popped out before I could stop them.

"I'm surprised Ms. Mitchell didn't tell you." The legal-minded Ms. Hurley shoved her clipboard and a pen in my direction. "It's nothing, really. It merely states that what happens at the club stays at the club, so no one has to worry about censoring themselves." A tiny smile lit her face. "It's to protect all our members, whatever their names.

Because no one likes a blabbermouth, do they, Ms. Kendricks?"

Was that supposed to be a threat? Because it sounded like a threat to me.

I took the pen from her hand and glanced at the form, which was brief and basically stated the "what happens here, stays here" policy with "dire consequences" resulting from exploiting the privacy of the Caviar Club gatherings or its membership without approval from the ownership, though it didn't say who the "ownership" was.

I signed the danged thing, scribbling illegibly, because I saw no way out. Besides, I wasn't exactly doing this on the up and up anyway, so if they wanted to sue me for telling Janet what I saw tonight, they could have at it.

When I handed the clipboard back to Hurley the Hun, she gave me a quick rundown of the rules, like never revealing to nonmembers the location of the parties, never inviting nonmembers to gatherings because only Belugas who've reached "tagger" level can do that.

And, "most importantly," she said, and poked her pen in the air for emphasis, "never, never enter the private room beyond the red velvet drapes. It's for top tier Belugas only. You can be terminated for such an offense."

"I wouldn't dare," I lied, wondering what was behind said velvet curtain, even before I'd seen it. Was that where the real action was? The kind of stuff worthy of blackmail photos, perchance?

"Ah, sorry, one more thing, Ms. Kendricks . . . "

I felt pinned into place again by the Clipboard Queen, just when I assumed I'd gotten clearance to take off. I feared for a moment she'd seen through my faux Cissy attitude and meant to toss me out on my keister.

"I'm afraid that Ms. Mitchell won't be attending tonight. She phoned a little bit ago and said to tell you she's sorry to have missed your debut at the club, but she's decided to spend some quality time with her husband."

Now *that* was a laugh riot.

"Thanks for the skinny," I said and turned away, smiling for real as I carefully tottered toward the silk-draped doorway.

Ah, so it was true. Cinda Lou had opted out of partying to cuddle up with her decades older and oodles richer husband.

How very wifely—and wise—of her.

The girl must've decided to reform *tout suite*, which meant she'd be out of my hair this evening.

Phew and double phew.

Lucky Break Number Two, I mused, and wondered how long my luck would last as I pushed back the silk panel and crossed through the threshold into the party zone.

I gave my eyes a minute to adjust as I dropped the drape behind me. The club was lit only by a few dimmed spots and loads of candles, arranged in elaborate standing candelabras of wrought iron and illuminating the faces of the thirty-odd people in the room in a muted glow.

Well, everyone looked better in candlelight, didn't they?

Although if the Caviar Club was limited only to the prettiest of the pretty, I wouldn't imagine any lighting tricks would be necessary.

A waiter all in black emerged at my elbow and offered me a glass of champagne, which I took instinctively. I didn't intend to drink it—or much of it—but I couldn't afford to look out of place, and everyone else in the room had glasses in hand.

As I took delicate sips of the bubbly, I peered over the rim of my glass at the smiling faces, listening to the eruption of laughter right and left, and I wondered if anyone was mourning Miranda. Did they even realize she was dead? Did they care?

Even worse, I imagined that whoever had pushed Miranda into the Great Beyond could be in this very room, drinking Moët Chandon and living it up.

The thought made me sick to my stomach.

"Ooh, aren't you a tasty little thing. I could just eat you up," a voice cooed in my ear, and I jerked around to face the source of the lecherous remark.

I met the fellow eye-to-eye, or rather, eyes to beady eyes.

He was no taller than I was in my sky-high boots, with a thick head of hair so overstyled that I figured he'd used at least a whole jar of gel, if not two. His two-day stubble merely made him seem dirty, not sexy. Ditto the red silk shirt opened wide enough for me to get a load of his chest hair. I had a good sense this dude had the DVD set of *Miami Vice* and every other show Don Johnson had ever been in.

"You must be new here, huh? 'Cuz I would've remembered if I'd seen you before," he said, his gaze roaming over every curve revealed by my knit dress. "I like my chicks natural, not buffed up or blown up, if you dig what I'm saying," he added, as if I'd take any of that as a compliment. "Natural is *hot*."

Considering that it had just taken an hour for Janet's stylist pal to doll me up, I hardly considered my appearance "natural."

But I calmly held my champagne flute and kept my trap shut.

When still I'd said nothing, he piped up: "Ah, so you're shy, eh? That's okay. I don't like women who talk too much, and so many of them do."

"What about men who talk too much?" I said. I couldn't help myself.

"So you're a funny girl, eh?" He rubbed the stubble on his chin. "A sense of humor is the true sign of beauty so far as I'm concerned."

My God, where did this guy get his lines?

"By the way, I'm Daniel Kingsolver. I've got my own online cigar store. I call it 'Not Just a Cigar.' You know, from that thing Freud said. Get it?"

"Oh, yeah, I get it." And I wanted to get rid of it as fast as possible.

He grinned, stunning me with his porcelain veneers, which had me suddenly craving Chiclets.

You are an ass, I wanted to tell him, and reminded myself why I was there in order to refrain from tossing my champagne.

"So, Danny, are there lots of local celebs in the club?" I took a gander and asked him.

His smile faltered. He shifted on his feet and tugged at the gold hoop in his right earlobe. "Yeah, there are some big shots, but they hang out in the back room. They don't like to mix with the Sevrugas, unless there's a particularly delectable babe they don't mind smuggling in. Now me, I like hanging out with the real people, not the pretenders, if you know what I mean."

He actually winked at me.

I stood there for a long moment as I contemplated whether Daniel Kingsolver truly considered himself "real" vs. a "pretender." I found myself wondering, too, if his lame come-ons really worked on anybody.

I would have wagered that the dude went home alone this night . . . heck, every night.

"Are you allowed behind the red curtain, Danny?" I asked, because I didn't want to waste another minute on this tragic reincarnation of Don Johnson if he didn't have access to the back room at club gatherings. Because I was sure enough that's where Miranda had hung out.

The light left his eyes, and he shuffled on his feet.

"Um, not exactly, but I don't need to get back there to find a girl to get nasty with me, if ya know what I'm saying."

I cringed.

"Besides, I'm up for Beluga on my next evaluation, and they say third time's the charm, right?"

Who'd let this dog in?

Someone with a Don Johnson hangover from the 1980s?

Yeesh.

"Ah, excuse me, Danny, but I think I see a friend," I said, pretending to nod at someone across the room and quickly extricating myself from the presence of Dr. Fraud, the online cigar salesman.

I wedged my way between pairs and trios of Caviar Clubbers who were dancing—or, rather, grinding, which looked a lot like having sex without removing clothes—and others with heads together, confabbing, while the waiters wove around the room, dispensing champagne and retrieving empty glasses.

Despite only flickering candlelight and plenty of shadows, I did my best to take in all the faces, searching for anyone familiar, either famous or infamous, but only spotting a few women I was sure I'd seen modeling furs in last Sunday's full-page ad for Neiman-Marcus in the *Dallas Morning News.*

Big whoop.

I really wanted to do something good for Janet, not to mention poor Miranda, but I was beginning to have my doubts that I'd uncover anything earth-shattering for Jan to write about in her career-saving feature. Without getting past the red velvet curtain, the best story I could come up with would be about a girl geek turned beauty for a night getting hit on by a very cheesy Mr. Wrong.

I glanced back toward the *Miami Vice* devotee and felt relieved to see him hitting on someone else already. I took several baby sips of the sweet champagne, my toe tapping to the beat of the music and my gaze wandering over so many faces wearing that look of wanting, of desperation, I'd seen a thousand times. Heck, I'm sure I'd worn it myself once or twice. It didn't matter how it was packaged, whether it was online dating, the classifieds, or the Caviar Club. It was all about the same thing: pairing off.

Companionship, love, sex.

Take your pick.

I had never been as happy to be off the market as I was at that moment.

Sighing, I looked over my right shoulder, and my gaze stopped short.

A lanky dude with pierced ears and wavy brown hair to his shoulders approached, smiling shyly in classic Keith Urban fashion, and my cheeks heated up.

Hubba hubba, my hormones cried instinctively.

He was beautiful, indeed, and would've been high on my personal "yum" list B.M. (Before Malone). Only my life had changed since I'd met Brian, and so had my tastes. I had a button-down, hockey-loving, "I would never pierce my ears unless I were a pirate," briefcase-carrying boyfriend, whom I adored. I would rather walk naked down Central Expressway in rush hour traffic than cheat on him.

Though it couldn't hurt to flirt a little with this guy—heck, I'm sure Mata Hari had flirted plenty—and chat him up. I'd wager he was allowed past the velvet curtain. He might have even known Miranda and who she'd hooked up with

at past parties. So talking to him would be a mag-
nanimous thing, not selfish at all, right?

Gorgeous Dude had barely opened his mouth
to say, "Hey," when a hand grabbed my arm and
jerked me around, and I found myself standing
nose-to-jaw with a man I'd hoped never to lay
eyes on again.

"Surprised to see me?" Milton Fletcher said
dryly.

"Ack," I said, spilling my champagne on his
leather shoes.

And it wasn't even on purpose.

Chapter 18

"You!" I hissed at him, while droplets of pale gold from my champagne flute continued to plop onto his loafers.

They looked expensive, too, like Gucci or Bruno Magli. Heck, everything he wore appeared pricey, from his midnight blue velvet blazer over a tailored shirt with French cuffs (and cuff links!) to his artfully distressed jeans. I'll bet he'd even driven his Porsche tonight to enhance his uptown image. No beat-up Ford Taurus tonight, no siree.

"What in God's name are you doing here?" I ground out, not sounding the least bit glad to see him. Because, well, I wasn't.

"Um, hello to you, too, and thanks for the bubbly, but I normally like to drink it, not wear it." He reached for my hand and pried the glass from my fingers, though it was completely drained by then.

Darn it.

I wish I'd had at least a magnum more to spill. I wouldn't have minded sloshing my drink all over the front of his chichi jeans, too.

"Don't tell me you're a member of The C.C.," I said, and leaned in far more closely to him than I wanted to. The clean soapy scent of him filled my nose, and I found myself wishing he smelled repulsive, like patchouli cologne or baby spit.

He set my empty champagne flute on the tray of a passing waiter, freeing his hands to place them both on my hips, tugging me close as he whispered back, "I'm a lowly Sevruga tonight, darlin', as I suspect are you, because I can't imagine that you'd belong to this group of looks-obsessed partiers for real. Unless this whole debutante dropout, antisocial card you play is just to piss off your mother, and you're really as artificial as a Martha Stewart retractable Christmas tree from Kmart."

Whoa there, pardner.

Exactly who did he think he was?

Other than a former Navy SEAL who made a buck trailing cheating spouses to low-rent motels and taking pictures through the curtains.

"Excuse me?" I squawked.

"Oh, you heard me, all right," he said, his breath brushing my cheek. "You're not always who you appear to be, are you, Andy Kendricks? Cissy sees you as something of a good girl who detoured off the beaten path, but I'm not sure what to think. This afternoon, you were dressed in sneaks and ponytail, and now you're almost unrecognizable.

Though I'm not complaining. You look damned good when you apply the war paint."

If that was supposed to be a compliment, it sure didn't sound like one.

I refrained from biting his head off, instead blurting out, "You're a sexist pig, and you've got a stupid name to boot! So take a hike, Bubba Gump, and let me go!"

My voice seemed to rise above the Latin music, and a few of the clubbers schmoozing around us turned to glance.

"Everything okay?" a spiky-haired guy in a muscle shirt stepped forward to ask, and Milton laughed, shooting the dude an embarrassed smile.

"Everything's fine." He waved the fellow off. "Just having a little argument over how the Cowboys are playing this year. I say they're catching fire, and this cutie-pie here thinks they're going nowhere but the toilet."

Muscle Shirt nodded in that simpatico way that men did. "You've got my sympathies, buddy, 'cuz I'm with the chick. The 'Boys suck."

Then he left us alone to resume canoodling with two very blond women.

I glared at Milton. "Does Cissy know you're such a cad?"

"She's not paying me to be gallant," he shot back. "She's paying me to find out who shoved her friend's daughter past the Pearly Gates."

"That almost sounds believable," I said. "Coming from such a smooth liar. How'd you get into the party, huh?" I asked, this time lowering my voice. "Did you tell a bunch of fibs, like that you're Roger Staubach's long-lost son?"

"Shhh." He actually put a finger over my lips. "I'm actually going by Fletch Staubach, so if you could play along . . . "

The way he was grinning, I couldn't tell if he was joking or not.

I was leaning toward not.

"You can call yourself Doogie Howser and pretend you're a doctor tonight for all I care. Just act like you don't know me and leave me alone," I said, and tried to draw away from him.

But he held on.

If I could've conjured up a waiter at that moment, I would've grabbed another flute of champagne and tossed it on his head.

The harder I tried to get away, the tighter he held my hands in his and the closer he bound me to him, doing his best imitation of tasting my earlobe as he replied in a low voice, "I have a keen sense you're here for the same reason I am. Miranda DuBois, right?" he answered before I could deny it. "You're nosier than a hound dog and about as itchy. You can't leave this case to the police any more than your mother can. Am I on the money or what?"

Okay, so maybe he was partially right.

But my mother didn't know about Miranda's connection to the Caviar Club . . . or did she? Had she overheard that bit of my conversation with Janet in the den?

"Did Cissy tell you that Miranda was a Beluga until they kicked her out after her botched wrinkle treatment?" I asked.

"She wasn't sure about the connection, though she may have pointed me in this direction, yeah. Then I did a little sniffing around myself. I have a friend who's a producer over at Channel 5, and she let me have a few minutes at Miranda's computer before the cops showed up to haul away the hard drive. Miranda had downloaded her invitation letter, and I retrieved a few deleted instant messages from some married guy who called himself 'Big Dog.'" He raised his dark eyebrows. "They talked about meeting at one of the C.C. parties, so I put one and one together and came up with two. As in a pair of fish eggs who were hot for each other. I just need to find out who the guy is and if he's here tonight."

"And if he had anything to do with her death," I added for him, because that's the part he'd left unsaid.

"C'mon, admit it. You're as convinced as your mother that Miranda didn't snuff her own candle," he stated, and he seemed pleased when I sighed, "Yes."

"Well, I hate to agree with someone so disagreeable," Miltie went on, "but I think something's fishy in those waters, too, despite how things look. I talked to another pal at the medical examiner's office tonight, and he tells me it's likely the autopsy report will be issued as early as tomorrow."

"You have a lot of pals, don't you?" I muttered, but he didn't even break stride.

"Forensics says the only prints on the gun are Miranda's . . . on the bullet casings, on the trigger and pearl handle. I asked about other prints, as

Cissy told me about the, um, shooting incident at the Botox party."

"*Pretty* Party," I found myself correcting, though I'm not sure why.

"Anyway, if Miranda dropped her .22 and someone else picked it up, there should at least be another set of prints on the weapon, right?"

"And there wasn't," I offered, a tickle in my belly.

"No, there wasn't. So, if someone else picked the gun up, he was sure careful about handling it."

"Or she," I quietly added.

Despite the voices and music swirling around us, I heard little but the quickening beat of my own heart and Milton as he continued, "My buddy also tells me the site ramp angle—the way the muzzle was held against Miranda's temple—is a little high for a suicide, but not completely impossible. Still, I think it proves our point."

And there was still that missing laptop, I nearly said, but Milton spoke up before I could say more.

"So how about we call a truce, since we're both working toward the same end, eh? If you don't blow my cover, Andy darlin', I won't blow yours. You cool with that?" His eyes glinted, the devil clearly in them. "It might not be a bad idea if we did a little back scratching, too. Sharing ain't all bad, like we learned back in kindergarten."

Maybe Miltie and I had a similar goal in mind, but I had no intention of hanging on his elbow tonight. Not for love or murder.

"I'm an only child, Mr. Fletcher, so I don't do sharing well, or back scratching, either," I told him, because something about Milton Fletcher made me want to resist him, even if he made sense.

He rubbed his jaw. "Let me put it another way. If you play nice with me, I won't mention a thing to your very jealous boyfriend about seeing you here, dressed to kill and sipping Moët, because he doesn't know where you are, does he, sweet pea?" He drawled the latter, mimicking my mother, and I gritted my teeth. "Did you send him out to carouse with the boys?"

"No, he's not out carousing with the boys," I said with plenty of venom. "He's watching the hockey game, smarty pants, though it's got to be over by now, even if they went into a sudden death shootout."

"So he doesn't know where you are?"

"I didn't say that!" I snapped.

"Oh, yeah, you pretty much did." Miltie smirked.

He's lucky I didn't try that move on him I'd learned in self-defense.

"We trust each other," I said, not liking at all the way he was mocking my relationship with Brian when he knew nothing about it. "Though that's probably something foreign to you, isn't it? Considering your gainful employment depends on people *not* trusting each other. Now let me go."

A country western ring tone started playing, and I realized the noise was coming from the beaded purse.

I finally twisted out of his grip so I could reach

into the handbag, thinking at first it was Brian calling to see where I was; until I remembered I had Janet's phone and not mine. As if the ring tone wasn't evidence enough. I wouldn't have wanted him to hear loud music and cocktail chatter in the background when I picked up, that's for sure.

"That your boyfriend?" Mr. Nosy Private Eye asked.

"None of your bee's wax," I told him while I squinted close at the tiny screen, which said, ROSS CALLING.

I had no idea who Ross was, unless it was Mr. Perot wanting to get a hold of Janet.

So I turned off the cell and stuffed it back in the bag.

"Bet it was your home boy tracking you down."

"Wrong number," I told him, and snapped the purse closed.

He had me thinking of Malone, however, and wishing I were back at the condo. I reassured myself that in less than an hour I'd have dumped these clothes at Janet's and wiped the clown paint from my face; and I'd be heading north to Preston-wood in the Jeep, calling Brian on my own cell. I'd promise to be back at his side lickety-split, and that would be no lie.

"So what about it, Andy?" Milton Fletcher nudged my arm. "Want to play Nick and Nora to-night and see if two snoops are better than one?"

I glared at him, more irritated than I should have been. But he rubbed me the wrong way for some reason, like corduroy pants.

I was not about to join forces with Detective Fletch. I had some sniffing around to do on my own, and he'd only be extra baggage . . . and annoying baggage at that.

"How about you do a David Copperfield and disappear. I'll take care of myself," I told him in no uncertain terms. "So either you scram right now or I will."

"Wait a minute, Andy," he said. "I don't think you know what you're getting yourself into. There are some real players here, and I'd hate to see you taken advantage of. From what I hear, it's pretty hard-core in the back room, so don't get in over your head, kiddo. Your mother mentioned you could be reckless when you thought you were saving the world."

What the hay?

I was reckless, not to mention a gullible twit?

Puh-leeze! Who did he think he was, talking to me like that? My protector? My savior? Did he assume I was some dopey girl who didn't know how to watch her own fanny?

Give me a break, Jake.

"Later, Doogie or Roger Junior or whatever you're calling yourself tonight," I said, and I turned my back on him and started walking across the room, needing to be somewhere else, anywhere he wasn't.

I brushed past clots of pretty people smelling of expensive colognes and perfumes, ignoring the occasional hand that reached out to touch my arm or shoulder, attempting to draw me over.

I had a goal in mind, and it wasn't to mingle.

If I was going to get the real skinny on Miranda and the Caviar Club, I needed to zero in on the one person I recognized from Miranda's photos; someone who could very possibly have been involved with her romantically.

Someone who was already involved with another woman—a woman with access to sharp things like needles—and who should have kept his hands to himself.

I paused only once to rearm myself with an appropriate prop—meaning, I snatched another glass of champagne off a waiter's tray—which is when I spotted my target.

I saw Lance Zarimba's blond head just before it ducked behind the red curtain into the back room.

Yeah, I know, I know. Sevrugas weren't allowed past the velvet.

But this was an emergency. Janet needed to write a kick-ass feature exposing the Caviar Club and linking the late Miranda DuBois to it, which meant I had a ton of dirt to dig up this evening. As if that weren't enough, I didn't like people telling me where I couldn't go.

It only made me want to get there all the more.

And what was the worst they could do to me if I crossed through the velvet doors?

Toss me out? Revoke my temporary title of Lowly Fish Egg?

I wasn't Miranda DuBois. Being evicted from this silly club would hardly kill me.

So I downed the glass of champagne to give myself a jolt of courage, put the drained flute aside, and wiped my mouth with the back of my hand.

Here goes nothing, I mused and lifted my chin.

Then I took off after the dude who was Dr. Sonja Madhavi's main squeeze and who may well have been Miranda's lover. Oh, yeah, and possibly her killer.

If Dr. Miniskirt hadn't done the deed herself.

Chapter 19

No one stopped me as I entered.

If I'd expected to be grabbed and frisked, I guessed wrong.

Maybe it was the way I barged inside, snatching up a full glass of champagne from a passing waiter before I parted the curtains, my chin up, acting like I belonged.

My mother had always been expert at looking like she fit in—okay, more like she commanded the place, *any* place—so I mimicked that air of hers, practically daring anyone to tell me I wasn't supposed to be there the moment I stepped past the red drapes. That idiot Danny Boy had said the privileged Belugas sometimes smuggled in a "delectable babe," so I hoped to heaven I looked every bit as bedable as Suzy Bee had intended, even if it was all a façade made up of push-up bra, stiletto heels, and war paint.

Please, please, don't let me encounter Theresa Hurley. She of all people would recognize that I didn't belong. But I quickly pooh-poohed that thought.

The Keeper of the Clipboard would likely stand guard in the foyer of Bébé Gâté until the party was over. 'Cuz, God forbid, someone of average appearance got past the bald-headed bouncer and wandered in off the street. They'd probably have to call in the Pretty People Pest Control and fumigate for cooties.

Or, perhaps—and more likely—no one had tossed me out yet because they couldn't *see* who I was. I could hardly peer more than a yard ahead with any precision. All right, I was exaggerating. But it was awfully dark, so much so that I was afraid to go too far beyond the curtain I'd dropped behind me.

I didn't want to risk walking into somebody or spilling my champagne on anyone I didn't despise.

As my eyes better adjusted, I realized there was no electric lighting at all here, not even set to dim. It was strictly candle glow in the inner sanctum where the upper tier Belugas swam or cavorted or did whatever they did. No wonder Miranda's photos had all looked so dark.

I took a few tentative steps in, enough to assess a lengthy console table rigged with champagne in ice and plenty of tiny toast points and sterling bowls of roe. There was another large silver bowl that held some kind of square packets.

Was it candy?

I reached in, snagged a pack, and brought it nearer my nose.

The label was a bit difficult to decipher without direct light, but I soon picked out the large print on the front that touted the contents as a "glow-in-the-dark condom."

So these were the back room's party favors?

How very classy.

Not.

Though tempted to stash one in the Judith Leiber bag to take back to Janet, I didn't. I tossed it back into the pot instead and backed away.

When Janet had said the Caviar Club was for S-E-X, she hadn't been kidding. I'm guessing one-night stands were de rigueur for the members, if they were passing out condoms alongside the bubbly.

Yet another reason to be glad that I didn't belong.

I figured I'd need a long, hot shower to wash this place off my skin when I was done snooping.

Speaking of, how much longer would I have to lurk around here and take mental notes?

"One more glass of champagne's worth," I told myself. Then I was getting out, whether I'd seen anything worth reporting back to Janet or not.

When this flute I held was empty, it would be time to go.

Until then, it was my job to spy. And spy I would.

My ears still picked up on the thump of the bass from the music in the main part of the bar, although the Latin beat was much more muted;

but I detected something else I hadn't heard outside the velvet drapes: the voices seemed to whisper rather than to shout, and, oh boy, was that *moaning*?

And I mean the kind of moaning that sounded curiously like someone was playing an X-rated movie. Only I didn't see any television screens anywhere, just flickering candles and shadowy forms and fabric partitions separating me from God knows what.

I took a slow sip of champagne, the slide of bubbles down my throat adding to the faint buzz I'd gotten from my first glass. I had to nurse this sucker. If I drank too fast, I'd be positively giddy.

The entry area, where I stood, was deserted except for me. All the action seemed to be going on behind the partitions.

I started toward the nearest one and almost dropped my champagne when I walked into something solid reeking of bad cologne.

A man.

"Hey, there, sweetheart," a smooth voice whispered from the shadows around me, and I felt a hand slide possessively up and down my arm. "I was about to take off, but now I'll have to reconsider. How would you like to have a go with me under the canopy? It's not every day you run into a TV star like me, is it?"

TV star?

This could be the scoop I'd been looking for!

I turned and squinted up at the face that hovered above mine. The shadows created dark grooves on weather-beaten cheeks, and the hair

looked shiny with product. It was broad-minded,
I thought, for the Caviar Club to have allowed in
a dude who definitely looked well beyond middle
age.

Then something crackled in my brain, and I
gulped when I realized it was Dick Uttley, Miranda's former co-anchor on the Channel 5 nightly
news.

Egads.

Wasn't the dude in his late fifties, and he was
hitting on *me*? Obviously, he liked his ladies
younger by a couple decades (except for his long-
suffering wife, I mean). If the man had been messing around with Miranda before she died, he
obviously didn't seem overcome with grief now
that she was gone.

"Under the canopy?" I repeated, trying not to
sound as creeped out as I was feeling. "I'm sorry.
I'm new here. In fact, it's my first time."

"Ah, fresh caviar. Delicious." He laughed, as if
he'd made some hilarious joke. He took my hand
and tugged. "The canopy, my dear, is a spot where
you and I can get most comfortable. Perhaps I can
help break you in."

He laughed again, and I shivered.

I made note of the fact that he didn't even ask
my name before volunteering to "break me in."
How unchivalrous of him.

Somehow, I couldn't believe Miranda DuBois
would sink as low as having an affair with Sir
Dick. He was—how shall I put it?—yucky.

"This way, my sweet," Mr. Uttley uttered, and
quickly dragged me around one of the fabric

screens to somewhere quite a bit nearer the moaning noises, as they were louder and intermingled with subdued voices.

If only I had a flashlight to better see what was going on—then again, maybe I'd scorch my eyeballs and burn in Hell if I could—but the spotty candlelight did give me a good enough idea.

From the ceiling hung a gauzy web of netting, which I guessed to be the canopy that Dick Uttley mentioned. Below it, within the weblike folds, I could make out lots of moving parts atop a round mattress.

Body parts.

And some of them were glowing in the dark.

I thought of the party favors in the silver bowl and I gulped.

Good heavens, but there was an orgy going on, right in front of me. If it hadn't been so dark, I would've seen absolutely everything.

Ugh.

Call me a prude, but this wasn't my cup of tea.

In fact, if Uttley hadn't been clinging so tightly to my arm, I would've set off in a run.

"If I might unburden you of your clothes, my darlin', we can get on with it," Dick Uttley murmured in my ear. "Or get it on, anyway."

He leered, and I felt his hands move across my shoulder blades, toward the buttons that ran down the back of my dress, and I knew I'd never watch Uttley on Channel 5 again without wanting to shout *You old pervert!* at my TV set.

"Stop it," I said, batting at his arms.

Which only made him grin wolfishly. "Ah, you

like it rough, do you? Well, I can do that," he said, and grabbed at my hardly biblically proportioned breasts.

I reacted instinctively and, for the second time that evening, lost a glass of champagne.

Only this time it was no accident.

I tossed the bubbly right in Dick Uttley's face as he sputtered and screeched, "I should kill you, you little witch!"

He grabbed blindly at me, but I sidestepped him and turned to flee. I teetered and tottered on my high-heeled boots, moving as fast as I could around the gauzy canopy with the bodies writhing beneath, while Dick ranted and raged somewhere behind me. Thank goodness he was even slower.

I zigzagged around another of the partitions, my heart banging like conga drums in my chest. *Get me out of here!* my brain kept screaming as I pushed past people and candlesticks and the odd table or chair, ultimately running smack into the arms of another man.

Oooph.

I dropped the crystal handbag and it hit the floor with a clatter. I dared not even think how many of the tiny beads may have shattered on impact.

The dude I'd plowed into swayed against me, my shoulder having slammed into his chest, and I heard his grunt as he caught me around the waist.

Another lech, I thought instantly, and reached up to push him off; but he held on firmly. "Hey, hey, slow down," he said. "Are you okay?"

"Yeah, I guess," I murmured, my pulse continuing to race, "if okay means getting pawed by a cologne-drenched creep twice my age." I glanced up at him through the dim, seeing the outline of an oval face with a smooth pate.

It took a second for my brain to whir, and then I recognized Dennis Bell, the computer wizard who sold more desktops and laptops than all the others combined. Wasn't he married?

And he picked up chicks at the Caviar Club?

I guess being a rich geek made it a lot easier to get a little sumpin-sumpin on the side.

Hooey.

He let me go and bent down to retrieve the Judith Leiber bag from where it had fallen near my feet. The crystals caught the glow of candlelight and flickered. "You'd better kept a tighter grip on this"—he pressed the bag into my hands—"my wife has a few, so I know what they're worth."

"It's not even mine."

"Oh. Well, it's hard to lose what isn't ours to begin with, eh?"

"Yeah, sure."

Whatever that meant.

"You might want to duck into the ladies' room," Dennis Bell suggested, cocking an ear. "I think I hear that cologne-drenched creep, and he's headed this way."

With that, he walked off, heading toward the red velvet drapes, and I figured he was leaving. Maybe going home to that wife he'd mentioned, because it was hard to believe anyone would bring their spouses to a party meant for hooking up with other swingers.

I didn't have much of a chance to dwell on the guy, because I heard Dick Uttley's nasty voice, too, raised above all other sounds, saying something about "tossing that little witch out."

Being that I was the "little witch" in question, I figured it might be a good idea to scram altogether. Forget the ladies' room.

I was just about to make for the velvet curtains when I spotted a slick-looking dude coming through them.

Oh, Lord.

Milton Fletcher.

The conniving cur!

He was no Beluga!

Well, okay, neither was I. Still, I didn't like that he seemed to be turning up everywhere I went. It made me nervous, the way he was following me around, sticking his nose in my business, or Miranda's business, anyway. My nose had already butt in first, which made it rather crowded. One of us would have to go.

So I spun around, diving for the nearest door and throwing myself into a pitch-black room. I had a feeling it wasn't the loo, or someone would've left the lights on, wouldn't they?

No matter.

I figured I'd wait there a few minutes, long enough to slow down my pulse, and then I'd get out of the nightclub as fast as my stiletto-heeled boots would carry me.

Dirt or no dirt.

Janet could ream me out for all I cared. I was going home where I belonged.

My breaths sounded loud at first, doubly noisy, in fact.

Like I wasn't the only one breathing in the room.

A throat cleared—it wasn't mine—and I heard the tiniest click as a light went on, illuminating a blond-haired man with a pale mustache, sitting behind a desk, muscled arms leaning on the desktop.

"You hiding out, too?" Lance Zarimba asked.

My hand went to my heart and I made a little *eeep* sound.

"My God," I croaked. "You scared the crud out of me."

He smiled sheepishly, his wide shoulders shrugging. "Sorry. I didn't mean to. I just figured I was here alone."

I took a tentative step toward him. "In the dark?"

"Well, it wasn't much darker than out there." He swung a thumb in the direction of the door.

And I realized he was right.

"Plus it's quieter," he said. "All that shouting. What's old Dick pissed off about this time?"

"Me," I admitted.

"What'd you do? Swipe his Viagra?" Lance suggested. "Knock off his toupee? Call his wife to come and get him?"

I couldn't help it. Maybe it was nerves, but I burst out laughing.

Lance grinned all the wider and leaned back

in the desk chair, hands clasped at his flat belly, looking like he owned the place. For all I knew, he did.

"C'mon and sit down," he said, and gestured to a nearby chair. "You look amazing, by the way. I almost didn't recognize you. Andy Kendricks, right?"

"Man, you have a good memory."

"I told you you'd look like a million bucks if you just spent a little time in front of the mirror, didn't I? It was true."

"Okay, rub it in."

"I just did."

At the time he'd said it, I'd been more than a tad miffed. Then, it had seemed insulting. Now, I decided to take it as a compliment and let it go at that.

"Not a bad place to hide," I said, and walked over to the leather chair in front of the desk and settled into it, tucking the bejeweled bag at my side.

Sitting primly, hands on my knees, I looked around the room, at the French art deco posters and small bronze sculptures. There was a make-shift bar set up on the credenza behind the desk. I saw an open bottle of champagne in a silver bucket with spare glasses nearby, and I noticed then that Lance had a nearly empty flute perched atop the desk beside a goose-necked lamp.

All the comforts of home, I mused.

"Is this yours?" I asked.

"This office?" He bent forward, leaning over the desk again.

"The club," I clarified.

He looked confused. "The Caviar Club?"

"No, Bébé Gâté," I said, finding the direction of his thoughts rather interesting. Telling, even.

"Ah. No." He shook his head. "It belongs to a friend of mine. He lets us have parties here, so long as we let him join in."

He lets us have parties here.

Did that sound a little proprietary, or was my suspicious nature just in overdrive?

"Are you enjoying yourself?" His question caught me off-guard, and I wasn't sure whether to lie or be honest.

I settled for something in between. "It's been an *interesting* evening so far."

It reminded me what was going on outside, beyond the closed door, and I thought again of Miranda and the photo I had seen where Lance Zarimba appeared to have his tongue in her ear.

It made me wonder if Lance was as benign as he seemed on the surface. Or if he had a darker side, one that came out in his private life, when he wasn't downsizing pores at Dr. Sonja's boutique.

I reminded myself that quizzing Lance about Miranda was a big reason I'd come to the Caviar Club tonight. Then again, if he had something to do with her death, I wasn't so sure I wanted to hang out with him unchaperoned.

"You're not a member of the club, are you, Andy? I know you haven't been to a party before, have you?" he asked, and I shook my head. "You're a friend of Cinda Lou Mitchell's, right? She tagged you."

"Yes." I raised my chin and met his eyes, channeling my mother as best I could, not wanting to look freaked out, like I was up to something.

I felt suddenly nervous, like he was about to unmask me. It's a good thing I'd rolled on the Secret.

"Is there something wrong with that?" I asked, doing the narrow-eyed thing that my mother could do when making a point that always had me itching to slide under the table.

"Not when the girl getting tagged is as lovely as you. It's the whole reason behind the club, putting pretty people together. And you happen to be very pretty." He lifted his champagne glass and casually drained it.

"Is that how Miranda DuBois got in?" I found myself asking. "Was she tagged by a Beluga?" I even went so far as to say, "Maybe by you?"

Lance didn't answer.

"You liked Miranda a lot, didn't you?" I pressed on, daring to suggest, "I saw some pictures of you with her, so I know how close you were."

His eyes went wide, and I knew I'd struck a nerve.

"I'll bet Dr. Sonja didn't appreciate your, um, growing affection for another woman. Or was it just Miranda in particular she didn't care for? Is that why Sonja ruined her face?"

Way too quickly, he replied, "Miranda was a beautiful woman, one many of the members found attractive. As far as Sonja's being jealous of her, I imagine Miranda inspired jealousy in plenty of females."

Sometimes even generalities were revealing, I mused.

"Got it," I told him.

"Do you really?" His shoulders stiffened, and I noticed his hand close so tightly around his empty champagne flute that I half expected it to crack. "No, Andy, I don't think you do. I don't believe you understand what happened with Miranda at all."

"Why don't you explain, then, Lance," I said carefully, deciding it would be unwise to piss the guy off. He was twice my size, with arms as big as my thighs. "I'm all ears," I offered. "I'm sure you didn't do anything wrong. It was Sonja who hated Miranda, not you."

He stared at me stonily for a long moment, and I debated excusing myself and getting the heck out of there, as had been my intention a few minutes earlier. Sometimes it paid to listen to one's gut, and mine was grumbling pretty loudly.

Well, geez, if he was going to clam up, I wasn't going to hang around.

"Perhaps I should go," I murmured, and picked up the beaded bag.

I was halfway out of my seat when Lance stood up, begging plaintively, "Please, don't leave. I want to talk about Miranda with you. You're so different . . . so, well, normal compared to everyone else."

The different part, I bought.

But calling me *normal*?

If Malone had heard that, he would've laughed his head off. I was having trouble keeping a straight face myself.

Maybe Lance Zarimba wanted someone who could be straight with him. It sounded like he might be ready to knock that chip off his shoulder. Why shouldn't I be the one to catch it? Then I could hand it over to Janet for her story, before I washed my hands of this whole mess.

I sat back down, saying, "Thank you. I think."

"I mean it. You're easy to talk to, Andy." He got up with his glass, turned his back to me and refilled it before he glanced over his shoulder to ask, "Would you care for some champagne?"

"Oh, gosh, I don't know." I wasn't much of a drinker, and I'd already had a glass, nearly two. And I didn't want to be sloshed when I arrived back at the condo. Brian was likely worried enough about me already. Had he called my cell and talked to Janet? I only hoped whatever excuse she'd used wasn't so far out that he'd get worried and send a posse after me.

"Just one glass. C'mon," Lance insisted, keeping his back to me. "Please, stay, and I'll fill you in on my relationship with Miranda. I want you to see my side of things."

So he *did* want to get something off his pumped-up chest.

I was willing to bet that whatever guilt he felt was gnawing at him like a chain saw.

I heard the *glub-glub* of the bubbly being poured into a crystal flute, even though I hadn't agreed to anything yet.

"I really shouldn't—" But he cut off my protest.

"Please, Andy. Don't make me drink alone," he

said, which I found very funny, considering that's exactly what he'd been doing—alone and in the dark—before I barged in.

The guy was odd, no question about it; but perhaps he realized confession would be good for his soul. Besides, there were at least fifty people in the club, just beyond the closed door to the room. I felt pretty sure he wouldn't try anything, not when we weren't really alone.

When he finished fixing my drink, he came around the desk, carrying both champagne flutes. He proffered the one in his left hand then lifted the one in his right.

"A toast," he said, "to Dick Uttley."

"What?" Just hearing the name startled me.

"Without him chasing you in here, I wouldn't have gotten to see you again, all gussied up," Mr. Muscles smoothly said, smiling the most devilish smile, and I glimpsed some of the charm that must've attracted Sonja Madhavi . . . and even Miranda. "It was worth the wait, Andy, I can tell you that."

Feeling slightly embarrassed, I blushed and glanced down at my feet in the pointy-toed boots. I took a long, slow sip of Moët, managing to empty half the glass—what the heck, I was thirsty—intending to bolt once I'd finished.

But after a couple more swallows, I felt a big buzz hit my head. Okay, so I'd had at least a glass before, but several shouldn't have knocked me for a loop like that. Unless I was even more of a lightweight than I'd thought.

"You wanted to talk . . . about Miranda," I got

out, my voice sounding thick. I was tired, and the booze wasn't helping matters any.

"You went to school with her, didn't you?" Lance asked. "And with that society reporter, Janet Graham, too? The one who interviewed Sonja."

"Yes, I went . . . we all went . . . to Hockaday." The words came out more slowly than I'd intended. My thoughts were so muddied. I didn't recall ever telling him I'd been classmates with either Miranda or Janet. Maybe he'd done a little research of his own.

Then again, my head whirled like the Mad Hatter's Teacup Ride. I could have blurted it out and completely forgotten.

"You said you took Miranda home after the Pretty Party and that she let you in," he went on, asking more questions, when he was supposed to be handing me answers.

"Um, yes," I said, though it came out more like *Yezzzz.*

"Is that when you saw the pictures?"

"Saw the pee-chures," I murmured, and stared into the bottom of my champagne glass, suddenly seeing two of everything. I could hardly keep my head up.

"Andy, are you all right? Are you feeling ill?"

His voice sounded distant. I closed my eyes.

Without meaning to, I released the crystal flute, and it slipped from my hands, plopping down with a gentle thud onto the shaggy area rug.

What was wrong with me?

"My God, but it hit you fast. Some girls are so easy. Like I told Sonja, it never hurts to keep a few roofies on hand to help the ladies loosen up. Only your case is special."

Oh, hell, had he slipped me a mickey?

Did he plan to assault me? Right here in the office of Bébé Gâté?

"You're not here to party, are you? You're here to snoop, and I think you know too much already."

I tried to talk, but my mouth wouldn't move. My tongue felt glued to my palate.

"Miranda must've spilled it all to you before she died. Didn't she, Andy? Tell the truth now. It won't do you any good to lie."

"Troooth," I got out, slurring the word.

"That's why you asked so many questions this morning about Miranda's injections, isn't it?" he kept hounding, his anger echoing in my ears. "She told you I was there, didn't she? That Sonja messed her up because she thought I was obsessed with Miranda, and I didn't stop her. Well, if you think you can blackmail us, you're wrong. It wouldn't have worked for Miranda, and it won't work for you."

Blackmail?

Saw Sonja do what? Screw up the injections?

Because Lance was obsessed with Miranda?

So it was true.

What was he . . . how did she . . . good heavens, but my brain felt thick.

"Did you kill her?" I tried to say, but my lips wouldn't cooperate. It came out as mindless babble.

"What did you say? Andy? C'mon now, you can't possibly be going down so fast."

Lance's face seemed to zoom in, and I blinked, fighting to keep my eyes open and having trouble focusing.

The room swirled, all a blur.

The door clicked. Footsteps entered. Voices buzzed.

I tried to force my eyes open, but I couldn't make anything work.

"Let's get her out of here. Down the back stairwell, Lance, and be quick."

Hands reached for me, caught under my arms and hauled me up from the chair.

I didn't resist.

I was too far gone.

Chapter 20

A ringing phone nudged its way into my consciousness, playing intermittent bursts of some silly song. My eyes closed, I fought against the grogginess, focusing on the music, trying to get my brain to work.

What *was* that tune?

Save a horse, ride a cowboy.

Yeah, that was it.

But it wasn't my cell. Mine played Def Leppard.

It seemed to go on and on; until, finally, it stopped.

Without its noise, I could pick up more distant noises. I heard a woman's voice and then a man's, going back and forth, muffled as though behind a closed door. Though I strained to listen, I couldn't catch more than a few words here or there, and what I could hear wasn't exactly a news flash.

"Too risky not to do it . . . Miranda's big mouth . . . Cissy Kendricks's hiring a P.I. . . . police asking questions."

God, my head hurt. And my mouth was beyond dry and tasted like I needed a good brushing. My hair fell across my eyes and tickled my cheeks. I tried to raise a hand to wipe the hair from my face.

Only my right arm wouldn't move. I tried the left arm, and it went nowhere, too.

A wave of panic rushed through me.

Was I paralyzed?

Hmm, I could wiggle fingers and toes, even move my legs, so my guess would be no.

I was tied down, wasn't I?

My wrists strained weakly against restraints that felt like plastic tubing, but I couldn't get out of them. I'd been tied securely to the arms of the chair.

Despite how it hurt, I cracked my eyelids open. The room was so bright. A light beamed directly down from above, and I turned my head to the right, wanting to look away so I wouldn't be blinded.

I blinked hard to clear the cobwebs, willing my eyes to focus, and I glanced around me.

Where the heck was I?

The room looked familiar somehow, the walls a pale green, the noise of water trickling. The scent of herbs. Oh, gosh, was that tangerine? Smelled like the face mask Lance Zarimba had slathered on me that morning.

Ding-dong.

Hello!

I was back at The Pretty Place boutique, wasn't I?

Only I'd been strapped to one of those reclining chairs. Guess someone didn't want me to leave.

What was I doing there, for Pete's sake? And how long had I been there?

Minutes, hours?

I fished around my muddy brain for a memory to grab, something that would explain what had happened. After a few moments of mental constipation bits and pieces fluttered back. I remembered entering the bar in Deep Ellum, parting red curtains and seeing bodies writhing beneath a gauze canopy. I'd bumped into Milton Fletcher, hadn't I? And a man had threatened to kill me, so I sought refuge in a dark room, away from everyone.

No, wait.

I hadn't been alone.

That dude . . . the blond muscleman who did facials for Dr. Sonja.

Lance.

He'd been inside the room, almost like he'd been waiting for me.

Though that was impossible, wasn't it? Had he arranged for Dick Uttley to chase me, or for Dennis Bell, the Computer King, to suggest I hide in the nearest loo (though I'd picked the wrong door)?

Was I doing a bit too good a job at channeling my mother and her conspiracy theories? Or was there something to my paranoia?

For instance, did Lance know I'd be at the party?

He must have, I realized. How else would he have known Cinda Lou had tagged me? Because he did, and I hadn't told him.

What else had been odd (like there hadn't been plenty)?

I searched my foggy brain for answers.

Oh, yeah, when I'd asked him if he owned the club, he thought I meant the Caviar Club, hadn't he? And why would he jump to that conclusion, huh, unless it was the truth?

I'd drunk champagne, which he'd poured with his back to me. The bubbles had done more than tickle my nose. My brain had been slammed by an ingredient I'd wager Mr. Moët hadn't added to his libation.

Within ten minutes I'd lost my grip.

The dude had drugged me.

So it's hitting you, is it? Like I told Sonja, it never hurts to keep a few roofies on hand to help the ladies loosen up. Only your case is special.

Arrrrgh.

I could now count myself among the ranks of oblivious women who'd been slipped the date rape drug in their drinks. In my case, minus the "date" part. But at least I hadn't awakened naked to find myself in some skuzzy dude's bed after he'd had his way with me, thank heavens.

I mean, I wasn't naked, right? Whatever had gone on after I'd faded to black, I wasn't so sure of.

I swallowed hard and prayed that Lance hadn't doped up my bubbly so he could do *that* to me.

I lifted my head off the table as far as I could and glanced down the length of me.

My dress was still on, as were my boots. Nothing seemed less than intact.

Dropping my head back, I released a mental *Phew*.

I felt lucky.

Stupid, but lucky.

If one didn't count being bound to a chair in a needle-crazy doctor's office after hours in a deserted mall with an obviously loony aesthetician.

Let's get her out of here. Down the back stairwell, Lance, and be quick.

Not to mention the needle-crazy doctor, I realized, knowing I'd heard her voice back at the club just before I completely conked out.

What did they want from me?

That damned cell phone began to ring again, throwing out aborted bursts of "Save a Horse, Ride a Cowboy," and I craned my neck to the left to glimpse the white countertop and the shiny beaded purse lying atop it.

That was Janet's phone.

If I could just get to it; but struggle as I did against the ties that bound me, I wasn't going anywhere.

"Forget it," a woman's voice advised, and I turned my head gingerly, hearing Sonja Madhavi's high heels tap-tap their way into the room. Unfortunately, the shoes were attached to the evil doctor, who wasn't in her clean white smock; instead, she had on a slinky black minidress, sheer black stockings, and lots of red lipstick; dressed to kill. She looked every bit like she'd been at a party.

A Caviar Club party?

Her equally evil cohort, Lance Zarimba, followed her in and carefully closed the door.

I'd slowly begun putting two and two together. Maybe I was totally out of my mind, but I thought Dr. Miniskirt and her boyfriend ran the Caviar Club. They'd invited Miranda in, and then Lance had fallen for her, much to Sonja Madhavi's chagrin.

It all just fit.

"Sorry, Ms. Kendricks, but we can't take the chance that you'll run your mouth off to the police," she said. "You know far too much, and that's uncomfortable for me."

"Too much? About what you did to Miranda?" I babbled. One of my weaknesses. The babbling.

"Yes, that," Dr. Sonja snapped, and strode toward the cabinets nearer me.

I heard her rummage around, then caught the *snap* of something elastic-sounding. When she turned around, she was tugging on latex gloves.

Oh, great.

"You botched her injections on purpose," I said, my voice scratching, because hadn't Lance admitted as much back at the club? "You wanted your boyfriend to stay away from Miranda, so you made her ugly."

Like the villain in a Disney flick, she laughed. "So the poor delusional Miranda did talk to you before—"

"You killed her," I finished, and Dr. Sonja laughed again.

"Killed her? My God, but you have a wild

imagination." She stopped doing whatever she'd been doing at the counter and approached the chair where I reclined so uncomfortably. "I did no such thing."

I saw the needle in her gloved hand and flinched.

Was that for me?

My heart didn't just leap into my throat, it did a cannonball.

I wet dry lips. "If you didn't, who did?" I inclined my head toward Lance. "So he did it for you?"

Lance stepped farther into the room, shaking his head. "No, no, no"—he sounded like a petulant kid—"Sonja didn't do it, and neither did I. Miranda killed herself. You were at the Pretty Party. You saw how nuts she was."

"And I was with her afterward," I said, trying to stay calm when I wanted to pee in my pants. Er, my dress. "She wasn't suicidal. She wanted revenge, and she had the ammunition," I rattled on, figuring that as long as I was talking, Dr. Sonja wouldn't stick me with whatever was in that vial. "She had photos on her camera from the Caviar Club bashes, and she sent Janet Graham an e-mail saying she wanted to expose everyone . . . the members who were liars and cheaters. And the owners. That means you."

I saw Lance look at Sonja.

"You're the ones who started the Caviar Club, aren't you?" I said aloud what I'd only assumed until then. "You handpick the membership, maybe even from your own patient list, so you can throw

together the prettiest women with the most powerful men in the city."

"It's a dating club," Sonja shot back. "Nothing
illegal about that."

"It's a sex club," I countered. "I saw it with my
own eyes tonight. And maybe that isn't even illegal, but it's not exactly kosher. At least, I'm sure it
would be frowned upon by a good deal of Dallas
society—half of them your clients—if word got
out. And that's how Miranda was going to bring
you down, was it not? If she didn't get you for de-
stroying her face first."

Sonja rounded the chair, pausing near my feet,
no doubt so I could see her suck the vial's contents
into the syringe. "Miranda was unstable. Any of
the women who saw her take a potshot at me at
The Pretty Party will vouch for that."

"But Lance knows what you did," I said. "And
how do you know he won't crack?"

"Because I won't!" he growled, and Sonja
hushed him.

"Lance is very loyal to me," Dr. Miniskirt
insisted. "Besides, he knows who butters his
bread."

"Lance is so loyal that he went after another
woman?" I piped up. "Miranda had photographs
of him with his tongue in her ear. And she had
lots more pictures even more incriminating," I
went on, though I didn't know that for sure. I'd
only glimpsed a handful, including the one of
the dark-haired dude embracing her. "She probably had notes on her laptop, too. But if you took it
after you murdered her, you should know that."

Again, Dr. Evil and her henchman exchanged glances, and neither appeared any too happy.

"What laptop?" Lance asked, perspiration beading on his forehead.

"The one that was on the coffee table at Miranda's before she died. It somehow vanished before morning."

"Not my concern." Sonja shrugged, and Lance mimicked her with a shrug of his own.

Why did I get the feeling they were truly clueless?

"Enough." Sonja tapped the syringe and sighed. "Don't worry, Andy, I'm not going to do you in. I'm just going to give you enough Rohypnol, on top of what Lance gave you, to make you totally forget tonight . . . and, well, probably the last few nights as well. Isn't that lovely? You won't remember Miranda's last night any more than you'll recall this one. And we'll make sure you're found somewhere safe. Don't worry about that, either. We're not criminals, Lance and I."

No?

I pressed my back into the chair, willing myself to disappear. My whole body trembled. The chick was insane.

"This might sting, but just for a second," she said.

Which is when I let out a hellacious scream and kicked a pointy-toed boot at Dr. Sonja, catching her arm and throwing her off-balance.

Lance lunged in my direction as the door sailed open and a dude in a midnight blue blazer and jeans flung himself into the room. He pointed a gun at Lance and yelled, "Nobody move a damned muscle unless you want a slug up your ass."

Lance stopped just shy of landing on top of me.

Dr. Sonja was still scurrying to recover her missing syringe.

"I called the police as soon as I glimpsed you being helped out the back door of the club. I followed you here, and the cops are right behind me," Milton Fletcher said, and sure enough, as soon as he stopped to take a breath, Deputy Chief Anna Dean strolled in with a couple of uniformed officers, unstrapping the handcuffs from their belts.

"You have the right to remain silent," Anna Dean began, reciting the Miranda, and Miltie the Detective tucked his gun into the back of his jeans and walked straight toward me.

"You okay, Andy? Didn't I tell you you'd be safer working with me than if you went solo?" he lectured.

I'd been pawed by Dick Uttley, trapped in a room with Lance, and drugged once—nearly drugged twice for good measure—and now *this*?

Couldn't I have been rescued by anyone but Milton Fletcher, the Navy SEAL turned P.I. turned pain in the tush?

I would've rather been saved by Cissy, for Pete's sake.

Only mealy-mouthed girls in very grim fairy tales dream of being rescued by smart-mouthed dudes who drive Porsche Boxers.

Oy.

"Your mother was right about you, Andy," he continued yapping as he worked to untie my wrists. "You *are* reckless. Lucky for you, I like that in a woman."

If I hadn't already felt like throwing up, that would've done it.

Unfortunately for Miltie, my weak stomach chose that moment to heave. So I leaned over the side of the reclining chair and spewed recycled champagne all over his fancy Bruno Maglis.

Chapter 21

I sat in the passenger seat of Milton's Porsche Boxer, still shaken but a whole lot steadier than a few minutes before. He'd put his velvet blazer over my shoulders and turned up the car's heat.

Still, I shivered as he told me, "I got a call from a buddy in the HPPD right after I took off from the club. He said the crime lab recovered the chip from Miranda's damaged cell phone. They got the data off it, Andy, and they traced the text messages from the guy who called himself Big Dog to a phone number that showed up plenty, both as sent calls and received. They're not so stuck on their suicide theory anymore."

"Who?" I asked, croaking like a frog that needed a Ricola.

"Who what?"

"Who's the Big Dog? He's their prime suspect, right?"

"I didn't say he was a suspect, but he's a person of interest, all right. It's some dude named Armstrong. Anna Dean said they'll bring him in tomorrow morning, first thing."

"Why not sooner?" Call me antsy, but I wanted whoever killed Miranda put away ASAP. Then my life could get back to its usual state of slightly less than crazy.

"Geez, Andy, it's late, and they're a little busy booking Dr. Madhavi and her boyfriend on kidnapping and assault charges."

"The police aren't charging them with murder, are they?"

"No."

Despite everything I knew, I felt disappointed. It wouldn't have been hard for me to watch Dr. Sonja and Lance Zarimba take the fall. But I also felt in my gut that neither Sonja nor Lance had shot Miranda. Not with a gun anyway, just with strategically placed nerve-damaging Botox injections. Which was bad enough.

"C'mon, Andy. I should take you home. You want to call your boyfriend and tell him what's going on?"

Tell Brian?

Oh, God, no.

Seriously, how was I going to explain this to him? I hadn't even told him I was going out, much less that I was dressing up like a high class hooker to infiltrate a local sex club. Which reminded me that I hadn't called Janet to tell her what was going on, and she was doubtless frantic, too.

I needed time to collect myself, get my brain working again. It still felt incredibly slow-witted, and my thoughts were all jumbled. Probably why my reactions were on time delay.

Some dude named Armstrong.

"Wait a minute." I would've slapped my brow but my head ached too much. "Did you say Armstrong?"

"Yeah, so what?"

"What's his first name?"

Milton aborted his attempt at shifting out of Park and let the Porsche idle again. "I believe it's Jonathan."

Jonathan Armstrong?

Sister Mary Merlot!

My eyes bugged.

That was Delaney's husband.

The handsome guy in the family portrait that I'd glimpsed on my way out of the Pretty Party.

I'd never met him face-to-face, but I'd heard stories of how Delaney had chased him all over UT-Austin until she'd worn him down. Or maybe her having a bun in the oven before graduation had done the trick. Whatever, I'd constantly been told he was the love of her life and the "perfect guy," the kind they didn't make anymore.

So the perfect man hadn't been so perfect after all?

He'd been going to Caviar Club sex-fests and sleeping with Miranda DuBois.

Whoa.

Slow brain or not, it was all starting to make sense.

"*That's* who was having an affair with Miranda?" I said aloud. "That's the guy she was in love with who was unavailable?"

I would've bet money at that point that Jonathan Armstrong was the dark-haired man in the photograph with Miranda, the one I'd glimpsed on the screen of her laptop.

Yowza.

"Sure looks like it." Milton reached inside his shirt pocket to bring out a folded note. "My pal gave me a heads-up on the final text message sent from Armstrong to Miranda, because it's not being made public yet for good reason. The Big Dog apparently told her: 'Done thinking. Love you. I am yours forever.' It was dated the evening she died, Andy. Sent a few minutes after midnight. She responded with: 'I love you, too.'"

"You're kidding me?" I stared at him, flabbergasted.

That sounded an awful lot like Jonathan had decided to leave his wife for Miranda, even with her messed-up face.

Since Miranda had apparently gotten his message that night and responded likewise, there's no way she would've killed herself. No way in hell. She would've had everything to live for, right?

On the other hand, if Jonathan had told his wife he was leaving her, what would that have done to Delaney? Uptight, control-freak Delaney Armstrong who'd undergone every procedure Dr. Sonja had in her arsenal to attempt to stay youthful and attractive for the only man she'd ever loved.

Her perfect guy.

Oh, boy.

If I knew Delaney, she would've been mad enough to kill.

But she would never have hurt her beloved Jonathan. No matter what he'd done. *No, siree, Bob.* She would've pinned the blame on Miranda completely.

I pulled Milton's velvet jacket tighter around me, realizing how easy Miranda had made it for Delaney. The former beauty queen had stormed into Delaney's own house the night of a party, so there were plenty of witnesses to Miranda's crazy behavior, namely her taking a shot at Dr. Sonja.

"Jonathan Armstrong's wife had to have been the one who took Miranda's gun," I said, thinking how Delaney must've seen it as the answer to her prayers. "Delaney could've picked it up during all the brouhaha and no one would've been the wiser. She also had the keys to Miranda's duplex, because Miranda had left her car in front of the Armstrongs' house."

It would've been so easy for Delaney to let herself in after I'd left. A drunk and snoozing Miranda wouldn't have known what hit her until it was too late.

Dear God.

I reached over to Milton and clutched his arm. Ignoring his "Oww," I asked, "Can you take me to Delaney Armstrong's house right now? Please,

Fletch, I need to talk to her. I've known her since kindergarten. If she did this . . . if she murdered Miranda in cold blood, I want to hear her say it out loud."

"Did you actually call me 'Fletch'?"

"Will you or won't you?" I squeezed his arm more tightly.

He looked at me, incredulous. "You actually think she's going to confess just because you want her to?"

"Maybe." If I played a mean Angela Lansbury, like in *Murder, She Wrote,* or did a really good Matlock impression. "Heck, I don't know. I just have to do it."

"The police won't be any too happy with you."

"Anna Dean hasn't been happy with me since she met me. So, are you driving me?" I still had a good grip on his arm, and I wasn't letting up. "Or should I call a cab? Because one way or the other, I'm going."

He grimaced. "If you let go of me, yes, okay."

So much for him being a tough guy.

I let him go.

"It's on Bordeaux." I pulled on my seat belt. "And drive this phallic symbol as fast as you can, please."

"Phallic symbol?" he repeated, and shook his head. "Whew, Andy Kendricks, you are one strange girl."

"Thank you," I said. Like I hadn't heard that one before. Kissing up wouldn't get him anywhere. "Now step on it, Navy SEAL."

I leaned back against the seat and released a huge sigh, ignoring the headache and the tightness in my now empty gut.

What the heck was I doing?

Probably my second really stupid act of the night, besides going to the Caviar Club party and drinking tainted bubbly.

I didn't even know if Delaney would answer the door. It was already past midnight. She was probably asleep, without a clue what was about to happen to her. Although, I guessed that knowing her husband loved another woman had probably put a major crimp in her life.

As it put a fatal crimp in Miranda's.

What if she did confess to me? What then?

Honestly, I didn't know, and I didn't care. Perhaps I was as reckless as my mother and Milton Fletcher seemed to believe, because I was riding on pure emotion at the moment.

All I was certain of was this: I wanted to look Delaney Armstrong in the eye and have her tell me whether or not she killed Miranda.

Though, deep inside, I think I already knew the answer, no matter what she said.

She had the Big Three all wrapped up: motive, means, and opportunity.

Knocking off Miranda DuBois meant saving her marriage, holding her family together, and continuing to pretend that her life was oh-so perfect.

Delaney was merely following the secret formula known as the Way of the Park Cities Woman.

Their motto: If it's broke, fake it.

Well, all but the murder part. Most Park Cities women didn't kill their husbands' mistresses, so far as I was aware. But one never knew.

"Andy? Which way from here?" Milton asked, cutting into my rather depressing thoughts.

I directed him toward the 4200 block of Bordeaux, where the Armstrongs resided in a most elaborate English manor. Back when Delaney and Jonathan had tied the knot, Delaney's daddy had bought her two side-by-side lots and had the existing homes torn down so he could build his darling daughter her six-million-dollar dream home.

Unfortunately, Delaney had decorated it herself, without the aid of an interior designer, which accounted for all the flocked wallpaper, poofy window treatments, and bordello style furnishings with plenty of tufting and fringe.

Considering what her husband had been doing during his off-hours, I decided she didn't have any better taste in men.

Within minutes Milton was guiding his sports car into the circular front driveway. Except for gas lamps burning on either side of the front door, I didn't see any lights on in the house.

Oh, well.

As soon as the Porsche stopped moving, I reached for the door handle; but Milton caught my arm and said, "Hey, not so fast, lady."

"*What?*" I was anxious to get going and half afraid I'd chicken out if he stalled me too long.

"You can't just barge in there and accuse a woman of murder without some kind of backup."

He unleashed his seat belt so he could reach behind him and retrieve a leather case, which he jammed on his lap, opening it up so one flap wedged against his chest and the other was against the steering wheel. First, he retrieved a pair of funky looking sunglasses, which he shoved at me.

"I don't think these things work very well at night," I told him, wondering what he'd been drinking.

"They're not ordinary sunglasses." He snatched them back from me. "It's got an MP3 voice recorder with a built-in microphone." Stabbing his arm back into the mouth of the briefcase, he emerged clutching a rather large pen. "This baby has thirteen hours of playback," he said, and I stared at him.

"You think I'm taking a giant pen in there with me? Should I clip it to my blouse?" I asked dryly. "Or prop it behind my ear? Maybe Delaney won't even notice."

Okay, enough. I caught my fingers in the door handle again, about to pull open the red tin can, when Milton slapped the briefcase closed and returned it behind the seat.

He fumbled with the chunky silver watch on his wrist, ultimately removing it and handing it to me. "It's got a built-in digital recorder. I'm pressing the Play button now, see? The memory holds nine hours, and you're already rolling."

Already rolling?

Before I could say anything, he grasped my hand and forced the watch onto my wrist, where it dangled rather like a Newfoundland's collar on a Chihuahua.

"You want me to wear this thing?" I balked.

"No, *Andy*, I want you to use it." He looked straight at me, as serious as I'd ever seen him. "If you're intent on confronting Delaney, then you're not going in there without it. Or else I'm coming in with you. Take your pick."

What kind of choice was that?

"I won't be long," I said, and got out of the car. I didn't want Inspector Gadget to force any other goodies on me.

My high-heeled boots click-clacked loudly on the cobbled drive, and I was glad I'd kept Milton's jacket on, as the night was cold. I could see well enough before me, thanks to the glow given off by the gas lamps.

I stepped onto the front stoop and sucked in a deep breath before I pressed a finger against the light of the doorbell, hearing the chimes and hoping Delaney might still be awake. If she was guilty, surely she wouldn't be sleeping well, right?

A light went on above my head, and the door quickly opened.

An older woman's turban-wrapped head poked out. "Miss, it's late," she said, and I realized it was the Armstrongs' housekeeper.

"Please, get Delaney," I told her firmly. "I need to speak with her, and, no, it can't wait till morning. If you don't bring her down, I'll call the police. It's that important."

"But, miss—"

"It's all right, Benita," I heard Delaney say. "I'll take care of Ms. Kendricks. I believe I know why she's here."

The housekeeper's head disappeared, and Delaney stood in front of me, holding the door wide open. "Get in here, Andy, before you wake the whole house," she ordered, glancing past me at the red Porsche in the driveway. I did as commanded, hurrying past her into the foyer. She shut and locked the door. "This way."

She gestured to her left, taking me into the living room where Miranda had dinged her Picasso. I followed her shadowy figure as far as the archway, waiting as she stooped to switch a table lamp on before I entered. I didn't want to trip over an ottoman and land on my face. Or worse still, on Milton's watch.

As she stood, she crossed her arms tightly over her purple silk robe. Her bare face almost startled me. Without her makeup, Delaney had no visible eyelashes, and her eyebrows were too thin to be seen. "Have a seat," she said, but I shook my head.

"I think I'll stand. I'll only be here long enough to get something off my chest."

"It's about Miranda, isn't it?" Her already-too-tight features tightened.

"Yes." I ignored the hollow pounding in my chest and threw everything I had at her. "The police got the data from Miranda's cell, and they know your husband was having an affair with her. But you already knew that, didn't you?"

She glared, saying nothing.

"Which is why you wanted Miranda dead, and, bless her dumb soul, she gave you the perfect chance to do it. You took her gun when she dropped it at the Pretty Party. Only you realized no one saw you do it. So what better way to get rid of her than to use her own keys to get into her duplex when she was alone, sleeping off the booze, and use her own gun to shoot her?" I paused, giving her an incredulous look. "You saw the photo on the laptop, didn't you? The one of Miranda and Jonathan. So you took the laptop with you. My God, Delaney, how could you kill her? And don't bother to deny it, not to me. It won't work. No matter how this ends, I'll know in my heart it was you."

"Stop it." She raised a hand, as if about to deny every word, as I would have expected.

Then she lowered her head, shaking it, and clasped her hands together. She didn't rant or shout, but answered in a most subdued voice, "I'm thirty-one years old, and I've done everything in my power to look as young and pretty as I possibly can. Have you ever had a C-section, Andy?"

"No," I said. She knew I hadn't.

"Have you ever had folds of your belly hanging down so you need surgery in order to please your husband? Or realized the love of your life looks at every big-breasted woman in the room wherever you go, until you buy yourself a couple DDs of your own?"

"No," I said again. For Pete's sake, she could glance at my chest and realize I hadn't.

"Younger females are so aggressive these days." She sighed and touched her cheeks. "They don't have any compunction about sleeping with married men, and it's way too tempting.

They haven't lived enough yet for the years to show up on their faces, and their mothers apparently never taught them about wearing underpants. They're all a bunch of sluts, Andy, and that's what I've had to compete with. Don't you understand?"

I saw her eyes fill with tears, but I wasn't about to move.

I might've felt compassion for her once. I didn't now.

She was a killer.

"Miranda wasn't twenty years old, Delaney. She was our age. It wasn't her fault that Jonathan liked to stray outside your marriage. Though it probably hurt even worse when you learned about her, more than the others, I'd guess. Because she wasn't twenty-something . . . heck, she wasn't even perfect, not after what Dr. Sonja did to her. And still, Jonathan wanted to be with her." That was it, the crux of it all. "Even though she was imperfect, he still loved her, and he was going to leave you. That's what did it, isn't it? His text message to her, the one he sent after midnight, after your Pretty Party. You read it somehow. That's what killed you."

"No"—Delaney was shaking her head, the tears falling steadily, her voice a mere hiccup—"it's what killed her, Andy. I tried so hard to be the kind of woman he'd want, but he chose Miranda. Even with the drooling mouth and twitchy eye. He chose her, don't you see?"

I saw all right.

I saw a woman who'd gone to extreme lengths to keep a man who didn't want to be kept. Who didn't love her, and maybe never had.

"But it's all over now, isn't it?" Delaney said, wiping her cheeks with the sleeve of her kimono.

"Yeah, Delaney, it's all over."

I felt Milton's watch, dangling from my wrist, and wondered if she realized just how right she was.

Epilogue

★ It had been a week since Miranda DuBois died.

Milton Fletcher had received his final check from my mother for his work on the case. The pathologist Mother had flown in from Los Angeles was given a return ticket and sent home on a departing plane.

Debbie Santos had returned from South America and properly buried her daughter in a lovely private ceremony at Sparkman-Hillcrest Memorial Park, where beauty maven Mary Kay Ash had also been laid to rest. I think Miranda would have appreciated the irony of that.

The Highland Park police had arrested Delaney Armstrong for Miranda's murder, and someone from ARGH (Abramawitz, Reynolds, Goldberg, and Hunt), my boyfriend's firm, was representing her. They were offering a plea of not guilty by reason of insanity, which I guess fit the case well enough. Trying to stay young and pretty for a lifetime in order to please a man was definitely inspiring of insanity in my mind.

As for Janet Graham, she wrote a smash-bang feature for the *Park Cities Press*, exposing the Caviar Club and its owners, Dr. Sonja Madhavi and her beau Lance Zarimba, noting the pair's arrest on kidnapping and assault charges and mentioning Dr. Sonja's alleged intentional disfigurement of Miranda DuBois. She linked it all to Miranda's murder and the downfall of Delaney Armstrong, a Hockaday graduate, heiress, and soccer mom.

Even the young gun taking over the helm of the newspaper couldn't convince his board of directors to oust the venerable Society pages editor for his inexperienced chippie girlfriend after that.

So all was well, right?

The bad guys were going to court.

Janet had kept her job (and earned a raise).

Milton Fletcher was out of my hair.

Cissy had turned her focus back to her ladies' group teas, alumnae luncheons, and charity balls, and ceased meddling in the HPPD's business.

And Brian Malone had forgiven me for skipping out on him during the Blues-Stars game, which the Blues miraculously won in a shootout; though he threatened to take me to the dentist and have GPS chips soldered to my teeth if I ever did anything like that again.

The best part of it all was his admitting aloud how much he loved me and wanted us to be together, even suggesting he give up his apartment and permanently move in with me.

Weeee.

I promised I would stick by him like glue—at least, on the weekends—and I held true to my word, lolling in bed until noon the next Sunday, while Malone slipped from beneath the covers and offered to fix me breakfast.

"I like my toast brown, but not burned, and no butter, just blueberry spread, and I'll take orange juice, too," I told him as he pulled on his sweatpants and hurried from the bedroom, as if in a rush to get the toaster going and the juice pouring.

I closed my eyes and happily rested my head on the pillow for another ten minutes, until I smelled food and opened them again to find Malone entering the room, a tray in hand.

I scooted up against the headboard into a seated position as he plunked the tray over my knees, and it took my eyes a second to realize there was more than just breakfast on my plate.

In the center of two slices of toast sat a robin's-egg-blue box.

I opened my mouth and mutely gazed at my boyfriend. My heart was going mach five, at least, and I realized instantly what was coming.

He smiled furtively and plunked up the box, got down on bended knee beside the bed and said, "Andy, I—"

Whack!

I heard the bang as the front door of the condo burst open, a voice trilling, "Andrea! Andrea? I saw your car, and Mr. Malone's, too, so I know you're here!" Footsteps thudded, bracelets jangled, and the scent of Joy perfume permeated the air. "It's past noon, and your drapes are still drawn, and the Sunday paper's still lying on your stoop."

Oh, God, it was my mother.

Brian stopped mid-sentence and blinked dumbly at me, his train of thought obviously smashed to smithereens.

Dang that Cissy!

Hadn't she heard of calling first?

She must've used her key to the place, one I'd given her "for emergencies only," which I thought had meant if I were lying dead on the floor, not answering my phone, or if a hurricane blew half of Dallas away—not for interrupting what could possibly be the most important moment of my life.

"Andrea!" She burst into the bedroom, seemingly unmindful of the fact that I was in bed with a breakfast tray on my lap, with my shirtless boyfriend kneeling on the floor with a Tiffany box in his hands, surely about to propose to me.

Like the Attention Diva that she was, she pushed her way in, striding toward the bed in her chinchilla coat and matching hat, thrusting her hand into my face the instant she was close enough to wiggle fingers beneath my nose.

"Guess what?" she asked, though I could've seen the sparkle of the huge honking diamond solitaire on her third left finger even if it hadn't been a mere inch away from my eyeballs. Strange thing was, the ring was new, not the one she'd been wearing since she'd married my father all those years ago.

"I'm engaged," she announced, before I managed to get the word dislodged from my throat. "Stephen proposed at brunch this morning, and I said yes! Can you even believe it?!"

She was beaming, like a schoolgirl showing off her first corsage, and I felt such mixed emotions that I wasn't sure what to say or do.

Did she *always* have to one-up me?

"Well, aren't you going to congratulate me?" she said, pouting. Then she looked over at Malone, still on bended knee, and quipped, "Dear boy, did you drop something?"

Yeesh.